THIS DIARY BELONGS TO:

Nikki J. Maxwell

PRIVATE & CONFIDENTIAL

If found, please return to ME for REWARD!

(NO SNOOPING ALLOWED!!!☹)

ALSO BY
Rachel Renée Russell

Rachel Renée Russell

Double

DORK

diaries

3

SIMON AND SCHUSTER

First published as an omnibus edition in Great Britain in 2015 by Simon and Schuster UK Ltd
A CBS COMPANY

Simon & Schuster UK Ltd
1st Floor,
222 Gray's Inn Road,
London WC1X 8HB

Dork Diaries: Dear Dork first published in Great Britain in 2012
by Simon and Schuster UK Ltd, a CBS company. Originally published in 2012 in the USA
as Dork Diaries: Tales from a Not-So-Smart Miss Know-It-All, by Aladdin,
an imprint of Simon & Schuster Children's Publishing Division.

Dork Diaries: Holiday Heartbreak first published in Great Britain in 2013
by Simon and Schuster UK Ltd, a CBS company. Originally published in the USA in 2012
as Dork Diaries: Tales from a Not-So-Happy Heartbreaker by Aladdin,
an imprint of Simon & Schuster Children's Publishing Division.

Copyright © Rachel Renée Russell 2012 & 2013
Book design by Lisa Vega

A CIP catalogue record for this book is available from the British Library.

ISBN 978-1-4711-2276-7

www.simonandschuster.co.uk
www.simonandschuster.com.au
www.dorkdiaries.co.uk

3 5 7 9 10 8 6 4

Printed and bound by CPI Group (UK) Ltd, Croydon, CR0 4YY

Dear Miss-Know-It-All,

I think my arch-nemesis is
spreading rumours about me. Help!

OMG!!! Does your arch-nemesis have
a name that starts with "Mac" and ends with
"Kenzie"? Maybe YOU can give ME advice!!

Your friend,

(a.k.a Crush-itis
and BFF
drama expert)

(a.k.a. Nikki Maxwell)

Miss Know-It-All

How can Nikki help everyone else
with their problems when shes
can't solve her own??
Find out in DEAR DORK...

<u>OMG</u>! I CANNOT believe I'm actually going to go through with this!

It's supposed to be just a little prank. But I have to admit, I'm a little worried. I really need to think about the consequences of my actions.

Because if something goes wrong, there's a chance SOMEONE could actually end up . . . DEAD!

<u>YES</u>, that's correct. DEAD ☹!!

Namely . . . ME! Because if my parents find out about this stupid stunt I'm planning to pull, they're going to KILL me!

It all started when Chloe, Zoey and I decided to have a sleepover during our winter break from school.

We excitedly counted down the seconds to midnight . . . "TEN . . . NINE . . . EIGHT . . .

SEVEN . . . SIX . . FIVE . . . FOUR . . .
THREE . . . TWO . . . ONE . . ."

HAPPY NEW YEAR!!!

CHLOE, ZOEY AND I CELEBRATE!!

I was really looking forward to a brand-new year. Mainly because last year was filled with SO much drama.

What better way to start things off than with me and my two BFFs having a WILD and CRAZY New Year's Eve pyjama party at Zoey's house?

We pigged out on pizza, double-chocolate cupcakes, M&M's and ice-cream sundaes, and then washed it all down with soda.

Soon we were giggling hysterically and bouncing off the walls from a major sugar buzz.

We were having WAAAY too much FUN painting our nails funky colours and playing TRUTH OR DARE to watch some lame disco-ball thingy drop in Times Square on TV.

"Zoey! Truth or dare?" Chloe asked, locking her eyes on Zoey with an eager grin.

"Truth!" she answered.

CHLOE, ZOEY AND ME, EATING JUNK FOOD
AND PLAYING TRUTH OR DARE

"I have a really good one!" Chloe squealed. "It's

SOOO romantic and from my FAVE book! Okay, who would you rather kiss, Deadly Doodle Dude or Hunk Finn?!"

"Oh! That's easy!" Zoey giggled. "I pick Hunk Finn. He's the sensitive artist type and supercute."

"Yeah, but Deadly Doodle Dude is so . . . morbidly . . . beautiful and intensely . . . doodley," Chloe gushed.

That's when I almost choked on my pizza.

I know my BFF is a hopeless romantic, and I love her to death. But sometimes I worry that her TEETH might be BRIGHTER than SHE is.

Crushing on a DOODLEY guy is just so . . . WRONG!

I mean, is that even a REAL word?!

If I was going to create the perfect guy, he would be KIND, have a good sense of HUMOUR, and be adorably CUTE (just like my crush, Brandon). . .

ME, MIXING UP THE INGREDIENTS TO MAKE
MY DREAM GUY

"Your turn, Nikki," Zoey said, and turned to me. "Truth or dare?"

"Oooh! I have a really good one!" Chloe exclaimed.

A wicked grin spread across her face as she whispered in Zoey's ear.

Zoey's eyes got as big as saucers. "OMG, Chloe! Nikki is going to DIE if we ask her that!" she shrieked through her giggles.

I scrunched up my face and nervously chewed my lip.

Answering a truth about a fictional guy was fun and exciting.

But answering one about a REAL guy could be totally EMBARRASSING.

And I was hoping to AVOID discussing ONE guy in particular, if you know what I mean.

Which meant I didn't have a choice.

"DARE! Nobody's been brave enough to try a dare, so I'll do one. Give me your hardest!" I challenged Zoey.

She tapped her chin, in deep thought.

Then suddenly a sly smirk appeared on her face. "Are you SURE about that, Nikki? Requesting a truth might be A LOT easier."

"Or maybe NOT!" Chloe said smugly.

"Yes, I'm sure. DARE!" I blurted. "Bring it!"

Sometimes I really wish my brain worked faster than my big, fat mouth.

Because it was quite obvious that Chloe and Zoey were up to some mischievous, evil-genius stuff!

But there was just NO WAY I was going to voluntarily SPILL MY GUTS about Brandon in a game.

Until I heard Zoey's dare. . .

I just stared at Zoey and gasped. I couldn't believe my ears.

"OMG!" Chloe exclaimed. "That's so dangerous and

9

sneaky . . . and totally the BEST dare ever!! You
GOTTA do it, Nikki!"

I immediately broke into a cold sweat.

"I d-don't know, guys!" I stammered. "I mean, what
if I get caught?! I could get in really big trouble! I
guess I'm just a big . . . CHICKEN! Sorry to ruin all
of the fun."

"Don't feel bad, Nikki. I gave you a supercrazy dare.
Only the CCP (Cute, Cool & Popular) kids do stuff like
that. Chloe and I are chickens too!" Zoey admitted.

"I KNOW that's right! Buck! Buck! Buck-aah!" Chloe
clucked.

I think Chloe and Zoey said those things just to
make ME feel better about NOT doing that dare.
They're definitely the BEST friends EVER!

To vent our frustration, we played the "Chicken
Dance" song and danced and clucked for nine
minutes. . .

CHICKENS "R" US

Afterwards, we just sat there staring at each other, wishing our lives were a lot more — I don't know — EXCITING or something.

It was strange because the more I thought about all of the mean stuff MacKenzie had done to us, the more TICKED OFF I got.

There's only so much public humiliation, vicious

teasing, malicious gossip, ruthless sabotage and mean-girl backstabbing that a person can take.

I'd had quite enough of people who went out of their way to make my life totally miserable.

"People" being snobby, shallow, evil girls like, um . . . MACKENZIE HOLLISTER!!

Calling her a "mean girl" is an understatement. She's a DOBERMAN in lip gloss and designer jeans. And for some reason, she HATES MY GUTS!

MacKenzie having to clean up a few rolls of toilet paper is NOTHING compared to the very long list of horribly rotten things she's done to US.

And she's hurt other people too. It was HER fault Brandon almost moved to Florida.

"You know what, guys? I'm STILL pretty angry about MacKenzie locking us in that storage closet right before we were supposed to skate in the Holiday on Ice show!" I fumed.

"Yeah! If she'd had her way, we'd still be in there!" Chloe griped. "Until someone found our skeletons!"

ME, CHLOE AND ZOEY,
NOT LOOKING VERY CUTE AFTER BEING
LOCKED IN THAT STORAGE CLOSET FOR
THREE VERY LONG YEARS!!

"You're right! And THAT was the last straw! I've changed my mind about the dare. I'm going to do it! But only if you guys come with me," I announced.

"We've got your back, girlfriend!" Zoey said. "This isn't a dare anymore! It's PAYBACK! I'll get the toilet paper!"

So right now I'm locked in Zoey's bathroom, writing all of this in my diary.

And instead of doing the sleeping part of our sleepover, we're secretly planning the Great Toilet Paper Caper.

The good news is Miss Thang (also known as MacKenzie) is FINALLY going to get just what SHE deserves ☺!!

The BAD news is IF my parents ever find out about this, I'M going to be DEAD MEAT!

I can't believe it's only thirty-seven minutes into the new year and I'm already FREAKING OUT.

One thing is very clear.

THIS year is going to have WAAAAAAY
more DRAMA than LAST year.

Have you ever had a REALLY bad feeling about something?

And inside your head a little voice is screaming, "NOOOOOOOO! Stop! Don't do it!"

Well, that little voice was warning ME that our Great Toilet Paper Caper was going to be a complete and utter

DISASTER!!

But did I listen? Of course not!

Although, I have to admit, part of me wanted to just call the whole thing off.

Sneaking out into the cold, dark night to wreak havoc on the world sounded exciting. But we could have had just as much fun staying inside doing all of the normal sleepover stuff.

You know, stuff like . . .

Crawling into my warm and cozy sleeping bag and PRETENDING to be asleep.

While my BFFs giggle uncontrollably and pour water on my hand to try and make me pee my pants.

GIGGLE, GIGGLE!!

GIGGLE, GIGGLE!!

GIGGLE, GIGGLE!!

ME, PRETENDING TO BE ASLEEP

Stealing Chloe's overnight bag and raiding Zoey's underwear drawer while they're both busy brushing their teeth.

Then secretly stuffing everything in the freezer.

ME, SECRETLY STUFFING CHLOE'S AND ZOEY'S CLOTHES IN THE FREEZER

Taking turns SCARING ourselves to death by telling superSPOOKY stories in the dark by flashlight.

. . . THEN THE GHOST FLOATED ACROSS THE ROOM, MOANING, "ZOEY!! NIKKI!!"

But another part of me — a very dark and primitive side—wanted DESPERATELY to get even with MacKenzie.

The thought of being a teen rebel with a cause seemed so COOL. At the time, anyway.

Although I'd been to MacKenzie's house before, purely by accident (OMG! THAT'S a long and gut-wrenching story!), I didn't realise she lived only a few doors down from Zoey.

I felt a little better about the whole thing knowing we didn't have to walk very far in the dark.

Zoey and I found torches and gathered up rolls of toilet paper.

But Chloe was no help whatsoever.

She just sat in front of the mirror humming "Girls Just Want to Have Fun" while making-up her face to look like a bunny.

"Um . . . Chloe. . ." I gawked at her in confusion. "You realise we're not going to a costume party, right?"

"Hey! I know what I'm doing," she assured me. "If we get caught, do you think the cops will arrest an adorable little bunny and throw her in jail? Of course not! But I'll definitely come and visit you and Zoey in the slammer."

Okay! NOW I was starting to get a little worried.

As we trudged through the snow to MacKenzie's house, it was pitch-dark and eerily quiet. All we could hear was the crunching of the snow underfoot and our heavy breathing.

I had to resist the urge to turn around and run screaming back to my warm and safe sleeping bag.

Finally we reached MacKenzie's house, and it was just like I had remembered.

GINORMOUS!!

Suddenly my stomach felt superqueasy.

Only, I didn't know if it was all the junk food I'd eaten earlier that night, OR the fact that I was very close to finally getting a meet-'n'-greet with some of my favourite rap artists who were doing time in prison.

As a fellow INMATE ☹!! YIKES!!

"Come on! Let's get this done before somebody sees us," I whisper-shouted.

Zoey took six rolls of toilet paper out of her backpack and tossed them to Chloe and me.

Chloe and Zoey ran towards a huge tree on the left, and I ran towards one on the right.

Then we frantically tossed the toilet paper over the branches until the two trees looked like towering six-metre mummies.

OMG! It was such a RUSH!!

ME

72725

25

It was the most FUN we've had together since . . .
um, yesterday.

Suddenly the porch light flicked on ☹!!

"OH, CRUD! Someone's coming outside!" I shouted.
"HIDE!!"

We quickly dove into some nearby bushes and then
cautiously peeked out.

The front door opened, and we saw a figure walk down the sidewalk.

"Hurry up and go potty already, Fifi! It's freezing out here!" said a very familiar voice.

It was MACKENZIE ☹!!

OH, CRUD! I'm going to have to finish writing this diary entry later. I'm trying to vent about some VERY personal and private stuff and my MOM just barged into my bedroom without even knocking!

She said that for Family Sharing Time, we're all going with Brianna to see the latest Princess Sugar Plum movie.

And then we're having dinner at Queasy Cheesy.

AGGGGHHHHHH! SPLAT!!

That was me BARFING!

I don't know which I HATE more, Princess Sugar Plum movies or Queasy Cheesy!

I guess I'm STILL traumatised by that time MacKenzie videotaped Brianna and me dancing at Queasy Cheesy and put it on YouTube.

Gotta STOP writing in my diary even though I don't want to!!

TO BE CONTINUED . . .

So, where was I before I was so RUDELY interrupted (tapping chin, trying to remember)?

Oh! Right in the middle of the Great Toilet Paper Caper!

"Hurry up and go potty already, Fifi! It's freezing out here!" MacKenzie complained to her poodle.

Although her humongous garden had more landscaping than a city park, that stupid dog decided to PIDDLE on EXACTLY the same BUSH we were hiding in.

OMG! We didn't move a muscle. We didn't even dare breathe!

"What's wrong, Fifi? There's nothing there but bushes. Let's go back inside now."

We breathed a collective sigh of relief. WHEW!

Then, without warning, Fifi darted under the bushes and lunged at us, barking like a rabid pit bull.

"Bark, bark, bark! Bark-bark! Bark! Bark-bark!"

"AAAAAAAAAHHH!" we screamed as we fell over each other trying to scramble out of the bushes.

Of course, we scared the juice out of MacKenzie. She gaped in horror and screamed even louder than us. "AAAAAAAAAHHH!!"

Realising that MacKenzie had actually seen our faces, we just clung to each other and screamed louder. "AAAAAAAAAHHH!!!"

Which freaked MacKenzie out even more and made her scream louder yet. "AAAAAAAAAAHHHH!!"

All of that barking, freaking and screaming in the bushes went on for what seemed like FOREVER.

AAAAHHH! AAAAHHH!

BARK, BARK, BARK!

"NIKKI?! CHLOE?! ZOEY?!" MacKenzie finally sputtered. "OMG! You guys nearly scared me to death! WHAT are you doing out here in the middle of the night?!"

"Um, would you believe we were taking a little walk and got lost in your bushes?" I asked.

"NO! I wouldn't!" she said, folding her arms and glaring at us.

"I didn't think so. . ." I muttered. "Well, it was nice chatting with you. But we really must be going—"

"Not so fast! YOU have some explaining to do. WHY are you snooping around my house? And WHY is the Easter Bunny here on New Year's Day?!"

~~The Easter Bunny~~ Chloe, Zoey and I just stared at the ground.

Hey, I may be a coward, but at least I'm an HONEST one. I felt morally obligated to tell MacKenzie the truth.

"We . . . um . . . were sort of in the middle of toilet-papering y-your house," I stammered.

"You were WHAT?!" MacKenzie turned around and finally noticed the streamers of toilet paper dangling from her trees. "No way! Nikki, I can't believe you would actually—"

"It's NOT her fault. It was MY idea," Zoey said in my defence. "I dared her to do it."

"Yeah, but the Truth or Dare game was MY idea," Chloe said, hanging her head. "That makes ME totally responsible."

"Come on! Do you REALLY think I'm STUPID enough to actually believe you naive little dorks could pull off a majorly deviant prank like this?" MacKenzie sneered.

Our mouths dropped open in shock.

"Um . . . YES! We think you're STUPID! And NO! We're NOT so naive that we couldn't pull off a prank like this," I shot back.

"Yeah, right! You can't even LIE convincingly," MacKenzie scoffed.

Then she gave us the evil eye, like we were something her poodle had just left on the pavement.

MACKENZIE, GIVING US THE EVIL EYE

That's when it dawned on me that she didn't believe a single word we were saying. I was . . . FLABBERGASTED!

"Obviously, some really cute guys did this to get

my attention! Boys are SO obsessed with me."

MacKenzie giggled and batted her eyes like she was flirting with some invisible crush only she could see.

"Hmmm . . . I bet it was Brady and some of the football jocks. Or maybe Theodore and his nerdy band members. . ."

Then she put her hands over her heart and swooned.

"OMG! I think I know who did it! BRANDON!!" she squealed. "Nikki, you must be SO jealous that he toilet-papered MY house and not YOURS! Eat your heart out, hon!"

"MacKenzie, I have seven words for you. YouNeedToGetAClue.com!" I said, staring right into her beady little eyes. "But since we made this mess in your garden, I guess it's only fair that we clean it up."

Suddenly she narrowed her eyes at me.

"You came over here in the middle of the night to clean up the toilet paper in MY garden?! But WHY? I bet you didn't want me to see it. Then I would never know that Brandon is CRUSHING on me! Is that it?"

I rolled my eyes at her. "No, MacKenzie! Brandon had nothing to do with—"

"You're LYING! It's MY toilet paper! So don't even think about touching it! If Brandon went to all this trouble, he must REALLY like me. And that's why you're hanging around here trying to UNDERMINE my love life!"

ME?!! Undermine HER love life??!!

SORRY! But I'm WAY too busy undermining my OWN love life. Which is why I don't have one.

MacKenzie thinks the whole world revolves around her, and I wanted to burst her little bubble SO badly. But talking to a SNOBBY AIRHEAD like her is a lot like eating a can of SARDINES . . .

POINTLESS and NAUSEATING!

← MACKENZIE

SARDINES →

"Whatever, MacKenzie!" I sighed. "Believe what you want. We toilet-papered your house! We're TIRED!! And we're going HOME!!"

Chloe, Zoey and I picked up the empty cardboard toilet paper rolls strewn across the garden and headed towards the pavement.

Hey, we were vandals, but we WEREN'T litterbugs!

"PUT THOSE BACK! THEY'RE MINE!" MacKenzie

screeched. "Or I'll call the cops! It's illegal to take stuff from private property. LOSERS!"

Chloe, Zoey and I froze and looked at each other in disbelief. Then we tossed the cardboard toilet paper rolls BACK into her garden.

It was pure INSANITY!

"Oh! And by the way . . . HAPPY NEW YEAR!!" MacKenzie chirped, all happy and friendlylike.

Did I mention that girl is SCHIZOID?

We walked back to Zoey's house in complete silence. The entire experience was just . . . SURREAL!

Suddenly Chloe started to snicker. Then Zoey caught the giggles. Finally I did too. We were laughing so hard we were practically staggering down the pavement.

"Thank goodness MacKenzie didn't believe us.

Otherwise, she'd probably be burying our dead bodies in her back garden," I chuckled.

"Hey! We tried to tell her the truth. But her ego is so huge it has stretch marks." Zoey snorted.

In spite of everything, I think my BFFs and I learned two very valuable life lessons that night.

1. Revenge is NOT the answer and

2. No one can make a complete FOOL out of MacKenzie better than . . . MACKENZIE!

The Great Toilet Paper Caper was an epic FAIL!

But, personally, I'm just happy we made it out of there alive.

It looks like my new year is off to a really good start!

☺!!

Guess what I got in the mail today?!

An invitation to . . .

BRANDON'S BIRTHDAY PARTY!!

SQUEEEEEEE ☺!!

I was so happy I did my Snoopy "happy dance".

Brandon's birthday party is on Friday, January 31, and I can hardly wait!

Chloe, Zoey and I are invited, but MacKenzie isn't. I have to admit, I feel a little sorry for her ☹.

40

NOT!! Too bad, MacKenzie ☺!

She was SO SUPERjealous about Brandon's party that she actually tried to HYPNOTIZE him into giving her an invitation by smiling, batting her eyes and twirling her hair. But it didn't work.

Anyway, I don't have the slightest idea what I'm going to get Brandon for his birthday. But at least I have enough money saved up to get him something nice.

I was thinking about taking him out to dinner at a quaint little Italian restaurant. And we could share a romantic plate of spaghetti like in my favourite Disney movie, *Lady and the Tramp*. SQUEEE!

Speaking of restaurants, Brianna and I went to this brand-new place in the mall called Crazy Burger. They make these HUGE gourmet burgers that are supposed to be delicious.

However, after placing my order, I wasn't so sure the food was all that healthy . . .

I wanted to say, Um . . . NEVER MIND!

But I was absolutely STARVING!

I was SO hungry I could have eaten that foam-rubber burger right off the top of his ridiculously tacky hat.

Plastic googly eyes and all.

And get this. Those ridiculous hats were for sale for $7.99. But WHO in their right mind would even buy one of those things?!

Anyway, that burger was superyummy and juicy. Brianna loved hers too.

Hey! Maybe Brandon and I could have a fancy, candlelight dinner at Crazy Burger for his birthday!

NOT!

☺!!

Today I received some exciting news from Trevor Chase, the producer of the hit television show *15 Minutes of Fame* and the judge of the Westchester Country Day Talent Showcase.

Back in November, I put together a band called Actually, I'm Not Really Sure Yet. And yes! I know it's the craziest band name ever. We were supposed to be called Dorkalicious. But MacKenzie stuck her big nose in my personal business and pretty much messed up everything.

Her dance group won the WCD Talent Showcase and a chance to audition for the TV show.

But Trevor was so impressed with MY band that he asked us to record an original song that we'd written called "Dorks Rule!"

Can you believe THAT?

Anyway, I was just hanging out in my bedroom

writing in my diary when I finally got the follow-up call that he'd promised . . .

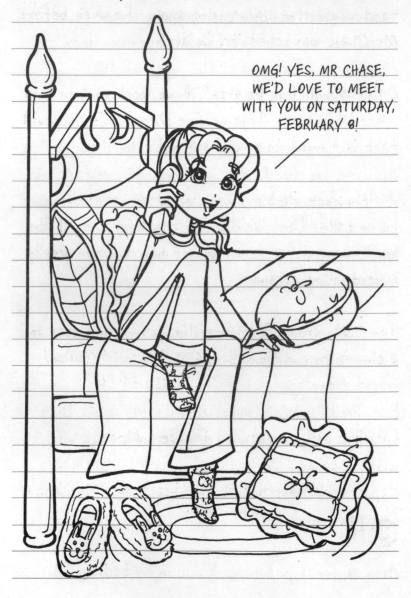

I called Chloe, Zoey, Brandon, Violet and Theo and gave them the fantastic news! We decided our band would start practising again the week before Mr Chase was scheduled to arrive.

OMG! Wouldn't it be great if we went on tour and opened for Lady Gaga or One Direction?! We could take this music thing and run with it.

Just imagine what our lives would be like if we became pop stars. We'd be on the covers of all the teen magazines and maybe even have our own really cute-smelling perfume.

The best part is that Brandon and I could star in a blockbuster movie called *Middle School Musical*. About two dorks in LOVE! SQUEEEEE!!

I smell an Academy Award for Best Movie!

Hey, it could happen. Eat your heart out, MacKenzie!

!!

Today was the first day of school after our two-week winter break.

I have to admit, I was NOT looking forward to seeing MacKenzie.

I guess I was just SUPERworried about Chloe, Zoey and me getting in trouble for toilet-papering her house.

Would our parents be called to the school?

Would we get detention?

Would we be suspended?

Would we be arrested?

However, I would have gladly chosen ANY of these horrible outcomes over listening to MacKenzie BLAB on and on and on about her nonexistent SECRET ADMIRER. . . !!!

NIKKI! I DON'T KNOW WHAT YOU LITTLE TROLLS WERE DOING AT MY HOUSE THAT NIGHT. BUT I'M WARNING YOU, KEEP YOUR NOSE OUT OF MY PERSONAL BUSINESS!

That girl was all up in my face like bad breath.

"MacKenzie, I already apologised and offered to clean up everything. But as I explained before, Chloe, Zoey and I were just goofing around."

"You liar! You're just jealous because Brandon is my secret admirer! Sorry, but he likes ME and not YOU! It's not MY fault your face looks like it caught on fire and someone tried to put it out with a fork!"

"Well, it's not MY fault you're such an AIRHEAD that if you open your mouth I can hear the ocean!" I shot back.

"I'm warning you, Maxwell. Just back off!! Or you'll be sorry. You don't belong at this school anyway."

When MacKenzie said those words, a cold chill ran down my spine. But she was absolutely right!

I DIDN'T belong at her school. Unfortunately, I was attending on a bug extermination scholarship that my dad had arranged.

MacKenzie is the ONLY student who knows my embarrassing secret. And if the other students find out, I am going to just . . . crawl into . . . my locker and . . . DIE!

MacKenzie gave me a big smile as she hurled one final insult.

"Oh, by the way, I LOVE what you did with your hair today. How did you get it to come out of one nostril like that?"

Then she slammed her locker shut and sashayed away. I just HATE it when MacKenzie sashays.

By lunchtime the whole school was gossiping that Brandon was crushing on MacKenzie.

The story was that he had spent an entire hour toilet-papering her house as a practical joke to get her attention. Then he'd left a dozen roses and a box of Godiva chocolates at her front door, rung her doorbell and run away. Nikki Maxwell was SO jealous that she had showed up in the middle of

51

the night with her BFFs to try and take down the
toilet paper so she could ruin MacKenzie's surprise.

OMG! That entire story was SO ridiculous, I
was pretty sure no one would believe it. Besides,
MacKenzie had no proof WHATSOEVER . . .

Except her framed photograph of it all!

She was so proud, she'd actually taken a picture of her house with her mobile. I heard she had even posted it online!

And during lunch, all the CCP girls were crowded around and swooning over her photo like it was a baby picture of Justin Bieber or somebody.

But I was more worried about Brandon than anyone. He had enough stuff going on in his life without MacKenzie and me creating additional drama.

I just hope all of this idle gossip won't damage our friendship.

Although, I have a really bad feeling that damaging our friendship is EXACTLY what MacKenzie is trying to do.

☹!!

AAAAAAAAAAAHH!

(That was me screaming!)

Right now I'm having a complete meltdown!

WHY?

Because when I went to breakfast this morning, I saw a strange man in a fancy business suit standing in our kitchen.

And get this!

My mom handed him a cup of coffee and then gave him a big, fat kiss.

Right on the lips!

I was about to scream, "MOM! WHAT ARE YOU DOING?! YOU'RE MARRIED TO DAD!!"

54

But then I realised the man WAS my dad!

I have to admit, he cleans up really nicely.

"Dad, you look great! What's the occasion?" I asked as I took a huge bite of my strawberry Pop-Tart.

"Well, dear, due to Maxwell's Bug Extermination's great reputation, I just might have an exciting new business opportunity." Dad beamed proudly.

Hey, I didn't want to rain on his parade, but the guy rides around town with a two-metre tall plastic bug on top of his van.

I mean, just how GOOD could his rep actually be?!

I'm just sayin'!

He continued, "I have a meeting this morning with the owner of the most successful property management company in the city, Hollister Holdings, Inc."

At first I just stared at my dad with my eyes practically bulging out of my head.

Then I choked and sputtered . . .

OMG! DAD! DITH YOU JUTH THAY "HOLLITHER"?!

It felt like a huge chunk of pastry had got stuck inside my throat. Or maybe pure dread and a massively severe anxiety attack were stopping me breathing.

"Yep! I'll be meeting with Marshall Hollister. Your mom says his daughter goes to your school and she's a really good friend of yours."

Suddenly I felt really light-headed, and the room started to spin!

"But, Dad! How do you know it's a business meeting? Maybe he wants to talk to you about something else, like . . . um, I don't know! Something kind of surprising or shocking, that could involve lots of, you know, um . . . toilet paper . . . and trees. . ."

"HUH?!" Dad looked at me, totally perplexed. "I don't even KNOW this guy. What ELSE would Moneybags Marshall want to talk to me about but a business deal?"

"I—I don't have the slightest idea!" I stammered.

That's when I looked deep into my father's eyes and desperately pleaded with him:

"DAD! PLEASE! DON'T GO TO THAT MEETING!

I HAVE A REALLY BAD FEELING ABOUT IT!
IF YOU REALLY LOVE ME, YOU WON'T GO!
PLEASE, PROMISE ME!"

But he must have thought I was just joking around
or something, because he chuckled and kissed my
forehead.

"Boy! You and your mother are more nervous about
this meeting than I am. But don't worry, I'm a
shrewd and savage shark when it comes to business.
I'm TOTALLY in control. Just call me MR BIZ!"

"Well, Mr Biz!" My mom giggled. "Your tie is
floating in your coffee and you have jam in your
moustache. I think a shrewd and savage shark needs
to run upstairs to wash his face and change his tie!"

Dad fished his tie out of his coffee and stared at
it in total disgust.

"Aww, shucks! This is my really pretty POWER tie!
Now it's RUINED!" he whined like a five-year-old.

MY DAD, THE SHREWD AND SAVAGE BUSINESS SHARK

It was quite obvious! MacKenzie had finally ratted on me, and now HER dad wanted to talk to MY dad.

Which means at some point in the immediate future, my parents are going to KILL ME!!

I was torn as to whether I should pack my suitcase and sneak away to become a teenage bag-lady BEFORE or AFTER school.

But the least I could do was try to warn my BFFs, Chloe and Zoey, that MacKenzie's dad was probably going to be contacting THEIR parents next.

So it's settled.

I'll run away AFTER school.

☹!!

WHAT in the world is going on around here?!

MacKenzie has been superNICE to me for the past two days!

And even though HER dad had that meeting with MY dad yesterday, she's STILL bragging to everyone that Brandon toilet-papered her house.

Which makes no sense WHATSOEVER!

And weirder yet, my dad and mom haven't uttered a single word about me being . . .

1. in REALLY BIG TROUBLE,

2. a MAJOR DISAPPOINTMENT to them, or

3. a POOR ROLE MODEL FOR MY YOUNGER SISTER, BRIANNA

. . . and it's driving me completely NUTS!

I started thinking they were using some kind of Dr Phil-inspired "parental reverse psychology" thing on me as punishment. Just to watch me squirm.

Because, I swear, I'm feeling so NERVOUS and so GUILTY right now I'm ready to confess what I did, give myself a stern lecture, take away all of my own privileges and then ground MYSELF for the rest of the year.

But as soon as I got home from school today, it all started to make sense.

My dad was out in the front garden with all of this fancy new high-tech extermination equipment.

OMG! He had an X-14 Bug-B-Gone Power Sprayer with twenty-four assorted EZ Snap-on Nozzle Tips, a BreatheMore Ventilated Face Mask, a PowerPack UltraLight Double Canister Backpack and a poly-cotton-blend blue designer uniform by Tommy Hilfiger.

Dad had filled the sprayer with water and was

playing with it like a little boy trying out a new Super Soaker water gun or something.

However, the thing that totally freaked me out was NOT the shiny new blue van parked nearby, but the company NAME plastered across it. . . .

WOO-HOO! THIS IS POWER!!

HOLLISTER HOLDINGS, INC

← DAD

That's when I realised my dad had pretty much sold his soul to the devil!

As far as I was concerned, the Maxwell family was now OWNED by the Hollister family.

Dad waved at me and smiled. "Hi, honey! How was school today?"

"Horrible! Dad, where did you get all of this new stuff?"

"Oh, it's not mine. Yet, anyway. That meeting with Marshall Hollister yesterday went really well. He owns seven apartment complexes and four office buildings and plans to expand this year. His pest-control technician just retired and he wants me to stand in for a few weeks until he finds a new guy and trains—"

"So it's just temporary?!" I interrupted. "Thank goodness!" I could feel a weight lifting off my shoulders.

"Marshall said he's heard good things about my

extermination work at your school from his daughter. And he says she HATES everyone. Even him!" Dad chuckled.

"But what about YOUR customers? How are you going to have time to run your own business AND work for Mr Hollister?"

"Actually, he said I could set my own hours. And I get to use his new van and all of his fancy equipment. But the best part is the extra income. Working for Mr Hollister is a fantastic opportunity, and I plan to take full advantage of it."

That's when I had the most horrible thought!

What if my dad quits his job to work full-time for Mr Hollister?!! Then I'd lose my scholarship at WCD and have to transfer to a new school!!

Maybe that was MacKenzie's master plan?!! I felt my heart drop into my boots.

I could NOT believe my dad was ruining my life like

this! But I knew this was NOT really about him.

It was about that big blowout I'd had with MacKenzie on New Year's Eve.

And now Dad's fairy godfather, Moneybags Marshall Hollister, had appeared out of thin air and offered to turn him into a bug-zapping Cinderella.

DAD'S FAIRY GODFATHER

OMG!

DAD →

It was MACKENZIE who was ruining my life!! As USUAL!

"Don't worry, dear. I'm completely in control. Just call me—"

I finished his sentence. "Mr Biz! The shrewd and savage business shark, right?"

"Right!" Dad said, giving me a big hug. Then he went back to spraying water on his pretend snow bugs or something.

And I went straight to my bedroom and cried for an entire hour.

Now I'm sitting on the edge of my bed sulking. Which for some reason always makes me feel a lot better.

I'm just totally bummed about the possibility that I might have to leave my friends at WCD.

WHY is my life just one deep . . . dreary . . . cesspool of . . . heartbreak and . . . disappointment?!

ME, GAZING INTO THE CESSPOOL
THAT IS MY LIFE!

Judging by how much my dad is loving his new job, I'll probably be transferring for SURE!

I guess my only option is to try and hold on to my bug extermination scholarship for as long as possible.

Which is going to be next to impossible with MacKenzie out to destroy my life.

AAAAAAAAAAAAAH!!

That was me screaming in frustration!

I'm supposed to be in my first class right now.
But instead, I'm hiding out in the girls' toilets,
writing in my diary, and trying NOT to have a
nervous breakdown.

I just had a big fight with MacKenzie, and now this
whole Great Toilet Paper Caper thing has turned
into a major FIASCO!!

It all started when I stopped by the office to
get a copy of our WCD student handbook. I was
SUPERworried and was dying to find out what the
school policy was on pranks.

And guess who was the student office assistant?

JESSICA ☹!! Who, BTW, is MacKenzie Hollister's
BFF. Jessica is supposed to work in there only

ONE hour a day during her study hall.

But I'm starting to suspect she SECRETLY lives in the school office or something. . .

I just knew Jessica was going to blab all of my personal business to MacKenzie.

But she didn't have to, because the very last person I wanted to see was sitting right there with Jessica, gossiping and doing her nails . . .

MACKENZIE ☹!!

Maybe I'm just paranoid, but it seems like those two girls are forever popping up in my life at exactly the WRONG time!

Like some kind of living, breathing, talking, gloss-addicted, um . . . PIMPLES!

I wanted to turn right around and run out of that place screaming. But instead, I cleared my throat, smiled and said really friendlylike, "Um, sorry to interrupt you guys. But I'd like a copy of the student handbook, please."

Jessica looked up from polishing her nails and just glared at me like I was something that had just crawled out of the sewer. I could tell she was SUPERannoyed when she said . . .

NIKKI, CAN'T YOU SEE I'M BUSY? MY NAILS WON'T BE DRY FOR AT LEAST ANOTHER TWELVE MINUTES! COME BACK NEXT WEEK.

JESSICA, → DOING HER NAILS

I could not believe Jessica actually said that right to my face. She's, like, the WORST office assistant EVER!

That's when MacKenzie glared at me all evil-like. Then she grabbed a handbook from the back counter and very rudely tossed it right at me . . .

"Actually, Jessica, Nikki really needs a handbook right now so she can read the part about how student pranks and destroying personal property are an automatic suspension from school. It's on page one twenty-eight. Read it and weep, Nikki!"

My hands were shaking so badly, I could barely hold the book. I turned to page 128 and quickly read the page.

"Wait a minute!" I said. "It says right here, 'Student pranking and practical jokes are discouraged and punishable by after-school detention. Purposely destroying property may result in a suspension from school.' No one destroyed any property, MacKenzie."

"Well, I think you DESERVE to be kicked out of school! Putting toilet paper in trees is not so bad. But EGGING a house can damage property. And I thought I saw eggs all over the place that night. Didn't you see them? Those eggs probably damaged my property."

"OMG, MacKenzie! You know good and well there WEREN'T any EGGS. And WE didn't throw any. . . !"

"Well, SOMEBODY did! And if it wasn't you guys, maybe it was . . . I don't know . . . my secret admirer. . . ?!" she said as an evil grin spread across her face.

"I can't believe you're actually accusing Brandon of toilet-papering your house AND throwing EGGS?!! How can you just LIE like that?! Especially knowing he could be suspended from school!" I screamed at that girl.

MacKenzie stared at me with her beady little eyes for what seemed like FOREVER.

"Actually, Nikki, I'm sure I could totally forget about the whole egg thing if someone was able to get me and Jessica invitations to Brandon's party. . ."

Then she batted her eyes at me all innocentlike.

I was so shocked I almost fell over.

I could NOT believe my ears!

I had to restrain myself from reaching over and SLAPPING that girl SILLY.

I would never, ever egg anyone or anything because it's wrong.

But right then I was so MAD at MacKenzie for being such a deceitful, manipulative, pathological LIAR that I couldn't help but imagine what I'd love to do with a dozen eggs. . .

Girlfriend, these eggs look so CUTE on you!

"Okay, MacKenzie. And what if someone DOESN'T come up with invites. . . ?" I asked.

"Oh, I don't know. Maybe I'll just write about the entire event in my little gossip column — er, I mean Fashion and Current Events column for the school newspaper. Once Principal Winston finds out, SOMEONE is going to be suspended! That's for sure. So it's YOUR choice."

Hey, you do the crime, you do the time. Toilet-papering MacKenzie's house was wrong, and I don't

78

mind doing after-school detention for it. I totally deserve that.

But no one threw eggs or destroyed her property.

And MacKenzie making up malicious LIES to get us suspended unless we cough up party invites is just WRONG on so many levels!

Losing my WCD scholarship because my dad decides to work full-time for MacKenzie's dad is really BAD! But the possibility of Brandon getting kicked out of school because of MY stupid prank would be horrendously UNFAIR!

There's just no way I can let this happen.

There has to be SOMETHING I can do to stop MacKenzie?!!

AAAAAAAAAAAAAAAHHH!

That was me screaming in frustration.

AGAIN! ☹!!

I barely got any sleep last night.

I just lay there, wide awake, trying to figure out how to stop MacKenzie.

I realise I could simply ~~ask~~ BEG Brandon to invite MacKenzie and Jessica to his party.

But then it would be MY fault if those snobby

little drama queens RUINED his birthday.

I wouldn't blame Brandon for wondering whether I was a true friend of his or just a mindless little puppet for MacKenzie.

So, my ONLY option is to try and get a position on the school newspaper.

That way, I can at least try to stop her from printing stuff in her gossip column about Brandon, Chloe, Zoey and me that could get us kicked out of school.

If I keep a really close eye on MacKenzie, I can shut her down BEFORE she makes any trouble, by reporting her to the newspaper adviser.

The BAD news is that I know nothing whatsoever about writing for a school newspaper. Except for maybe THREE things:

1. It has writing, and I'm seriously addicted to writing in my diary.

2. It has comic strips and cartoons, and I'm seriously addicted to drawing.

3. It has my crush, Brandon, ~~and I'm seriously addicted to him.~~

However, the GOOD news is that there's a meeting next week for students interested in joining the newspaper staff.

I'm just praying all of this works!

During gym I casually mentioned my plan to Chloe and Zoey, and they thought it was a wonderful idea.

Of course, I purposely left out the part about me needing to join the newspaper because MacKenzie was ruthlessly plotting to get all of us kicked out of school by spreading lies and untruths!

And when I explained to them that I was really worried because the only serious writing I'd ever done was in my diary, Chloe and Zoey assured me that I'd do just fine.

They said only an insanely untalented person could obsessively write in a diary like I did and STILL be a superCRUDDY writer.

It was SO SWEET of them to compliment me like that.

I think.

I got really emotional and my eyes started to tear up a little during our deep knee bends. . .

ME, GETTING SUPEREMOTIONAL DURING OUR DEEP KNEE BENDS

And get this!!

Chloe and Zoey said they would help with my newspaper projects.

I can ALWAYS count on them to be there for me. I'm SO lucky to have BFFs like Chloe and Zoey!

They also mentioned how joining the school newspaper would be the perfect opportunity for Brandon and me to spend more quality time together.

OMG! I hadn't really thought about THAT ☺!!!

I bet MacKenzie is going to be SO jealous!

And it was Chloe and Zoey's brilliant idea for me to ask Brandon to help me find a position, since he's SUPERfamiliar with the newspaper and the way it works.

He's going to be shocked and surprised when I pop up at the newspaper office during lunch on Monday.

We haven't really talked much this week because he's been unusually quiet.

I'm sure he's heard all of the ridiculous gossip about him toilet-papering MacKenzie's house and leaving her lavish gifts because he's crushing on her.

But the CRUELEST thing about all of this is that MacKenzie is actually setting Brandon up to take the blame for something I did, unless I compromise our friendship and arrange for her to get invited to his party.

I really want to set the record straight and tell everyone what REALLY happened that night.

But the last thing I need right now is to get into World War III with MacKenzie. Especially when the casualties could end up being people I really care about.

Like Chloe and Zoey.

And Brandon too.

And OMG! I almost forgot. Even my DAD!

Anyway, I can't imagine Brandon and me working together on the newspaper.

EVERY. SINGLE. DAY!

SQUEEEE!! Who would have thunk such an awful situation could turn out so . . . GOOD?!

For once, I'm actually looking forward to going to school on Monday.

I can't wait to tell Brandon my plans.

And once I join the newspaper staff, I'll be able to watch MacKenzie like a hawk so she can't stir up trouble.

The only thing that STILL worries me is my writing skills. Because I AM joining a NEWSPAPER.

I mean, this could be as disastrous as signing up for an ice-skating charity event when you don't even know how to ice-skate. DUH!

I remember the time I had to write my secret family recipe for Crispy Squares in our class recipe book back in primary school. The recipe book was a Mother's Day present.

My grandma said that recipe had been in my family

for sixteen generations. Apparently my ancestor, who was a Pilgrim, served it as the official dessert at the very first Thanksgiving feast back in 1621.

So I was more than a little SURPRISED when, a couple of months ago, I was reading the back of a cereal box and found the EXACT SAME RECIPE!!

ME, READING OUR SECRET FAMILY RECIPE ON THE CEREAL BOX

Can you believe that?!

OMG!

Especially after all of that stuff my grandma had said about it being in our family since 1621.

I was SHOCKED and APPALLED that people could actually be so blatantly DISHONEST!

Whatever happened to honesty and integrity?!

I mean, that huge cereal company should be ASHAMED of themselves for STEALING our secret family recipe for Crispy Squares and plastering it all over their cereal boxes like that.

I personally think we should consider taking legal action or something.

However, since my writing skills weren't that good, the secret family recipe I wrote back in second grade was actually ~~a little~~ A LOT different from the one on the cereal box. . . .

Nikki's ~~N̶i̶k̶k̶i̶~~ Crispy Squares

(Secret Family Recipe)

~~ingridintz~~ Ingredients

1. 4 cups Crispy Rice Bits cereal
2. One stick Butter
3. Something else (but I forgot what it was) ☹!

Directions

Place all ingredients in a pan Cook over low heat. Cool and eat.

ENJOY! ☺

THE FAMILY RECIPE I WROTE BACK IN PRIMARY SCHOOL

It was actually kind of embarrassing because I accidentally left out one of the main ingredients from the recipe.

Hey, I was ONLY seven years old!

Although, if it's supposed to be a SECRET recipe, WHY would you BLAB all of the ingredients?

Anyway, my yummy butter-fried Crispy Squares had a lot LESS calories than the ones slathered with those sugary-sweet melted marshmallows.

Hmmm, now that I think about it . . .

Maybe my first article for the WCD school newspaper could be my delicious secret family recipe for Crispy Squares.

NOT!!

☺!!

I can't believe it snowed another eight centimetres today!

I'm just so sick of this snow, and it's only January. I don't know if I can survive two more long, dreary, cold months of winter.

For spring break, MacKenzie and most of the CCPs will be going on holiday somewhere that's warm, sunny and exciting.

But not me! I'll probably be stuck at home helping my mom with SPRING CLEANING ☹!!

I'd give anything to be relaxing on a sunny, warm beach in Hawaii right now. How cool would THAT be?!

So when Mom insisted that I take Brianna outside to let her play in the snow, I grabbed some sunglasses and beach toys and decided to make lemonade out of lemons! Right in our garden . . .

94

95

Suddenly the weather felt so tropical, I almost got a sunburn just standing there admiring our work.

All Brianna and I needed were our swimsuits and a beach towel, and we could have joined in on the fun in the sun, surf and snow.

Am I not BRILLIANT?!

☺!!

Today is the big day! I plan to drop in on Brandon and ask him for help with joining the newspaper staff.

I wore a really cute outfit that my grandma bought me during her last visit. Chloe and Zoey said I looked really smart and professional.

I think they were right, because while I was at my locker putting on lip gloss, MacKenzie stopped by to get lunch money and eyeballed me all evil-like.

I knew she was dying to ask me why I was so dressed up. But I just ignored her.

I definitely wouldn't be surprised if she actually tried to spy on me.

Hey, the little weasel has done it before!

I decided to channel my inner "smart reporter" so I would feel more confident.

A pencil behind the ear for emergency notes and flair? Check.

Shimmery Savvy Girl lip gloss? Check.

Spearmint-fresh breath for interviews? Check.

Notepad for capturing my brilliant thoughts (and awesome doodles)? Check.

Intellectual-looking and slightly uncomfortable pumps? Check.

I was trying my hardest to be a sassy, journalistic girl genius and NOT the slightly illiterate writer I felt like inside.

Finally, I took a deep breath and headed down the hall and into the newspaper office.

I scanned the room for Brandon, and as usual, I recognised his shaggy hair behind one of the computer monitors.

OMG! I suddenly felt very queasy and light-headed. But in a really GOOD way ☺!!

Mostly I was worried that throwing up the strawberry-banana smoothie I had chugged at my locker for lunch would undermine my "smart reporter" image.

"Nikki!" Brandon smiled, waved, and gestured for me to come over. "What's up?"

"Actually, I just decided to sign up for the newspaper. And since the new members meeting is after school today, I thought maybe you could help me find a position and give me some tips. Since you're a SUPERtalented photojournalist and stuff," I said, blushing profusely.

Brandon blinked in surprise. "No way! You're kidding! Right?"

"Hey! I've got a pad of paper and a pen, and I'm NOT afraid to use 'em!" I teased.

BRANDON AND I DISCUSS ME JOINING THE SCHOOL NEWSPAPER!

"Very cool! I'd be happy to help you out, Nikki. I can't wait to read your first article."

"Um . . . thanks!" I plastered a big smile across my face, but inside I was a nervous wreck.

Sure, I'm a scribbling whiz kid when it comes to my diary. But writing boring, serious, newsworthy-type stuff, NOT so much.

I needed to pull off a major miracle or the only thing Brandon was going to get out of any article I wrote was a really good . . . NAP.

Brandon quickly pulled up on his computer a list of the open positions and started reading them aloud.

"Well, let's see. There're six open positions right now. Assistant fashion editor, sports, news . . . Hey, look at this! We need a photo layout artist. YOU'D be perfect for that!"

"OMG!" I squealed. "That means we could spend a lot of time together! Er, I mean, time t-together . . .

you know, w—working on those photo layout, um, thingies. . ." I stammered.

"Now, THAT would be way cool!" Brandon brushed his bangs out of his eyes and gave me a crooked smile.

I just HATED when he did that to me. I had a massive Roller-Coaster Syndrome attack right there in front of him. It was SO embarrassing!

I lost total control and actually screamed,

"WHEEEEEEEEEEEEE!"

But I just said it inside my head so no one else heard it but me.

That's when he kind of stared at me and I stared back at him. Then we both smiled.

And after that I couldn't help but stare at him, and of course he stared back at me. Then we both blushed.

All of this staring, smiling and blushing seemed to go on, like, FOREVER!

BRANDON AND ME, STARING, SMILING
AND BLUSHING

Brandon and I spent the rest of the lunch hour just hanging out and talking.

He even showed me some of his photos he planned to enter into a national competition next month.

And get this! We actually walked to bio together!

I can't wait to tell Chloe and Zoey how well everything went.

Although working on the newspaper is going to be fun, I have to remember to stay focused on the real task.

Shutting down MacKenzie!

Hey! That girl started this war, but I'M going to FINISH it!

I'M THE CHAMP!!

Right now I'm SO frustrated I could just . . .

SCREAM!!

But all I can do is sit here in my geometry class totally lost (as usual), pretending that:

1. I care about irregular quadrilaterals and

2. my life is NOT the vapid waste dump that it IS.

About seven new people showed up for the newspaper meeting. A half dozen staff members came to answer questions and serve as mentors, including Brandon and MacKenzie.

I really liked our journalism intern. Mainly because she was actually SANE (unlike our adviser). She started the meeting by saying, "Hi, everyone. I'd like to welcome our new members and thank you for coming today. My name is Lauren Walsh. I'm a senior at Westchester Country Day High School and a journalism intern. Mr Zimmerman, our adviser, will be here in a few minutes. He requested that I have all the new people sit in the front, so let's do that right now."

MacKenzie huffed and rolled her eyes at the prospect of having to give up her seat to a newbie. "This is SO lame! I'm NOT moving."

That girl is SUCH a drama queen. I was like, "Come on, MacKenzie. Just lose the attitude. Are you THAT attached to your desk? You're acting like you're about to put up matching curtains or something!"

But I just said that inside my head so no one else heard it but me.

Soon a middle-aged man in jeans and a wrinkled blazer shuffled in.

He carried an empty jumbo-size coffee cup, and he had a messenger bag over his shoulder that was so full he left a trail of papers on the floor.

MR ZIMMERMAN

His hair was messy, and the stubble on his face was
so long it was about to grow into a hippie beard.

He took a seat at his cluttered desk and just stared at us in disgust.

It was like we were something unpleasant he wanted to scrape off the bottom of his shoe.

Then he popped a few sweets into his mouth from the Scooby-Doo PEZ dispenser sitting on his desk.

After munching loudly on the sweets for what seemed like forever, he finally spoke, his eyes still glued on the kids in the front row.

"Lauren, WHO are these people?!"

"These are the students interested in joining the newspaper, Mr Zimmerman."

"And why are they sitting there staring at me?"

"Actually, they're seated in the front row, just like you requested," Lauren answered.

"Very interesting," he said drily. "Let me ask you something, boys and girls."

He got up and paced the floor.

"How many of you have NEVER worked for a newspaper before?"

Everyone in the newbie row excitedly raised their hand, including me.

"Okay. Then none of you have experience," he said, lowering his voice to barely a whisper.

The room was so quiet you could hear a pin drop.

"Well, today is your lucky day because I'm going to let you in on a little secret. You're about to experience firsthand how the real world of journalism operates."

We all leaned forward in our seats, straining to hear the pearls of wisdom Zimmerman was about to bestow upon us.

"Listen carefully, boys and girls, because I'm only going to say this once. . ."

YOU'RE FIRED!

Okay! There was no question about it.

Zimmerman was totally INSANE!

The room broke into a panic.

The girl with braces sitting next to me started to cry.

Lauren looked startled.

"Um, sir. . ." She ran to him and whispered something in his ear.

"What do you mean, 'They're only kids'?" Mr Zimmerman snarked.

I couldn't hear what Lauren was saying, but I could tell he didn't like it.

"I can't? Really?"

Lauren shook her head.

"I see." Mr Zimmerman sighed. "I'll need another coffee to get through this."

Lauren scribbled his order in her notebook and rushed out the door.

"Make it black," he called after her. "My wife says I need to cut back on sugar."

Zimmerman popped another PEZ candy and continued pacing.

"Listen up, kids. We have six openings," he said, handing a sign-up sheet to the guy at the end of the row. "I expect you to eat, drink and breathe journalism from this day forward, or you won't survive in this business. MY reputation is on the line here. And I DON'T want it tarnished! Am I making myself clear?!"

Although it was a yes-or-no question, all of us just stared at him blankly.

We weren't that afraid of working for the newspaper.

But we were TERRIFIED of this unshaven LUNATIC rambling about "survival".

When I got the sign-up sheet, I held my breath and peeked at it. I was the fourth person to sign it, and the photo layout artist position was STILL available.

I quickly scribbled in my name next to it.

I had to restrain myself from breaking into my Snoopy "happy dance."

I passed the sheet to the girl with the braces.

"I could tell you some stories about my days with the *Wall Street Journal*," Mr Zimmerman continued. "But I won't. My wife says I need to let that go . . . and so does my therapist. Now, where is that sign-up sheet?" he asked, looking around the room nervously.

"Right here, Mr Zimmerman," MacKenzie said, waving the page in the air. "I have it."

She sashayed to the front of the room and handed it to him.

"Thank you, Miss Hollister. Both your dedication and teamwork are duly noted!"

It was like MacKenzie had totally brainwashed the guy or something.

She smiled and sashayed back to her seat.

I just HATE it when MacKenzie sashays.

Zimmerman quickly read over the list of names.

"Hmm, I see one of you changed your mind about making this serious commitment. Good! I'd much rather you quit now than waste my time."

I tried not to stare at the girl with the braces. She looked like she was about to burst into tears again.

"I have very high expectations for all of you. And just remember, it's a jungle out there!"

Zimmerman called up the newbies one by one and introduced them to the newspaper staff person they would be working with.

I waited anxiously for him to call my name.

I was a little confused when Marcy, the girl with the braces, was assigned to work with MacKenzie as an assistant editor for fashion.

Since she'd been in tears for most of the meeting, I had assumed she was the person who had quit.

"Hi, I'm Marcy, and I just moved here last semester from Boise, Idaho! I can't believe I'm actually going to be working with you, MacKenzie!" Marcy gushed.

"And I can't believe I'm actually going to be working with YOU!" MacKenzie said, scrunching up her nose like she smelled a funky foot odour.

"I'm NOT a fashionista. But I did design and sew an entire wardrobe for my Barbie doll collection." Marcy beamed proudly.

"How quaint! For our first assignment, we're going to tackle an emergency makeover. Fab-N-Flirty Fashions is having a big sale," MacKenzie said as she scribbled madly on her notepad. "Let's meet at the mall immediately after school today."

"OMG! That sounds so exciting! WHO'S getting the makeover?" Marcy asked.

I felt really sorry for that poor girl.

Marcy hadn't quit just yet. But since she was stuck with MacKenzie, it was only a matter of time.

I gave her twenty-four hours. Or less.

I turned my attention back to Mr Zimmerman.

"And last but not least, we're going to pair the photo layout artist position with . . . let's see. . ."

Brandon! Brandon! Brandon! I screamed silently.

"Okay, how about . . . BRANDON."

YES!! I turned around and flashed Brandon a big smile. I could not believe we were actually going to be working together.

"Brandon, you'll be mentoring our new photo layout artist. . ."

ME! I whispered dreamily to myself.

". . . BRITNEY CHUNG," Zimmerman announced.

I felt like I had just been punched in the stomach.

Britney, a CCP girl, scrambled out of her seat and immediately started making goo-goo eyes at Brandon.

There had to be some kind of MISTAKE! I had signed up for PHOTO LAYOUT ARTIST!

And Brandon was supposed to be <u>MY MENTOR</u>!!

I was not at all surprised to see MacKenzie staring at me from across the room with this little smirk on her face. I wanted to walk over and slap it right off her—

OMG! I've been SO distracted writing about that crazy newspaper meeting that I haven't heard a single word my geometry teacher has said. . .

Wait a minute. . . !! Did he just tell us to clear our desks?!!!

Because we're having a POP QUIZ?!!!!!

RIGHT NOW?! NOOOOOOOO!!!

"What makes up an IRREGULAR quadrilateral?"

Um, how about CONSTIPATED quadrangles?!

Heck if I know!

I'm so going to fail this quiz.

Then my parents are going to do something completely crazy and irrational like take away my phone.

Somebody PLEASE help me. . .

☹!!

OMG! That meeting was a disaster!

In just thirty minutes my newspaper adventure had gone from a dream come true to a total nightmare.

"Okay, now that everyone's been assigned a partner, any questions?" Zimmerman asked as the room started to buzz with excitement.

"Uh, Mr Zimmerman. . ."

I tried talking a little louder.

"Excuse me, but I think you forgot m—"

"Just work closely with your mentor. And most important, DON'T SCREW UP MY NEWSPAPER!" he yelled.

In spite of the fact that I was waving my hand frantically, he looked right past me like I was invisible.

Then he started muttering. . .

Then Zimmerman walked to his desk, collapsed in his chair and started munching on sweets again.

Everyone else was busy working. But I just sat there like an idiot with no clue what to do.

OPTION 1:

Go up to Zimmerman and tell him he forgot to assign me a position.

Even though I was afraid he'd lose his temper and munch on my head like one of those sweet thingies for disturbing him.

OPTION 2:

Stay seated, smile mindlessly and fiddle with my pen until the hour was over.

Then find a secluded place and CRY like a BABY!

OPTION 3:

Pull a Zimmerman. Climb on top of my desk and yell at the top of my lungs like a maniac . . .

YOU FORGOT ME!!

However, since I'm actually a very shy person, I was leaning more toward Option 2.

I was trying to blink back tears of frustration when Brandon came over.

He gave me a warm smile.

"Welcome to the wacky world of newspaper! So, how's it going? I take it you decided against the photo layout artist position? I'm sure you'll like being an assistant editor."

"Um, actually, I didn't get an assignment at all. I think Zimmerman forgot me or something." The lump in my throat was so big, I could barely speak.

I guess that's when Brandon finally realised something was wrong.

Because suddenly his smile vanished and he kind of stared at me with this really concerned look on his face.

"I guess I should have warned you about Zimmerman before you signed up. He's not so bad once you get to know him. But sometimes he can be a little. . ."

Brandon made a face and glanced at our teacher to see if he was listening. But Mr Zimmerman was oblivious, busily reloading his Scooby-Doo PEZ dispenser.

". . . well, scatterbrained!"

Brandon's mouth whispered "scatterbrained," but his eyes screamed "PSYCHOPATH!!"

"You should let him know you haven't been assigned anything yet. If you don't feel comfortable, I'll tell him for you. I know he can be a little intimidating. . ."

"BRANDON! BRANDON!" Across the room his partner, Britney, was screaming like her hair was on fire. MacKenzie stood close by, whispering to her.

But Brandon totally ignored her.

"Looks like your mentee is in desperate need of some, um . . . mentoring," I said, rolling my eyes. "Listen, I really appreciate your offer, but I can talk to Zimmerman myself."

The last thing I wanted was for Brandon to ~~know~~ THINK I was a wimp and too scared to go up and talk to the teacher.

I mean, how juvenile would THAT be?! Especially since Brandon and MacKenzie actually liked the guy.

"Well, let me know if I can help out, okay?"

He hesitated for a moment, hoping I would change my mind. Then he shrugged and walked back over to his partner.

After giving myself a ten-minute pep talk, I finally gathered enough courage to approach Zimmerman's desk.

I stood in front of him for what seemed like forever, waiting for him to notice me.

But he just typed away on his laptop without looking up.

I cleared my throat and plastered a fake smile on my face. "HI, THERE!" I croaked. My voice came out way louder than I anticipated.

Mr Zimmerman cringed like I had just shattered a glass, then looked up at me.

"How can I help you, Sparky?" he said sarcastically.

Now that I had his attention, I totally lost my nerve. I opened my mouth but no sound came out.

"WHAT?!" he exclaimed, rolling his eyes. Then he whispered, "So . . . are you trying to communicate with me telepathically?"

That's when I totally panicked. "Um . . . can I go to the toilet?" I blurted out.

"Go ahead." He frowned. "You don't need my permission for that. Now SHOO! I'm very busy!"

"Um, okay, thanks. . ."

As I turned to run from the room, I just barely missed stumbling over the bin.

"Excuse me!" I said.

I don't normally make it a habit to talk to inanimate objects.

But right then I was a nervous wreck!

That's when I noticed the sign-up sheet inside.

And what looked like a crossed-out name.

I peeked at Zimmerman and wondered if he'd have a hissy fit if he saw me rummaging through his trash.

But he had resumed typing and didn't seem to notice I was still standing there.

Finally my curiosity got the best of me. I bent down and grabbed the sign-up sheet. . .

I took one look at it and gasped. Suddenly
everything made sense!

WCD NEWS

SIGN-UP SHEET FOR NEW MEMBERS

POSITION	NAME
ASSISTANT NEWS EDITOR	ALEX WESTLAKE
ASSISTANT FASHION EDITOR	Marcy Simms
ASSISTANT MOVIE REVIEWER	Chase Barrymore
~~PHOTO LAYOUT ARTIST~~	~~Nikki Maxwell~~
ASSISTANT COMICS PANELIST	Brian Lopez
ASSISTANT SPORTS EDITOR	Justin Smith
Photo Layout Artist	Britney Chung

WCD NEWS:
"THE WHEN, WHAT, WHERE AND WHY OF WCD!"

SOMEONE HAD CROSSED MY NAME OFF THE
SIGN-UP SHEET!!

And there was no doubt WHATSOEVER in my mind that the dirty, stinkin' RAT was:

MACKENZIE☹!!

So that's why I wasn't assigned a partner!

All I had to do now was explain to Zimmerman that my name had somehow been "accidentally" crossed out and then ~~ask~~ BEG him for a position.

I'd take just about anything.

Even . . . fashion.

Mostly because I needed to keep an eye on MacKenzie. Really badly!

I smoothed out the sheet and walked back to Zimmerman's desk.

"Um, excuse me, I really hate to bother you again, Mr Zimmerman, but something's wrong—"

"I *TOTALLY* agree with you!" he said, closing his eyes and rubbing his temples.

"You do?" I was starting to think maybe this guy wasn't so bad after all.

"YOU'RE supposed to be in the TOILET. But for some strange reason you're STILL standing here PESTERING me. That's just . . . WRONG!"

"Well, actually, I was on my way to the girls' toilets. But then I saw our sign-up sheet and—"

"Really?! How'd our sign-up sheet get in the girls' toilets?"

"Um, actually, it wasn't IN the—"

"Listen! I'm REALLY busy right now! I suggest you go back to the toilets and just try to ignore that sign-up sheet in there. It probably won't hurt you. Okay!"

"I'm sorry for making all of this is so confusing. But somehow my name got crossed off of the sign-up sheet. Everyone got assigned a position on the newspaper staff except—"

Suddenly Zimmerman's mobile phone rang.

He answered it and held up a finger to shush me.

I could NOT believe that man actually had the nerve to SHUSH me right to my face like that! I was SO mad I wanted to just, um . . . SPIT!!

"Zimmerman here. No, never! I'll go to jail before I reveal my source."

He grabbed the papers off his desk and began stuffing them into his already overflowing bag while yelling into the phone. "And just for the record, I have no idea how my socks got inside that microwave. . . !"

As he hurried away, I anxiously chased after him.

ME, CHASING MR ZIMMERMAN!!

I had finally caught up with him and was just about
to show him the sign-up sheet when . . .

SLAM!

That was the sound of the door he slammed right in my face as he rushed out of the classroom.

I just stood there blinking my eyes with the sign-up sheet dangling in my hand.

I looked around the room for help, but everyone was busily working with their partners on their projects.

Well, everyone except MacKenzie.

I could feel her beady little eyes staring at me from across the room.

But I didn't care anymore!

I'd had quite enough of the newspaper, thank you!

I grabbed my notepad and pen and was about to leave when she sashayed over.

LEAVING SO SOON?

But I didn't say a word. I just walked right past her.

"Well, it looks like YOUR day was a total waste of makeup," she snarled. "TOO BAD!"

I couldn't believe MacKenzie had so coldly and

cruelly crushed all of my hopes and dreams beneath the bloodred sole of her designer shoe.

That girl is beyond RUTHLESS!

First she UNDERMINED my WCD scholarship by convincing HER dad to offer MY dad a job at Hollister Holdings, Inc.

And now she's UNDERMINED my plan for getting on the school newspaper by crossing my name off the sign-up sheet.

What am I going to do now?!

My life is HOPELESS!!

☹!!

All day I've been depressed and feeling like a complete and utter FAILURE.

After that mental BEATDOWN by MacKenzie during the newspaper meeting, my self-esteem is pretty much pulverised.

Chloe and Zoey must have sensed I was really down in the dumps.

Because during our library session they kept needling me about WHY I had changed my mind about joining the newspaper staff.

FINALLY I broke down and told them the truth. Well, part of the truth, anyway.

MacKenzie had single-handedly got me kicked out before I'd even had a chance to get in.

And Zimmerman was a certified LOONEY TUNE!

Well, Chloe and Zoey weren't having it. And boy, were those two totally ticked off!

NUH-UH! We're NOT going to just stand by and let our kind, but socially challenged, BFF be picked on and treated like a snivelling pushover by some egotistical, fashion-obsessed diva.

Sorry, girlfriend! But even insecure scaredy-pants with low self-esteem totally deserve to be treated with kindness and respect, Nikki!

I just stared at them in disbelief! I could not believe they had actually said all of that stuff.

OMG! Those were two of the nicest compliments I'd EVER received in my entire LIFE.

I do not deserve friends like Chloe and Zoey.

They're, like, the BEST friends EVER!

They marched me right over to Zimmerman's classroom.

Then they both looked me in the eye and said if I didn't get in there and demand a position on the newspaper, they were going to kick my BUTT.

It was SO funny. Because of course they were joking.

I think.

As I stood outside Zimmerman's door, it was reassuring to know my BFFs had my back and were there gently cheering me on. . .

OMG! I was so nervous I was practically shaking. I felt like I was Dorothy going to visit that scary Wizard of Oz guy or something.

When Zimmerman saw me walk in, he just muttered, "So, I hope you finally made it to the toilets. . ."

"Actually, I didn't. I'm here because you missed me

when you assigned jobs at the last newspaper meeting. Somehow my name got accidentally crossed off the list or something. See, it's right here. . ." I handed him the paper.

"Is that so?" Zimmerman read it over and then glanced up at the board. "Looks like you're right. The only problem is there's no more room for you. I had two additional people join yesterday. And I made them Lauren's assistants. Now maybe she'll be able to get my coffee to me before it gets cold."

"There HAS to be something I can do!" I pleaded. "To be honest, I have this big problem, and the only way I can straighten it out is to get on the newspaper staff. My friends are counting on me and I don't want to let them down. PLEASE!"

"Hey, slow your roll, kiddo! I feel your pain. But I'm really sorry. . ."

Zimmerman popped three sweets into his mouth and munched on them loudly while checking his watch.

I could not believe this guy!

What a cruddy teacher! I had come to him with a problem, and he had the nerve to just sit there and ignore me like I was one of his empty coffee cups. . .

ME, AS ONE OF THE PAPER CUPS LITTERING
MR. ZIMMERMAN'S OFFICE

"Well, thanks for talking to me." I sighed loudly and turned to leave as I blinked back a wave of tears.

Zimmerman suddenly leaned back in his chair, stared into space and scratched his fuzzy chin.

"Hold on! I might have something for you, Sparky. But it's going to be a lot of work. We're going to bring back the WCD advice column. Just for you!"

"Advice column? Just for m—me?" I stammered. My anger melted and was quickly replaced by raging insecurity. I was back to a sniveling rookie. "You mean, I'll be doing this all alone? With no mentor?"

"That's right," he answered. "I have a feeling you have the spunk to pull it off. Either that, or you'll single-handedly destroy the newspaper's reputation and give me a heart attack. But you wouldn't do that to me, would you, Sparky?"

"Well, I dunno. . ." I gulped.

"Of course you wouldn't!"

"I'm not that good at dishing out advice. What if kids don't like my answers? They might get mad at me and say nasty things."

"There's always that possibility. So when you write, you might want to use a pseudonym."

"Um, okay. But I don't think I have one. Is that like a computer?"

Zimmerman chuckled. "Sparky, you remind me a lot of myself when I was just getting started. Not much knowledge, but a lot of heart. Nope, it's not a computer. It's just a pen name."

"Oh, I get it! Pseudonym is a brand of ink pens."

Zimmerman looked annoyed and popped two sweets into his mouth.

"Okay, let's start over. Now, pay close attention, Sparky. 'Pseudonym' is just a fancy word for writing with a phony name. You know, so your readers won't harass you, hunt you down, or send you gross stuff in the mail. You'd NEVER believe the stuff I've got in the mail from disgruntled readers. Of course Lauren and I will keep your identity a secret, and we'll tell the staff you're our new assistant."

"Oh! Now I understand. I'll need to make up a catchy name."

"Exactly! See that bottom drawer of my file cabinet? Your stuff will be under lock and key in a black metal box. Check there tomorrow morning and you'll find everything you need to get started."

"Thanks, Mr Zimmerman. You have no idea how much this means to—"

"Now get out of my classroom. I have something important to do. SpongeBob comes on in two minutes. You know, he's the last Great American Hero." He waved his hand to shoo me away. "Good luck, kiddo."

His Royal KOOKINESS had spoken!

Starting tomorrow, I was going to become the WCD

version of Dr Phil. But with hoop earrings, lip gloss, a few pimples and, most dangerously, no experience WHATSOEVER.

And if I screwed it up, it was gonna be . . .

OFF WITH MY HEAD!

MY HEAD →

I was SO excited, I did my Snoopy "happy dance" all the way back to the library.

Chloe and Zoey are going to be superproud of me.

Am I qualified to give advice to my peers? Of course not! I can't even decide on milk or OJ in the morning.

But when my gut tells me something, it's usually right. So I'll do my very best to help people NOT mess up their lives. Guts, don't fail me now!!

Eww . . . that sounded kinda gross, didn't it?

Anyway, I'm about to make a major comeback!

And not even the evil forces of the DIVA OF DOOM (also known as MacKenzie) can stop me.

☺!!

Today was officially my first day on the job as a staff writer for the WCD newspaper as my advice expert alter ego, Miss Know-It-All.

Mr Zimmerman made an announcement over the school PA system yesterday about the return of the advice column and instructed students to leave their letters to Miss Know-It-All in a special mailbox outside the newspaper room.

I couldn't wait to see how many letters I'd got. For once in my life, I was out of bed BEFORE my alarm clock went off.

I hopped into the shower, brushed my teeth and threw on some clothes. Then I ran to the kitchen to grab a granola bar for breakfast.

"Good morning, dear!" Mom smiled. "Up already?"

"Yep," I said, shoving the granola bar into my mouth. "I'm working on a newspaper project! Mom, do you think you could take me to school extra early?"

When I got to the newspaper room, Lauren was busy reading over both the print and online versions of the school paper before they were released for publication.

All newspaper staff had access to them too, which very conveniently allowed me to monitor MacKenzie's Fashion and Current Events column.

If she tried to publish anything untrue about me or my friends, I'd report her to Zimmerman so fast it would make her head spin.

"Good morning!" I said cheerfully. "I'm ready to get started on my advice column. What does my mail look like?"

"Hi, Nikki! Well, let's check your mailbox," Lauren said as she picked up a metal box right outside the door and set it on her desk.

The box was covered with a thick layer of dust.

"It looks like this thing hasn't been used in years!" she said as she brushed her dusty hands on her pants and unlocked the box with a key.

My heart pounded as I waited to see how many letters I'd got – ten, twenty, maybe even fifty. But it dropped when I saw what students had left for me in the box. . .

"OMG!" I gasped as I stared in disbelief at a broken pencil, a sweet wrapper, a wad of gum and a used tissue.

"Gross! Some kids are SO immature!" I fumed, trying to pretend I wasn't as disappointed as I felt. "This is NOT a rubbish bin!"

"I'm sorry," Lauren said. "But our reader feedback has been almost nonexistent. We're hoping your column will change things. But it looks like the paper is going to take some time to catch on."

I didn't want to say it, but I was worried our paper would never "catch on". Other than Brandon's amazing photographs, the articles were dullsville.

The one time I did read an issue, there was a page-long interview with the lunch lady on nutrition. Yawn!

First of all, how exciting could her interview be? Second, what would she know about nutrition, serving us imitation ham on a mouldy roll?

After Lauren left the room, I collapsed in a chair and blinked back my tears. I felt as worthless as that rubbish in my advice box ☹!

I decided to update Chloe and Zoey by text: "Bad news!! My Miss Know-It-All advice column was a total FLOP! No letters, just rubbish!"

I got the exact same text from both of them: "☹!"

I sighed and tried to swallow the huge lump in my throat.

At some point I was going to have to tell them the truth.

MacKenzie was going to make sure we were suspended from school for the Great Toilet Paper Caper and for egging her house unless WE convinced Brandon to invite MacKenzie and Jessica to his party.

Who would have guessed that MacKenzie's diverse talents include a keen fashion sense, pathological lying and blackmailing?

That girl was basically a middle school mafioso in lip gloss and hoop earrings.

It was quite obvious she really, really liked attending parties.

That's when I got a text from Chloe to Zoey and me: "Just finished COOLEST book ever. Shy girl decides to run for student council president and her opponent/crush becomes her campaign manager."

I knew Chloe LOVED to read, but I was in the middle of a MAJOR life crisis! For once, couldn't she just try focusing on ME instead of her stupid book characters?!

Then Chloe sent us both a third text: "Snarfing down breakfast. Zoey, call me right NOW! Nikki, meet us in the library in fifteen minutes!"

Just GREAT ☹!

Like I wanted to start off my disastrous morning sitting in the library listening to Chloe gush over yet another of her teen romance novels.

I was already in the library sulking and having a pity party for myself when Zoey arrived loaded down with empty shoe boxes and poster paper.

Chloe was not far behind, lugging a big bag stuffed with scissors, glue, paper, paint and glitter.

"What's g-going on?" I sniffed sadly.

"We're here to save our FAVE advice columnist, Miss Know-It-All. . ." Chloe explained excitedly, and gave me jazz hands.

"We came up with the idea of putting up posters with supercute help boxes all around the school," Zoey said. "So . . . what do you think?"

"I THINK . . . you guys are AWESOME!" I squealed.

Then I watched in amazement as my BFFs worked their magic with glitter and glue. . .

Thanks to Chloe and Zoey, I now have four
fabulously cool posters with help boxes AND a
catchy new slogan.

Luckily, we managed to get everything done and posted in the hallways just before students started to arrive for class. . .

One thing is for certain, Chloe and Zoey's chic marketing campaign for Miss Know-It-All really created a buzz.

By lunchtime, the ENTIRE school was gossiping about it.

And since the identity of Miss Know-It-All is a big secret, everyone was trying to guess who she was.

Not a single person would EVER suspect it was ME!

I just hope I start getting letters really soon.

Because if Mr Zimmerman cancels the advice column again due to lack of interest, I won't be able to stop MacKenzie from printing her pack of lies in the school newspaper, and we could all end up KICKED OUT OF SCHOOL!

!!

ARGH!!

I feel just like I'm back in Madame Fufu's beginning dance class again!

WHY?!

Because Brianna's dance school is having its annual fund-raiser to pay for all of those frilly little dance costumes they wear for recitals.

Each student has to sell sixty chocolate bars.

At first I felt kind of sorry for her.

Until my parents told me I had to go door-to-door in our neighbourhood to help Brianna and keep an eye on her. Now I feel sorry for ME!

"Hey! Why do I have to sell chocolate?" I grumped. "I don't need a frilly little dance costume!"

ME, WEARING A FRILLY BALLET COSTUME
THAT I *DON'T NEED* FOR A CLASS I'M *NOT IN*

But I guess they didn't understand my logic.

"What's a fundraiser?" Brianna asked as we trudged
through the snow in our driveway.

"It's what we're doing right now," I muttered.

I was exhausted, and I hadn't even made it out of our front garden yet.

Those two bags of chocolate bars seemed to weigh fifty kilograms each.

I started to wonder if each bar was actually filled with a nutty caramel centre or CEMENT.

"I don't get it!" Brianna said.

I sighed. "A fundraiser is when you sell stuff to get money for something important."

"We're going to get MONEY for these chocolate bars?!" Brianna exclaimed. "Goody gumdrops! I'm gonna use my money to buy me a baby unicorn!"

"No! You DON'T get to keep it. You have to give it to your dance school.

"That's not fair! Why should I sell stuff if I can't keep the money?" Brianna complained.

"Just . . . because! You're asking too many questions. Let's walk over to the next street so no one I know will see us – I mean, so we can cover more ground."

I rang the doorbell of the first house on the street.

"Just let me do the talking, okay, Brianna?"

"But they're MY chocolate bars!" she shot back. "You're NOT the boss of me!"

"You'll only mess things up! Just keep quiet so we can sell this junk to some unsuspecting fools and go home!" I yelled at her.

"Uh . . . can I help you?"

Brianna and I both jumped. A man was standing at the door in exercise gear that was way too tight around his stomach.

We hadn't noticed him there while we were fighting.
He had an irritated frown on his face.

"Oh, sorry!" I cleared my throat. "Actually, we're here to see if you would be interested in buying a delicious gourmet chocolate bar to support fine arts for children. It's only three dollars."

"Only three dollars?" The man laughed sarcastically. "You must think I'M some unsuspecting FOOL! No thanks. Besides, I'm on a strict diet . . . unless you're selling dark chocolate. . ."

"Actually, we are!" I said as I smiled and held up two bars. "Would you like the one with nuts or the one without nu—"

That's when Brianna rudely interrupted my sales pitch.

"WOW!! YOUR BELLY JIGGLES JUST LIKE SANTA CLAUS! ARE YOU GUYS RELATED?" she blurted out.

The man glared at us and turned bright red.

Then he said some not-so-nice words and slammed the door right in our faces!

"Brianna! Why did you have to open your big mouth?" I scolded. "Look what you did!"

"It was a compliment! Why'd he get so mad?" she asked, scratching her head.

Sometimes I wonder if Brianna is really that naive. Or does she just enjoy aggravating me in the hope that one day I'll burst an artery and drop DEAD so she can get my bedroom and new phone?

"Forget it!" I said, and took a deep breath to calm myself down. "Let's just go to the next house."

We went to another six houses and still no luck. Since it was starting to snow, I decided to call it a day and just go home.

Which was the smart thing to do, considering the fact that my toes and those stupid chocolate bars were pretty much frozen solid and liable to snap into little pieces at the slightest touch.

Since Brianna didn't sell a single chocolate bar yesterday, my mom insisted that we go back out again after we got home from church.

I was like, JUST GREAT ☹!!

When we got to the first house, I rang the doorbell.

"Keep quiet. Got it?!" I whispered to Brianna.

She nodded and pretended to zip her mouth closed.

The door slowly opened, and a skinny old lady with no teeth stood there scowling at us.

At least, I thought it was a scowl.

But I really couldn't tell because her mouth looked all sunken in, like she had just sucked on a lemon or something. . .

"Um, good afternoon, ma'am," I began awkwardly. "We were wondering if you would like to support fine arts for children by purchasing a chocolate—"

"SIC 'EM, TATER TOT!"

the woman yelled at the top of her lungs.

Brianna and I looked behind her, expecting to see a

giant Doberman with one of those collars with spikes on it.

Instead, a fat white cat with a pink bow poked its head out and glared at us.

MEEEOOOWWW!!!...

Then Tater Tot hissed, snarled and charged.

Brianna and I turned around and ran for our lives, screaming.

YOWL!!

AAAHH!

AAAHH!

← BRIANNA AND I RUN FOR OUR LIVES!

That cat probably chased us down the entire street. Although I wasn't exactly sure because I didn't dare look behind me.

Hey! Chubby cats are no joke! Especially when they're angry!

If you'd seen that crazy look in Tater Tot's eyes, you would have run for your life TOO!

Finally Brianna and I collapsed on a snowbank and lay there, trying to catch our breath.

"I don't . . . wanna . . . do this . . . anymore!" Brianna panted.

"Me . . . neither!" I huffed in response.

"Excuse me," said a voice from the pavement.

My body was paralysed with exhaustion, so I just lifted my head. A confused-looking bus driver stood above us, fiddling with her GPS.

"Sorry to trouble you, but I can't get this darn GPS to work! Can you tell me where the nearest petrol station is?" she asked.

"Sure," I answered, forcing my tired lips to move. "Just go down this street about a mile. It will be on the corner on the right."

Then I lifted my weary arm and pointed north.

"Thanks a million, hon." Suddenly the bus driver's eyes lit up. "Hey! Are those chocolate bars?"

"Um . . . yeah," I answered.

"Can I buy one from you? I'm starving!"

"You actually wanna buy one of these?" I asked, surprised. "Okay! We have an assortment of—"

"Hey, lady!" Brianna interrupted. "My sister says we're only supposed to be selling these to unsuspecting fools. But you kind of look like one to me. . ."

The bus driver lady gave us $3.00 and Brianna
grabbed a chocolate bar and handed it to her.

BRIANNA AND I FINALLY SELL A
STUPID CHOCOLATE BAR!

She tore off the wrapper and took a big bite.

"Wow! This is really good!" she exclaimed.

"I need to get rid of all of these guys! Do you want to buy fifty-nine more?" Brianna asked hopefully.

"I don't think so, sweetheart," the lady chuckled. "But I've got a good idea. Why don't you offer them to the passengers on my bus? They're on their way to the Westchester Hills weight-loss camp."

"Really?! Are you sure that won't be too much trouble?" I asked.

"Hey! They've been snacking on carrots, celery and water for the past three hours and could probably use some real food. Assuming, of course, they haven't morphed into rabbits and hopped off my bus by now!" She laughed and winked at us.

Brianna and I grinned from ear to ear. We were starting to think that maybe we'd hit the jackpot!

"Okay!" we said, and grabbed our bags of chocolate.

OMG! It was a CHOCOLATE MASSACRE on that bus!

People were screaming and waving money in the air
as they climbed over each other to get to us.

Then they bought two or three bars each and gobbled them up like they hadn't had a crumb of food in days.

We sold Brianna's entire two bags in less than five minutes. I was SO relieved that chocolate fiasco was FINALLY over.

On our way home, Brianna and I started thinking. Maybe we could go into business together and get rich selling chocolate bars at weight-loss camps.

I'd use my money for WCD tuition, and Brianna said she'd buy a baby unicorn.

I seriously thought about telling her that unicorns don't exist. But then I decided, NAH!!

After we make our first million, I'll probably just pay for a really good therapist for her. I'm just sayin'!

!!

Today in gym class we started practising for the President's Challenge physical fitness test, which is given each spring.

To make sure students had adequate time to train, our gym teacher gave us a handout back in the autumn with the names of the four exercises we were going to be tested on: curl-ups, push-ups, pull-ups and crunches.

My health and fitness are VERY important to me. So I've been doing these exercises at home every day to try to stay in shape.

Unfortunately, I just found out today I was doing ALL of them totally WRONG ☹!!

I'm SO disgusted! This is all my teacher's fault. She should have provided specific instructions on HOW to DO these exercises.

Now I'm really worried that I'm going to completely FAIL the presidential fitness test. . .

EXERCISE #1: CURL-UPS

CORRECT WAY →

Tones and strengthens
abdominal and back muscles.

Difficulty level: HARD

GROAN

← INCORRECT WAY

My CURL-UPS make my
hair curly and bouncy.
They are easy to do with
exercise equipment like a
curling iron. After fifteen
minutes of these, you'll look
superCUTE!

Difficulty level: EASY

EXERCISE #2: PUSH-UPS

← CORRECT WAY
Strengthens shoulder, arm, abdominal and leg muscles.

Difficulty level: VERY HARD

GRUNT

INCORRECT WAY →
My PUSH-UP ice-cream cup is good exercise for my tongue, lips and chin. The best part is that it tastes really yummy.

Difficulty level: VERY EASY

EXERCISE #3: PULL-UPS

CORRECT WAY →
Strengthens and tones arm
and back muscles.

Difficulty level:
NEXT TO IMPOSSIBLE

UGH

← INCORRECT WAY
My PULL-UPS are great
for socks, pants, tights, gym
shorts and anything else that
has a tendency to fall down
around your ankles. It exercises
fingers and improves balance.

Difficulty level: EASY

EXERCISE #4: CRUNCHES

CORRECT WAY →

Tones and strengthens back, arm and abdominal muscles.

Difficulty level: HARD

MOAN

CRUNCH

← INCORRECT WAY

My CRUNCHES are fun and easy to do. I just bite down really hard on a yummy, crunchy snack like crisps, nachos, pretzels, or apples, then chew. This exercises my jaw muscles and teeth.

Difficulty level: EASY PEASY

See what I mean?! I've wasted a lot of time and energy doing the WRONG exercises.

I'm thinking about filing a petition with the school board, requesting that students be given the choice to do either version.

At least MY exercises aren't superHARD and they DON'T make you all sore, sweaty and smelly like the ones from that presidential fitness program.

Anyway, while I was in the locker room getting dressed after gym, I was really looking forward to checking my new help boxes after school today.

UNTIL I overheard MacKenzie and a few of the CCPs saying the advice column idea is SO LAME and that only a TOTAL LOSER would write in to Miss Know-It-All.

Now I'm SUPERworried they might be right.

Because between classes I couldn't help but notice everyone walking right past my help boxes, ignoring them.

To make matters worse, I'm in a really GRUMPY mood and in extreme PAIN from doing all of those really difficult exercises the CORRECT way.

I'm so stressed out that I decided to wait and check my help boxes tomorrow. Even though I already know they're probably going to be EMPTY.

Oh! I almost forgot! I got even MORE bad news when I got home from school.

It looks to me like my dad has decided to work full-time for Hollister Holdings, Inc.!

Earlier today, he actually put his work van up for sale at a used car dealership.

I can't BELIEVE he just dumped Max the Roach at some used car lot!

That's just . . . . COLD!

At least Dad could have let us all say our goodbyes to him so we could have closure!

GOODBYE, MAX THE ROACH. WE'RE REALLY GOING TO MISS YOU!

And I'm pretty sure Max is going to miss us, too! I bet he'll be really lonely at that big used car lot.

Especially with all of those total strangers very rudely GAWKING at him all day long. . .

TOTAL STRANGERS RUDELY GAWKING AT
MAX THE ROACH!

POOR MAX!! He's going to need some serious therapy when he gets older.

OMG! I just had the most horrifying thought!

What if AFTER MacKenzie's dad hired my dad full-time, she made him FIRE MY dad!!

Then not only would I lose my WCD scholarship, but my entire family could end up HOMELESS!

SORRY!! But I've got a really, really, really, really BAD feeling about Dad working for Hollister Holdings, Inc.

☹!!

All day I've been SUPERdepressed.

I'm absolutely DREADING having to check the Miss Know-It-All help boxes.

I'm sure Lauren has already told Mr Zimmerman that the ONLY thing students were leaving for me was rubbish.

My column is probably in danger of being cancelled, and I haven't even answered my first letter yet.

Anyway, by lunchtime I felt like crying AGAIN.

But I didn't because I knew everyone in the cafeteria was just going to stare and whisper.

Unfortunately, I couldn't avoid the inevitable.

So instead of going to the library to shelve books, I decided to hide out in the janitor's closet until all the students were in class and the halls were completely empty.

My heart was pounding as I took a deep breath and stared at the rainbow help box in the hall near my locker.

Then I slowly removed the top, and . . .

There were two letters inside ☺!!

OMG! I was SO relieved.

Then I raced down the hall to check the striped box right outside the cafeteria.

There was a letter in there, too!

And there was one letter in the smiley-face box near the drinking fountain and — get this — TWO letters in the metal box outside the newspaper room.

I couldn't believe it!

Chloe and Zoey's very chic marketing strategy had actually worked.

Miss Know-It-All had got a total of SIX letters requesting advice!

I was so happy I did my Snoopy "happy dance" right there in front of the girls' toliets.

Because those letters were MINE!

ALL MINE!!

Then, like the big dork that I am, I actually gave
them all a very big HUG. . .

ME, LOVING MY LETTERS!

Miss Know-It-All is officially in BUSINESS.

And MacKenzie had better watch her back ☺!!

I stayed after school to work on my first batch of
Miss Know-It-All letters.

Dear Miss Know-It-All,

I don't normally do this sort of thing, 'cause I'll totally get called out for it. But here goes nothing. . .

I'm a popular guy and a star athlete and my girlfriend is a cute cheerleader. We have been together for two weeks. My life is pretty sweet, except that I keep my favourite hobby a huge secret from people because I am super embarrassed about it.

The truth is, I love to bake. After a gruelling day of football I like to just chill out and make red velvet cupcakes. One day my girlfriend almost caught me red-handed, but I lied and said my mom made them.

She said the cupcakes were the best she'd ever had. I want to tell her the truth, but I'm afraid she'll laugh and break up with me. What should I do?

—Cupcake Man

I suddenly remembered how shocked I was to find a cupcake cookbook in the boys' locker room when I was searching for my lost diary. The cookbook belonged to the football team captain, Brady Grayson.

"I can't believe he wrote this," I laughed to myself.
"How adorable!"

Dear Cupcake Man,

I say you should own your mad cupcake skills, don't hide them! There's nothing a girl wants more than a guy who's in touch with his sensitive side. Good for you!

You should bake more red velvet cupcakes for your girlfriend, since she likes them. But present them to her in a way that will knock her off her feet. You will so NOT get dumped if you tell her your secret with charm and humour. I promise. ☺

Best of luck,
MISS KNOW-IT-ALL

I was pretty happy with my answer. I just wished I could've got my hands on some of those yummy cupcakes.

195

The next letter was possibly a prank, but I
answered it anyway.

Dear Miss Know-It-All,

Help me out with this one!

"The railroad track between Town A and
Town B is 500 miles long. The blue train
is scheduled to leave Town A for Town B at
2 p.m. The red train is scheduled to leave
Town B for Town A at 3 p.m., but is delayed
95 minutes due to an engine problem. If the
blue train travels at 35 mph and the red train
travels at 50 mph, when will they meet?"

I hate maths word problems. Do you think you
could write down the answer on a sheet of
notebook paper for me and stick it in locker
number 108 before Friday? Thanks!

—Slacker Superstar

P.S. Make sure you show your work!

A few of my brain cells died just reading that letter!

I figured Slacker Superstar would get a higher score on his/her homework turning in a paper with Brianna's drawing of a giraffe than with MY help.

But I wrote my answer down on paper and stuck it in locker 108 as instructed.

Dear Slacker Superstar,

It took me a while, but I finally solved your very complicated math problem.

Here is the answer:

DO YOUR OWN HOMEWORK! And if you need help, try getting a maths tutor.

Best of luck,
MISS KNOW-IT-ALL

P.S. Please make sure you show YOUR work!

This next letter could have been written by me.

I guess I'm NOT the only older sister with a bratty little sister or brother who drives her totally nuts!

Dear Miss Know-It-All,

I have a little brother who drives me absolutely CRAZY! He's always getting into my stuff, embarrassing me in public and reading my diary. But that's not the worst of it.

Whenever I'm forced to babysit him, something gets shattered into tiny pieces, eaten (including my homework), or burns to the ground.

My parents always chew me out and tell me I need to take charge as his babysitter, but he won't do anything I tell him.

How do I keep my sanity and control a wild six-year-old?

—Big Sister Blues

Dear Big Sister Blues,

You have my deepest sympathy! I know how you feel because I have a sister just like that at home. All I can suggest is taking two paracetamol before babysitting and keeping the fire department on speed dial.

To be honest, I really don't know how to deal with younger siblings either. You don't need Miss Know-It-All's help! You need an animal trainer! And when you find one who doesn't run away screaming, would you do me a huge favour and give me his number?

Thanks,
MISS KNOW-IT-ALL

This next letter was a very deep and complex question most students ponder at some point in their lives. But it will forever remain unanswered. . .

Dear Miss Know-It-All,

What's in the meat loaf in the school cafeteria?

—Just Curious

Dear Just Curious,

Have you ever wondered why that month-old piece of meat loaf lying next to the bins outside has never turned green? Ever asked yourself where all the chemicals go after you do lab experiments in science class? I'm just sayin'! Not trying to put any of our lovely cafeteria staff on blast, but that meat is probably injected with more preservatives than Madonna's face! But let's look at the positive side. If you eat it, you probably won't look a day over thirteen years old when you graduate from college.

Bon appetit,
MISS KNOW-IT-ALL

Dear Miss Know-It-All,

Do girls really dig a guy who wears Buff Body cologne?

'Cause the commercial says supermodels will fall in love with you if you buy it, and that would totally rock!

—Desperate Dude

Dear Desperate Dude,

I'm just shakin' my head at this one. Commercials for boys are, by far, full of the most baloney I've ever seen. Those people are just taking you for a ride, Dude. If you had to choose between wearing Buff Body cologne or bug spray, PLEASE drench yourself in the bug spray! Buff Body reeks! Period.

Don't waste your money! Girls will be happy if you just shower every day. Besides, we tend to fall in love with our hearts, not our noses. It's just that simple.

Your friend,
MISS KNOW-IT-ALL

Dear Miss Know-It-All,

I'm crushing on my Hollywood idol, and some people think I'm obsessed. Who isn't crazy about him? He's only perfect, amazing, talented and SUPERcute!! I have all of his music and movies, millions of posters and every piece of fangirl merchandise out there. I'm president of his official fan club, so nobody knows him better than I do. And nobody's more perfect for him than I am!

My friends don't understand me either. At school, there's a guy named Alex who, I guess, kind of likes me. But I'm not interested because there's only one boy for me. My friends tell me I'm nuts for rejecting Alex, and that I need to get in touch with reality. But I just know that my dream guy and I are meant to be! Is it so wrong to be in love??

—Starstruck

Wow! Starstruck actually seemed to be really, really, um . . . starstruck! But who hasn't been in love with that supercute guy on the cover of your fave CD or starring in your fave teen sitcom? I decided to tell her the truth very gently.

Dear Starstruck,

There's nothing wrong with being in love, but sometimes people can mistake infatuation for love. You may think you know your idol because you've read about him. But you don't "know him", know him. Know what I mean? Sure, any girl would give her right arm to date him! But all they see is his celebrity image, not the real him. BTW . . . isn't he going steady with that cute Disney actress?! I don't think you need to give up being a fan, but why not crush on that nice guy in your maths class who makes you laugh? Love has a way of showing up where you least expect it!

Your friend,
MISS KNOW-IT-ALL

I can hardly believe that when the next newspaper comes out tomorrow, I will kinda, sorta be a published writer!

Wow! Mom is going to be so proud that she'll put my first column on the refrigerator next to one of Brianna's crazy drawings.

Hey, I'm just getting warmed up with this advice stuff.

But THIS is the totally mind-blowing part. . .

On my way out of the building, I checked all of my help boxes, and I'D GOT FOURTEEN MORE LETTERS!

SQUEEE!! Can you believe THAT?!!

So I'm going to wrap up this diary entry and get busy saving the world.

Miss Know-It-All's work is NEVER done!

☺!!

"Dear Miss Know-It-All."

I read the bold print at the top of my column over and over again. It felt like I was looking at an official article written by an official writer, who wasn't me. But it WAS me!

In the cafeteria, EVERYONE had their newspapers out, and they were reading my advice column on page 2.

"Have you seen 'Miss Know-It-All'?" Alexis, a cheerleader, asked her friend Samantha.

"I'm looking at it right now," she answered.

"Someone on our squad is dating a total sweetheart who loves to BAKE!" Alexis gushed. "How romantic is THAT?! And Miss Know-It-All gave him great advice! I SO envy his girlfriend!"

I just stood there in shock, listening to all of the chatter with a freakishly huge grin on my face.

ME

ME, SHOCKED AND SURPRISED THAT
EVERYONE IS READING MISS KNOW-IT-ALL

But I couldn't just stand there basking in my
success. I had work to do.

Out of my twenty-one new letters, this one caught my eye:

Dear Miss Know-It-All,

I'm a well-liked teacher who has been with WCD for over fifteen years. I would say I'm a fairly easy person to get along with. But for whatever reason, another teacher has it in for me! Sometimes I come to class and my whiteboard erasers are missing. This forces me to use my hand or sleeve to erase the board, and by the end of the day, I'm a rainbow-coloured mess. Then, in the hall, I hear other teachers snickering at me, which is humiliating.

To make matters worse, this crook also steals my lunch from the teachers' lounge. I can't teach on an empty stomach! But it's either that or buy food from the cafeteria, and that's not happening. Do you know what they put in that stuff??

Anyway, I need your help. How do I find out who is doing this to me and get the respect I deserve?

—Taunted Teacher

You learn something new every day! I had no idea that teachers had a pecking order just like kids. But whoever that person was, my heart went out to him/her. I was eager to help my elder dork outsmart this overgrown bully.

Dear Taunted Teacher,

Sheesh! Anyone who'd resort to stealing sandwiches from fellow teachers needs to get a life! And most importantly, a loaf of bread, some mayo and ham.

I know a thing or two about bullying, and it stinks. But you have to fight brawn with brain. Wouldn't it be funny if a certain someone packed a "special" lunch of baked beans, prune juice and bran, so when a certain thief ate a stolen lunch, a certain surprise would make their crime obvious? The good news is that the culprit would NEVER mess with you again. The bad news is that you'd NEVER be able to use the toilet in the teachers' lounge again either! Consider it a minor casualty of war. I'm rooting for you!

Your friend,
MISS KNOW-IT-ALL

I was really anxious to see how that situation worked out. If any of the teachers were replaced by a substitute in the middle of the day, I'd know they were suffering from "the chocolate pudding of wrath". (Wink, wink!)

Normally, I would never promote revenge. And yes, I SO regret the Great Toilet Paper Caper. Everyone knows I'm basically a peaceful, fun-loving, Disney-watching hippie!

But if someone stole food out of my mouth, I'd be taking OFF my earrings and putting ON my boxing gloves. I'm just sayin'!

Anyway, as lunch was ending, I noticed a huge commotion in the hallway. The cheerleaders were crowded around a locker, and I could see Brady Grayson with a coy smile on his face.

"Brady! OMG!" squealed a cheerleader in pigtails.

I buried my face in my maths book like I was totally engaged in it (yeah, right!) so I could get closer and sneak a peek at what was going on.

Brady had decorated his girlfriend's locker with red wrapping paper and ribbon to make it look like a giant gift. And when she opened it, everyone gasped, including ME. . .

Brady had followed Miss Know—It—All's advice, and her locker was filled with red roses and red velvet cupcakes. He'd even spelled out "You're Special!" with alphabet magnets.

"I have a confession to make." Brady blushed. "I made those cupcakes you like, not my mom. I love baking, and I hope that doesn't change anything between us."

"Oh, Brady! Don't be silly!" she gushed as she gave him a big bear hug.

There wasn't a dry eye in the crowd. I could barely keep myself together. I buried my face deeper in my maths book so no one could see where those crazy—sounding sniffle-hiccups were coming from.

I was so proud of myself, and Brady, too. With a little sound advice, Prince CHUMP had become Prince CHARMING!

And at that moment just a teeny-tiny part of me was SUPERenvious of Brady's girlfriend. But not for long, because Miss Know-It-All's advice blew up in my face! Later that day I received a letter that sounded like it was written by his girlfriend.

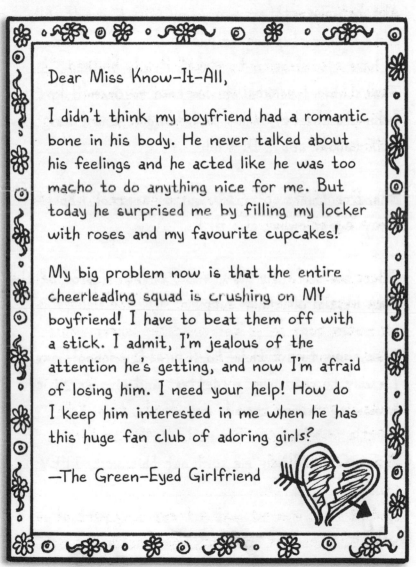

Dear Miss Know-It-All,

I didn't think my boyfriend had a romantic bone in his body. He never talked about his feelings and he acted like he was too macho to do anything nice for me. But today he surprised me by filling my locker with roses and my favourite cupcakes!

My big problem now is that the entire cheerleading squad is crushing on MY boyfriend! I have to beat them off with a stick. I admit, I'm jealous of the attention he's getting, and now I'm afraid of losing him. I need your help! How do I keep him interested in me when he has this huge fan club of adoring girls?

—The Green-Eyed Girlfriend

I was like, Just great ☹! My advice about the Brady cupcake thing had totally BACKFIRED!

And to make matters worse, my Miss Know-It-All letters were starting to pile up.

That's when I decided it was time to consult my favourite experts on human behaviour. And I was NOT talking about Dr Phil.

Whenever things got really out of control, I could always count on my two BFFs. . .

Chloe, the self-help guru, and Zoey, professor of chick lit and all things sappy!

I was going to ask them to stay after school next Tuesday to read over my letters and give me advice on how to answer them.

If anyone could help me sort out this mess, THEY could!

!!

Dear Miss Know-It-All,

I am thirteen and originally from Boise, Idaho. I just transferred to this school last term, and I already hate it. My experience with the people here so far has been terrible. On my first day, at lunch I sat at a table of girls who seemed to be fun and outgoing. I thought maybe they wouldn't mind me sitting with them. But boy, was I wrong!

When I introduced myself, everyone got quiet and just stared at me. I felt really awkward! Then I went to get some napkins, and when I returned, everyone was snickering. That's when I discovered my lunch was missing. It had been tossed in the rubbish along with my backpack!

I want to go back to my old school in Idaho or just not go to school at all! What did I do to deserve this?

—Missing Idaho

Had I been anyone else, this letter would have been challenging to answer. But no one was more qualified to give advice to a troubled and traumatised newbie than me. I knew exactly what to say.

Dear Missing Idaho,

I know being new isn't all sunshine and rainbows. I understand how you feel, because I've been through that experience before, myself. But don't judge everyone so quickly. Not everyone is a mindless clone, and you'll find there are kids who have attended WCD for years who also feel like they don't fit in. Only, these people may not stand out as much because they're quieter and more mature than the loudmouthed, attention-starved "popular" crowd. Hang in there! When I felt like giving up, I finally met my friends. And know that the snots who trashed your lunch are way more insecure than you. Be sure to talk to your parents or a teacher about what happened. And just remember, things will get better!

Your friend,
MISS KNOW-IT-ALL

I wanted to tell her all of my horrific tales about being tortured by the CCP girls and their goblin queen, MacKenzie.

But my letter would be so long, it would end up looking more like a book.

No! It would be a book SERIES!

I hoped my words would give Missing Idaho a little bit of motivation to hang in there and give WCD a chance.

I had a hunch who might have written that letter.

And I planned to keep an eye out for her and invite her to hang out with Chloe, Zoey and me during lunch next week.

!!

<u>OMG! OMG! OMG!</u>

<u>I just got a letter that's pretty much freaking me out! I think I know who wrote it. . .</u>

Dear Miss Know-It-All,

I met a girl last September and we immediately hit it off. She's cool, smart, funny and a talented artist. I'm beginning to think we could be good friends or maybe even more. But I'm really bad at expressing myself. And whenever I try to tell her how I feel, I panic and just end up staring at her like an idiot.

My biggest fear is how she'll react because I'm not really sure if she likes me back. I'm also worried she'll find out that I don't come from a wealthy family like all the other kids at this school. I haven't told anyone about that because I'm afraid they'll treat me differently.

Should I be honest with her and risk being rejected or keep everything to myself so we can stay friends?

—Shy Guy

What if Brandon wrote this about ME?! SQUEE!!

OMG!! I just had the most horrible thought! What if Brandon is writing about MacKenzie?!! Maybe he likes her and NOT ME ☹!

Dear Shy Guy,

PLEASE think things through carefully before you tell your friend you like her. It could be the BEST decision you ever made in your life. Or it could lead to immediate doom and despair! It's safe to say that if she is an awkward–yet–adorable shy girl, you have nothing to fear. You should TOTALLY tell her you like her! She probably definitely likes you too! But if you're crushing on a lip–gloss–addicted CCP with a personality faker than her glue–on eyelashes, I can only say this: DON'T DO IT! She's a mean, selfish SNOB, and you should run away SCREAMING (not that I know her)!

Your friend,
MISS KNOW–IT–ALL

P.S. Gook luck! You're gonna need it!

Okay, I admit my letter was a little biased. But you'll never guess what happened next. Shortly after my advice was published in the newspaper, Brandon actually asked me if I wanted to skip lunch and work on an extra-credit project with him in bio.

And while we worked, we had a serious chat.

BRANDON AND ME, HAVING A REALLY DEEP
CONVERSATION WITH EACH OTHER

He said there was a lot of stuff he wanted to share with me about his background, but he was a little nervous about it.

He said he felt SO comfortable around me because I was honest and truthful and comfortable in my own skin (unlike MacKenzie).

And I didn't pretend to be something that I wasn't because I was very secure. He actually said I was an inspiration to him and that he admired me and considered me one of his best friends at WCD.

OMG! I was SO flattered.

But then I started to panic when I realised he was TOTALLY WRONG about me.

I DON'T possess any of those good qualities.

As a matter of fact, Brandon doesn't really know the REAL me at all.

But it isn't HIS fault.

I am just the BIGGEST PHONEY at WCD. Maybe even bigger than MacKenzie!

After that conversation, I am SUPERworried about our friendship.

I am so NOT who he thinks I am.

But I REALLY, REALLY want to be that girl because he totally deserves to have a friend like her.

I'm just WAY too insecure and afraid he won't like the very dorky person that Nikki Maxwell really is.

Why is my life SO complicated?!

☹!!

Brandon's birthday is next Friday!

I've checked out all the hottest styles in *Copycat Couture* magazine and have selected the supercute outfit I plan to rock at his party.

I even went the extra mile and started gargling with that teeth-whitening mouthwash stuff every day! Even though it tastes like bleach and stings my tongue. *Copycat Couture* says guys are real suckers for that "I've just been to the dentist" look.

I've put a lot of time and energy into preparing for Brandon's big day. But there's one tiny thing I totally forgot about:

His birthday present! DUH! What was I thinking?!

Chloe and Zoey were smart and bought their gifts for Brandon weeks ago. Fortunately, they offered to go with me to the mall today to help me shop.

Unfortunately, Brianna was tagging along. And she was DYING to go to the grand opening of the mall's Kandy Kingdom play area.

"So, where should we start?" Chloe asked as we stared at the mall directory.

"There's a cool gadget store upstairs. Maybe we'll find something there," I suggested.

Chloe, Zoey and I walked toward the escalator, but I only heard two pairs of snow boots scuffling behind me, not three.

I turned around and saw Brianna standing six metres behind us, frowning with her lips poked out.

"Move it, Brianna! You're slowing us down!" I yelled.

"I wanna go to Kandy Kingdom! NOW!" She pouted.

I knew she wasn't going to move from that spot unless I gave in.

"Fine! We'll go, but we can only stay there for fifteen minutes," I said. "Now, where is this place?"

"We gotta take the Gumdrop Express!" Brianna exclaimed, pointing to a kid-size rainbow-coloured train choo-chooing down the hall. The driver was an old guy in a conductor getup.

"Are you kidding me?" I cringed. "There's no way we're riding that! What if someone sees us?"

"But just look at how cute it is!" Chloe squealed. "It'll be fun!"

"Can we ride it? PLEEEAAASE?" Brianna begged.

She and Chloe both made sad puppy eyes at me.

Getting tag—teamed like that was NOT fair!

"All right, already!" I groaned. "Just please stop doing that thing with your eyes! It creeps me out!"

The $90 in my purse was my entire life savings, and that dumb train was $5 per person. Even so, I figured $70 was more than enough for a nice present for Brandon (and ME, too!).

Zoey and I reluctantly squeezed into the back of the small train.

OMG! We were SO embarrassed.

We even covered our faces with our scarves so no one would recognise us.

Meanwhile, Chloe and Brianna sat up front, waving to bystanders and chatting with the conductor the entire ride to Kandy Kingdom.

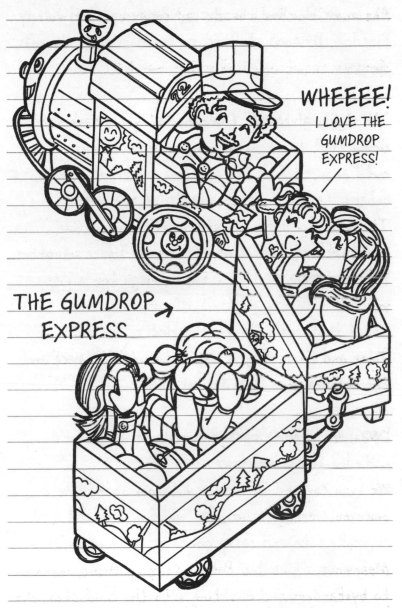

After we finished the train ride and visited Kandy Kingdom, Brianna started to complain that she was hungry.

"I'm starving! I want Queasy Cheesy!" she whined.

I was annoyed, but I've seen her tantrums when she's hungry. They can get really UGLY really fast!

I had to feed the little monster, so I spent another $19, plus a tip.

After that, we went to the electronics store and Chloe and Zoey helped me find an MP3 player and some video games Brandon might like.

I planned to come back for his gift after we'd visited a few more stores.

However, we hadn't got far when we spotted a pair of really cute and sassy boots in the window of a swanky department store.

OMG! They were HOT!

Even though we were supposed to be shopping for Brandon, we figured it wouldn't hurt to go inside to take a closer look.

While my BFFs and I were drooling over those boots, I suddenly discovered that Brianna must have got bored and wandered off or something.

Luckily, I spotted her pigtails in the cosmetics department across the aisle.

Brianna was sitting in a fancy chair in front of a mirror, applying makeup and humming to herself.

"Brianna, WHAT are you doing?!" I scolded. "You shouldn't be playing in that stuff. Besides, you're WAY too young for makeup."

Then she turned away from the mirror, looked at me and smiled.

OMG! I thought my eyes were going to actually rupture and bleed!

That pint-size Glamazon had glittery electric-blue eye shadow all the way up to her eyebrows, way too much blush on her cheeks and purple lipstick smeared around her mouth.

She batted her false eyelashes at me. Which, BTW, were crooked and hanging off her eyelids like skinny caterpillars.

"Don't I look beautiful, DAH-LING?" she purred, and posed like a model.

← BRIANNA'S MAKEOVER

I could think of several words to describe her makeup, but "beautiful" wasn't one of them.

"Sorry, Brianna! But you look like a cross between Miss Piggy and a zombie! Now put those makeup samples back where you found them! And clean your face so you won't scare the other shoppers. Or I'll have to put a bag over your head!"

"Meanie!" she muttered under her breath, and stuck her tongue out at me.

When I saw her shove a tube of lipstick back into its brand-new packaging, I almost had a heart attack.

"OMG! Brianna!" I yelled as I sorted through the small pile of the makeup she'd opened and used. "These AREN'T samples!"

"Um, what are samples?" Brianna asked, blinking mindlessly with her lopsided lashes.

"Don't you understand?!" I cried. "We have to PAY for all of this stuff! Otherwise, you'd be stealing!"

So there went the rest of my money for Brandon's gift!

ME, USING PRETTY MUCH ALL OF MY
CASH TO PAY THE SALESCLERK FOR THE
MAKEUP BRIANNA OPENED

I ended up spending almost ALL of it. I had a
whopping three dollars and ten cents left!

And we had to spend that on makeup-remover tissues to wash the gunk off Brianna's face. Thank goodness Chloe and Zoey were there to help me clean her up. They're the best friends ever.

But now that I'm flat broke, how am I going to buy Brandon a gift?

There's just no way I'm going to show up at his party with no present. That would be SO tacky.

Maybe I should just tell him the truth. I can't attend because I'm suffering from a severe case of BFS, also known as . . . Brianna Fatigue Syndrome!

Why, why, why was I not born an only child?

☹!!

SUNDAY, JANUARY 26

Answering all these Miss Know-It-All letters is starting to get a little exhausting.

So I've been racking my brain trying to come up with a way to get them all done in less than an hour.

I think I've finally come up with the perfect solution. A form letter! Also known as . . .

THE MISS KNOW-IT-ALL
QUICK-PICK ADVICE FORM LETTER

Dear: _____,
(INSERT NAME)

Reading your very
- ☐ sad letter
- ☐ disturbing letter
- ☐ crazy letter
- ☐ freaky letter

was so touching that it actually
- ☐ made me cry like a baby.
- ☐ scared the snot out of me.
- ☐ made me laugh so hard, I cried.
- ☐ made me so sick, I vomited.

I was once in a similar situation when I
- ☐ tried on my grandma's false teeth
- ☐ stepped on a poopy nappy
- ☐ ate an entire box of doggie snacks
- ☐ realised my breath smelled like liver and onions

and seriously thought about just giving up.

I realise that this problem is overwhelming, and you probably feel so
- ☐ nauseous   ☐ angry
- ☐ afraid   ☐ confused

that you want to

- ☐ dye your hair purple.
- ☐ eat a plate of fried worms.
- ☐ mud wrestle a very large pig.
- ☐ shove a hot dog up your nose.

Anyway, after careful thought and consideration about the issue you're having with

- ☐ your crush
- ☐ your parents
- ☐ your best friend
- ☐ your neighbour's dog

I feel the best advice would be for you to

- ☐ run away screaming.
- ☐ join the circus.
- ☐ take a relaxing bubble bath.
- ☐ get a new family.

This should help relieve the

☐ humiliation
☐ desperation
☐ aggravation
☐ constipation

you have been experiencing.

Just remember that no matter how

☐ gloomy
☐ smelly
☐ itchy
☐ rotten

things are right now, it always gets better.

I hope that this advice was helpful.

Your friend,

MISS KNOW-IT-ALL

Okay, I admit it STILL needs a little more work before I start sending it out to students.

But this will definitely save me a lot of time.

Am I not BRILLIANT?!!

ME, USING ALL OF THE TIME I SAVED ON ADVICE LETTERS TO PLAY GAMES ON MY PHONE!!

I had a bad case of indigestion, and it wasn't from those microwavable wing-ding thingies I'd munched on a few hours ago.

I was having second thoughts about this whole newspaper thing.

My advice column requires me to write dozens of essay-length letters to my troubled and tormented peers, giving them sound, unbiased and intelligent advice.

The thought of ME being Miss Know-It-All is still HILARIOUS.

Hey, I'm the last person I'D ever want to take advice from!

I'd been sitting at my desk, staring at the huge pile of letters to Miss Know-It-All for so long my butt was actually numb. . .

ME, SITTING THERE STARING AT MY HUGE
PILE OF LETTERS FOR SO LONG THAT MY
BUTT WAS NUMB

I didn't know where to begin!

"Why is this so hard?" I groaned, and covered my
face with my hands.

I had no idea how I could be SO exhausted from doing nothing. But I was.

That's when I thought I heard a giggle behind me. But when I turned around, no one was there.

All of the stress and lack of sleep was obviously making me delirious.

When I turned back to my laptop, I was a little freaked out to see two scribbled-on eyes, a crooked mouth and a hand all up in my face.

"HI!!! I'm Miss Penelope, and I can't find my snow boots! I think I left them in here!" Brianna said in a high, squeaky voice that could have shattered glass.

"Don't EVER sneak up on me like that!" I snapped. "You almost scared the wing-dings out of me!"

But Brianna and Miss Penelope both just smiled and stared at me like very evil mannequins or something. . .

BRIANNA AND MISS PENELOPE NEARLY
SCARE THE WING-DINGS OUT OF ME!

"Have you completely lost it, Brianna? Miss Penelope
doesn't even have FEET!"

"Does TOO!" she said, and stuck her tongue out at me.

"Just get lost, already! And tell Miss Penelope to STOP leaving her invisible junk in my room!"

I don't think Brianna heard a word I said. Her very short attention span was already diverted to my computer screen.

"Whatcha writing?" she asked.

"Stuff for the school newspaper," I muttered. "Now, why don't you both go outside and play in traffic."

"Ooh! You're a newspaper writer guy?!" Brianna gushed, obviously impressed. "I wanna be one too! Can I write something? Pretty please!"

"Believe me, Brianna, I'd love to give all this work to you, but I don't want to get fired," I said. "Besides, you're just a kid. The only thing you know about a newspaper is where to find the funny pages."

"Nuh-uh! I know lots of stuff about a newspaper!" Brianna said, giving me a dirty look. "If you won't let me write, Miss Penelope and I will make our OWN newspaper!"

"Fine," I said. "You two can do whatever you want. Just stop bugging me so I can try and get my work done."

"You're gonna be sorry! We'll show YOU who the best newspaper writer guy is!" Brianna fumed.

Then she and Miss Penelope stormed out of my room.

Ugh! . . . Did I just make things worse? I wondered. When Brianna is bent on doing something, she usually makes my life miserable until she gets her way.

After another hour of writing (and barely finishing three letters), I went down to the kitchen for another snack.

"Paper! Get your paper here! Hot off the press!" Brianna shouted, walking into the kitchen with Dad's newsboy cap on and a stack of spiral notebook pages under her arm. "Anyone want a newspaper?"

I rolled my eyes. "By 'anyone' you mean me, right?"

"Oh! I didn't see you there, ma'am," Brianna said, staying in character. "Care for a paper? You can keep up with all the latest news and gossip about the Maxwell family. And I'm giving it away to my next customer for absolutely FREE!"

"Okay." I humoured her. "I guess I'll take one of your newspapers if it's free."

"And guess what, Nikki? Me and Miss Penelope's newspaper is A LOT better than YOURS!" Brianna bragged shamelessly.

Then she proudly handed me a copy.

246

I hated to admit it, but Brianna was right. Other than Brandon's excellent photography, most of the WCD newspaper is beyond CRUDDY.

Brianna's little "newspaper" was called the _Some Times_ and was written in crayon.

"Brianna! Don't you mean to call it the Sun–Times, like that famous Chicago newspaper? You spelled it wrong."

"Nuh–uh!" she answered. "It's called the *SOME TIMES*! Because some times it's *GOOD* news! And some times it's *BAD* news!"

Okay. You ask a silly question, you get a silly answer.

Brianna's handwriting was so sloppy! I could barely read the first headline:

PRESIDENT PENELOPE PASSES NEW LAW FOR ICE CREAM BEFORE DINNER!

Yeah, right!

I smirked to myself. Not if Mom has anything to say about it.

I was slightly impressed that Brianna had actually illustrated her lead news story. Very CUTE!!

Then I read the headline on the next page:

BIG HAIRY GRIZZLY BEAR WITH STINKY
BREATH FOUND IN NIKKI'S ROOM!!!

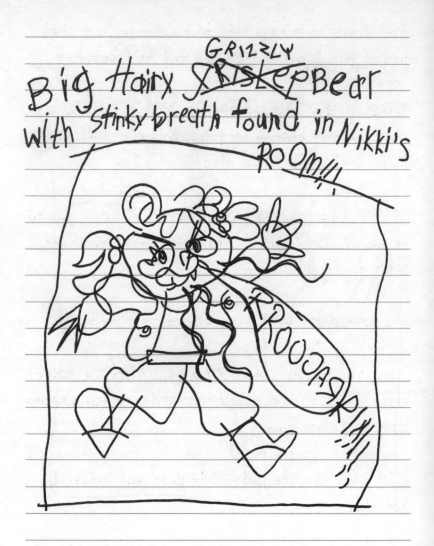

Next to the article, there was a picture of an
angry, cross-eyed bear with jagged teeth and stink
fumes coming out of its mouth.

And it was wearing a light blue warm-up suit that looked just like the one I had on!! NOT so cute!!

"What is this?" I cried angrily. "Why is there a crazy grizzly bear in my room, Brianna? AND WHY IS IT DRESSED LIKE ME?!"

"OOPS! I forgot that was in there," Brianna giggled nervously. "Gee, look at the time! Gotta finish my paper route. BYE!"

She dashed out of the kitchen and up the stairs.

"Hey! You better come back here, or the big, hairy grizzly bear's really gonna get ugly!" I yelled, chasing Brianna to her room.

Lucky for her, she locked her door just before I got there.

I was so mad at that little goofball in barrettes. She was about to experience an episode of *When Animals Attack!* up close and personal!

Brianna's been in her bedroom awhile, so I can only imagine she's up to no good and probably working on the next issue of that tacky piece of rubbish she calls the *Some Times*.

ARGH!! Sometimes I really want to strangle that girl!

But now that I think about it . . .

I wonder if Brianna would be interested in a newspaper job working for the Miss Know-It-All advice column.

NOT!

☹!!

It took me FOREVER to finish all my letters for my advice column.

I was SO happy when I finally posted the final one for editorial review. And as usual, my column created quite a buzz.

But by lunchtime all of the help boxes were running over. AGAIN!

To try and control the overflow of letters in the hallways, the school secretary took a large cardboard box, scrawled the words "Mail for Miss Know-It-All", and set it right outside the office door.

It was mind-blowing. By the end of the day I had a box full of 216 letters.

I was SO happy that Chloe and Zoey agreed to stay after school and help me sort and answer them all. I don't know what I would do without them!

This is us BEFORE answering the letters.

MAIL FOR
MISS KNOW-IT-ALL

This is us AFTER answering the letters.

MAIL FOR
MISS KNO...

But the most exciting news today came from Mr Zimmerman himself.

Just as we were finishing up, Lauren rushed in to tell me that Mr Zimmerman wanted to see me ASAP. Although I was finally starting to get used to him, he still made me SUPERnervous.

I didn't have the slightest idea why he wanted to talk to me. Unless MacKenzie was stirring up some kind of trouble.

Maybe she had finally submitted that article about the Great Toilet Paper Caper with all of those lies about her house being egged.

OMG! What if Mr Zimmerman gives the article to our principal? And the principal calls our parents?!

Chloe, Zoey, Brandon, and I could get kicked out of school ☹!!

My heart started pounding, and I broke into a cold

sweat. I knocked on Zimmerman's door, and he asked me to come in.

"Thanks for stopping by, Nikki. Please have a seat. I must admit, I was really shocked and surprised when I heard about what you'd done. And Lauren tells me you had two of your friends helping you."

"I'm really sorry, Mr Zimmerman. It's not as bad as it seems. I can explain!"

"Young lady, there's no logical or reasonable explanation for what you've done! Not only is your advice column the most popular thing in our newspaper, but it's increased our readership by 42%! I KNEW you had it in you! Congratulations, Sparky!"

I just stared at Zimmerman with my mouth dangling open. "Um, that IS great news, actually. Thanks!"

Then the weirdest thing happened. Zimmerman's eyes started to tear up a bit as he held up a large certificate with a red ribbon around it.

"Each month I select an MVP from the newspaper staff. It's my pleasure to award this certificate to you based on your outstanding contribution to the WCD newspaper as the advice columnist Miss Know–It–All. May you live long and prosper, Sparky!"

MR ZIMMERMAN PRESENTS ME WITH A CERTIFICATE FOR MVP OF THE MONTH!

OMG! I was SOOOO happy!

But more than anything I was relieved.

Me and my friends weren't in trouble after all.

And now Miss Know-It-All is an award-winning columnist!

EAT YOUR HEART OUT, MACKENZIE!!

There was even more good news.

Because I was getting swamped with letters, Mr Zimmerman suggested that I select and answer only six to eight letters a day, just like a real syndicated advice columnist. EASY PEASY!!

So now I no longer have to kill myself trying to answer two hundred letters a day. WOO-HOO!

!!

I should be asleep right now. But unfortunately, I'm wide awake, trying NOT to freak out!

I knew I should have just waited and checked my help boxes after school like I always do. But I didn't have time today because I STILL needed to get Brandon a birthday present.

That's when I decided to request a hall pass from geometry class. Since the hallways were usually totally empty during class hours, I could gather my letters and keep my identity a secret.

I had made my rounds around the school and had only one box to go.

I crept up to it like a ninja, and in a flash, snatched off the top and stuck my hand inside to grab my letters.

But that's when I ran into a major unexpected complication. Namely . . .

MACKENZIE CATCHES ME TAKING LETTERS
OUT OF MY HELP BOX!

"Nikki, WHAT are you doing?! Aren't you supposed to
be in the toilet?"

"Um . . . I was on my way there right now, actually.

But it's none of your business. Who do you think you are? The TOILET POLICE?!"

"Well, who do you think YOU are? Miss Know-It-All? I'm sure she wouldn't appreciate you snooping around in her letters like—"

That's when MacKenzie stopped midsentence and stared at me VERY suspiciously.

"Wait a minute! Are YOU Miss Know-It-All?!"

"No way! I wrote a letter to her because I need her advice. I was just putting it inside the box."

"So why is the top off and your hand inside? Couldn't you just drop it through the slot?"

"Actually, I had to take the top off because . . . you know, um . . . the little slot thingy was . . . clogged up."

MacKenzie looked at the top. "The slot doesn't look clogged to me."

"Of course it doesn't! I just UNCLOGGED it. DUH!"

I slammed the top back on the box and glared at MacKenzie.

Then we both walked back to class.

But get this! She started staring at me really evil-like and whispering to Jessica.

And everyone knows Jessica is the biggest gossip in our school.

Since she works in the office, she gets all the juicy inside information straight from the teachers and staff.

I actually think Jessica must have blabbed to MacKenzie about Mr Zimmerman naming me MVP of the month or something.

Because when I saw her at my locker after class, she was SO mad, fire was practically shooting out of her ears.

Personally, I think MacKenzie is just SUPERjealous because:

1. Brandon's party is in two days and she STILL doesn't have an invitation.

2. She suspects I'm Miss Know-It-All, and MY advice column is way more popular than HER very LAME fashion column.

3. Zimmerman gave ME the MVP award.

4. Brandon and I are becoming really good friends.

I just knew that girl was going to say something to me by the way she was looking me up and down like that.

And boy, was I right.

She slammed her locker shut and suddenly got all up in my face like acne cream or something.

I just looked at that girl like she was crazy. . .

LISTEN, NIKKI! I'M SICK AND TIRED OF YOUR LITTLE MIND GAMES!

MACKENZIE, GETTING ALL UP IN MY FACE FOR NO REASON!

"Jessica tells me Zimmerman gave you a little award. Congratulations! But I wouldn't get too comfortable around here if I were you. I have a meeting with Principal Winston tomorrow morning about a little toilet paper incident. Personally, I think the three perpetrators deserve a permanent suspension."

"It's about time you FINALLY figured out it was me, Chloe, and Zoey and NOT Brandon," I said.

"Are you kidding? I'm NOT stupid! I knew it was you guys all along. I was watching you clowns through my bedroom window the entire time."

"You actually saw us?! Then why didn't you try and stop us before we toilet-papered your house?!"

"Why would I want to interrupt your little shenanigans? Especially when I could use it against you guys to get you thrown out of this school? Like I'm going to do tomorrow!"

"So, why did you blame it all on Brandon if you knew it was us all along?" I asked.

"I knew he wouldn't want me to get you and your

little friends in trouble. And I was going to keep you out of it as long as he played along and agreed to hang out with me and invite me to his party. Everyone says we'd make such a CUTE couple! But he wasn't interested. Guys are fickle like that!"

MacKenzie was using ME to try to manipulate HIM into a relationship. AGAIN! But I totally trusted Brandon and knew he was a true friend.

"MacKenzie, you're a sick little cookie! I can't believe you're playing all of these mind games just to get an invitation to a party!"

"You say that like it's a bad thing! Anyway, I can hardly wait for you to leave so my BFF, Jessica, can move in to your locker. When Winston kicks your butt out of here, we'll FINALLY be rid of the very foul stench in this hallway."

I just stared into her beady little eyes and didn't say a word.

I'd been through SO much drama trying to stay

at WCD. And NOW I was about to get kicked out because of the Great Toilet Paper Caper?! A harmless prank! That MacKenzie had milked for all it was worth.

But more than anything, I felt really bad for Chloe and Zoey. They were getting dragged into this mess only because MacKenzie was trying to hurt ME!

I knew I needed to find my BFFs and warn them, but right then I just felt exhausted and overwhelmed.

The past month has been one wild roller-coaster ride. And it was about to come to an end. As it derailed, crashed and crushed all of my hopes and dreams into tiny pieces.

Later that night I had the most awful nightmares one after another.

But only ONE of them was horrible enough to actually wake me up. . .

After MacKenzie talks to Principal Winston tomorrow, I'm pretty sure I'm going to get in really big trouble. And maybe even kicked out of school.

If that happens, not even my bug extermination scholarship can help me stay at WCD.

And to make matters worse, when my parents find out about all of this, they're going to KILL ME!!

All I can do right now is bury my head in my pillow and have a really good cry.

My situation is HOPELESS!

I GIVE UP!

☹!!

When you're waiting for something HORRIBLE to happen, time seems to slow down. Which means the school day drags on and on and on.

I am so exhausted I can barely keep my eyes open. That's because I was up most of the night either crying or having nightmares.

My life feels so out of control.

Right now I'm supposed to be in the janitor's closet getting a refill for that hand sanitizer thingy in the library.

But I've been so stressed out all day that I need to write in my diary really, really bad.

If I don't take time to vent about what just happened, I feel like I'm going to . . .

EXPLODE!!

I've been a nervous wreck all day, wondering if MacKenzie was actually going to carry out her threat and report us for the Great Toilet Paper Caper.

Since it was getting towards the end of the school day, I started thinking she was just playing more mind games. Maybe she had decided NOT to go through with it after all.

But sure enough, while we were shelving library books, the office secretary sent down three passes for Chloe, Zoey and me to meet with Principal Winston right away.

I SO wished we hadn't toilet-papered MacKenzie's house like that. Now we were going to have to suffer the consequences.

Chloe, Zoey and I hung our heads as we silently walked down the hall to the office. It felt like we were going to our executions or something.

The worst part was not knowing whether our

parents had been contacted or whether they were going to be there at the meeting.

When we entered the office, the secretary smiled and asked us to have a seat right outside the principal's office.

"I have to run a quick errand," she said, "but I'll be back in a few minutes. Principal Winston is still on the telephone, and as soon as he gets done, he'll meet with the four of you."

Four of us?! That's when we turned around and saw MacKenzie sitting there staring at us with her beady little eyes.

We took a seat right across from her.

Then we tried our best to ignore that girl.

OMG! We were so SCARED it was pathetic.

But MacKenzie just sat there with this little smirk on her face.

I think she was enjoying watching us squirm.

Talk about AWKWARD!! . . .

CHLOE, ZOEY AND I WAIT
NERVOUSLY FOR OUR EXECUTION!

But more than anything, I wanted to slap that little
smirk right off her face. And I seriously thought
about doing it too.

Hey! If it was left up to MacKenzie, Winston was going to give us the worst possible punishment, like being kicked out of school.

So by slapping her silly, what did I have to lose? I'd just be expelled for TWO things instead of ONE. But I decided NOT to do it.

Suddenly the door opened and Marcy rushed in.

"OMG! I can't believe I have all of you together!" she gasped. "Mr Zimmerman wants me to do an investigative reporting piece on a controversy at school. I heard through one of my sources about an incident that happened between you guys a few weeks ago."

"YOU DID?!" the four of us responded, and blinked in surprise.

"Yes, and it's unbelievable! This story is breaking news and will be on the front page tomorrow. I'm hoping it's going to get picked up by the local press, and maybe even AP national. MacKenzie, I'm here to interview you and get YOUR side of the story."

This was NOT good news for us.

"You want to interview ME?!" MacKenzie asked as she smiled, batted her lashes and slathered on five layers of Wretched Revenge Red lip gloss.

Then, being the drama queen that she is, she sniffed and dabbed at fake tears. "OMG! It was just so . . . so . . . traumatising! But I'm willing to share my very tragic story with the entire world. So, Marcy, why don't you, um . . . call Brandon so he can get a close-up photo of my pure anguish?"

That's when I threw up in my mouth a little. Chloe and Zoey just rolled their eyes. That girl was SO full of RUBBISH her breath smelled like the city dump!

"Do you mind if I tape this interview?" Marcy asked. "I'd like to have a permanent record."

"Sure!" MacKenzie answered.

"That'd be great!" Marcy said. "Now let's get started. . . . MacKenzie, I heard from a VERY reputable source that not only did you STEAL Nikki, Chloe and Zoey's costumes for the *Holiday on Ice* charity event, but you LOCKED the girls in a dark storage closet at the arena as well. What is your response to this allegation?!"

MARCY INTERVIEWS MACKENZIE!

OMG! At first Chloe, Zoey and I just stared in shock.

Then we couldn't stop snickering.

MacKenzie looked like she'd seen a ghost or something.

But the funniest part was that her lips were moving but there was no sound coming out. Probably because she knew that every word she said was going to be recorded.

That's when Principal Winston finally opened the door to his office. "Good afternoon, girls. Come right in. I believe you requested this meeting, Miss Hollister?"

MacKenzie looked at Principal Winston and us. And then she looked at Marcy.

We looked at MacKenzie and Principal Winston. Then we looked at Marcy too.

Marcy looked at Principal Winston and MacKenzie. Then she looked at us.

Only, I could have sworn she winked.

All of this looking at each other went on for what seemed like FOREVER!

Suddenly MacKenzie cleared her throat.

"Actually, Principal Winston, I just wanted to have a little meeting to . . . you know . . . ask you about . . . um, the. . ." She looked around the office nervously and spotted an apple on the secretary's desk. ". . . the APPLES . . . in the . . . cafeteria. We really need more apple stuff! Like apple dumplings, apple pie, applesauce, apple turnover, apple . . . um, everything!" MacKenzie said nervously.

I couldn't help but imagine her standing there like an airhead with a huge tray of apple snacks. . .

AN APPLE SNACK FOR YOU, AND AN APPLE SNACK FOR YOU! EVERYONE GETS AN APPLE SNACK!

"Don't you agree, Nikki?" MacKenzie asked, and batted her eyelashes all innocentlike.

I shrugged. "No, not really."

I was NOT about to bail her out of this one.

Principal Winston looked highly annoyed and scratched

his head. "Miss Hollister, you actually requested this meeting to discuss adding more apples to the cafeteria menu?"

"Um, yes! Apples . . . ROCK!" MacKenzie said, and smiled really big.

"Well, okay then. I'll mention your idea to the head cook. Now, if you girls don't have any other pressing matters to discuss, I do have quite a bit of work I need to tackle," Mr Winston said, glancing at his watch.

"There's nothing else I want to discuss," MacKenzie rambled on, "and I'm pretty sure there's nothing else my good friends here want to discuss either. Right, girls?!"

We all just folded our arms and gave her a dirty look.

Then she continued. "Thank you for your time, Principal Winston. Now you get right back to work. We know you're busy, busy, busy! And we're all going back to class. Right, girls?! And we're going to study, study, study!"

Just like that, our meeting with Principal Winston was over even before it got started.

When we finally got back to the library, we did a group hug! Only this time it included Marcy. . .

↑
MARCY

OMG! Chloe, Zoey and I were SO relieved that fiasco was OVER.

We thought for sure our parents were going to be called in and we were going to get expelled from school or worse.

We couldn't thank Marcy enough for helping us out of that big mess.

"You guys are the only friends I have here," she said shyly.

"Well, we consider YOU a friend too!" I said.

"Unequivocally!" Zoey said.

"Absolutely!" Chloe added, and gave her jazz hands.

That's when my curiosity got the best of me.

"Actually, Marcy, what I really want to know is this: HOW did you find out about MacKenzie stealing our costumes and locking us in that storage locker?"

"Every investigative reporter has their secret sources. And mine is a SUPERreliable one!"

Then she held up a very familiar newspaper. . .

We cracked up laughing.

Apparently, Brianna has been handing out her *Some Times* newspaper to kids in her class. And Marcy's little brother had brought one home.

I could NOT believe Brianna was actually putting all of our personal family business in the streets like that. But thank goodness she had.

Another strange thing was the timing of Marcy's interview with MacKenzie. PERFECT!

"I was in the girls' toilets and overheard MacKenzie bragging to Jessica that she had scheduled a meeting with Winston to get you guys kicked out of school," Marcy explained. "MacKenzie also said she was pretty sure your dad was going to close his business to come work full-time for HER dad. And as soon as he did, she was going to convince her dad to transfer him to the other side of the state just to get rid of you."

I felt like I'd just been hit in the face with a bat.

So that was the master plan!

If my dad stopped working for WCD, I would lose my scholarship. But to make sure I was permanently out of her hair, MacKenzie was going to convince her dad to transfer my dad to the other side of the state?!

Which meant we'd have to move.

And if he refused to move, he'd end up UNEMPLOYED! After he'd pretty much liquidated his own successful business and sacrificed the WCD scholarship he'd arranged for his daughter.

I felt SO SORRY for my dad! He probably had no idea he was dealing with such RUTHLESS people.

That's when I noticed all three girls staring at me.

"Nikki, are you okay?" Zoey asked. "You don't look so good."

"Actually, I DON'T feel very good. I think it was

that leftover Casserole Surprise we had in the cafeteria," I lied.

I could NOT believe I had gone through ALL of this drama for the past month only to find out in the end that I might STILL have to leave WCD!!

I blinked back my tears.

Then I prayed my dad WASN'T planning to quit his job to work for MacKenzie's dad full-time.

But after he'd got rid of his van last week, the likelihood of that happening seemed very high.

At least things had turned out okay for Chloe and Zoey.

But the thought of having to say goodbye to them and Brandon was just . . . heart wrenching!

They say "Life is like a box of chocolates".

But my box is full of the yucky, gooey, smushed, cherry ones!

And that STINKS!!

☹!!

OMG! OMG! OMG!

All I can say right now is . . . OMG! I don't even know where to BEGIN!!! My day was just so . . . OMG!!

Even though I didn't get expelled from school yesterday, everything was still pretty much a disaster.

I knew that as long as my dad was working for MacKenzie's father, my life was going to be a major DRAMA FEST!

Brianna and Miss Penelope woke me up by jumping in my bed and screaming, "Wake up! Wake up! Dad has a really fabulous surprise for us. Come outside and see it!"

I was like, JUST GREAT ☹! He was probably going to announce he'd taken that job with MacKenzie's dad and we were moving. There was probably a huge moving van parked outside or something.

I quickly put on a sweater over my pj's and trudged out into the cold morning air. Brianna was right! It was a FABULOUS surprise. . .

DAD, MAX THE ROACH, AND OUR RAGGEDY OLD VAN WERE BACK WHERE THEY BELONGED!

I never thought I'd be so happy to see all three of them together again.

Dad explained that although he liked working for Hollister Holdings, he preferred being his own boss. And he liked having a flexible work schedule so he could spend more time with his family.

He said working for Mr Hollister had inspired him to try and expand his OWN business, Maxwell's Bug Extermination.

That's when Mom told Dad that he had proved to both her and the world that he was a shrewd and savage business shark after all.

We were all so proud of my dad that we tackled him and gave him a big hug and a kiss.

So it looks like my bug extermination scholarship won't be in jeopardy after all.

MacKenzie's going to blow a gasket when she finds out.

She is such a control freak!

But at least she's not controlling my dad anymore.

Anyway, later this evening when I was getting ready for Brandon's party, I found out at the last minute my mom had to stand in for a sick parent and be the driver for Brianna's dance class car pool.

Mom was all like, "Nikki, dear, I'm STILL planning to take you to Brandon's party. But we have a teeny-tiny complication regarding your transportation HOME. So your dad has agreed to help."

I could not believe my own mother would LIE right to my face like that. Sorry, Mom! But it WASN'T a teeny-tiny complication.

IT WAS A SUPERSIZED, GIGANTIC, HUMONGOUS BLOB OF A PROBLEM!!

WHY?

Because my parents casually informed me that I was going to be picked up by—wait for it, wait for it . . .

DAD and Max the Roach.

Even though I was happy Dad was no longer working for Hollister Holdings, there was just NO WAY I was going to let Brandon see me getting into that wacky-looking roachmobile.

And even worse, he finally would know what a huge PHONEY I am.

Why couldn't DAD drive for Brianna's dance class?!

Then, instead of brutally traumatising ME for LIFE, Dad could take Brianna and her little friends joyriding. It would be more fun than DISNEY WORLD!!

BRIANNA AND HER FRIENDS, JOYRIDING IN
THE ROACHMOBILE

That's when I made a VERY difficult decision. I was
NOT going to Brandon's party ☹! Even though I had
a present for him, after getting this week's allowance.

And being the honest person that I am, I planned to tell Brandon and all my friends the truth: Something had come up at the last minute.

Namely, my LUNCH! I was so SICK of my life ☹!!

I had picked up the phone to break the bad news to Chloe and Zoey when my mom knocked on my bedroom door and stuck her head inside.

"Nikki, dear, would you please write down the time you need to be picked up from your party along with the address and telephone number and give it to your dad? He doesn't have the best memory and gets lost going to the mailbox."

But before I could tell her I'd changed my mind about the whole party thing, she closed my door and disappeared into the hall.

I just sighed and dialled Zoey's number.

Actually, Dad NOT finding the house would be a really GOOD thing because—

Suddenly a little lightbulb clicked on in my brain, and I had a stroke of pure genius.

Brandon's party was going to be at Theo's house because he had a cool, arcade-style games room with an awesome sound system. The address was 725 Hidden Lake Drive. But what if Dad parked and waited for me somewhere else? At ANOTHER address? Then no one at the party would see me getting into the van with him and Max the Roach.

PROBLEM. SOLVED. ☺!!

I quickly hung up the phone.

Then I scribbled all of my party information for Dad.

Just like Mom had instructed.

Except I kind of fudged on the address-and-phone-number part:

PICK UP NIKKI
AT 10:00 PM

710 HIDDEN
LAKE DRIVE
TELEPHONE:
555-0129

Was I not brilliant? ☺!!

Anyway, Brandon's birthday party was just as fun as
I had imagined.

It was really cool hanging out with all my friends.

I even surprised myself and had a total change of heart about ~~asking~~ begging Brandon for that extra invitation for someone to attend his party, namely . . .

MARCY

Sorry, MacKenzie and Jessica ☺!!

Chloe and Zoey kept me laughing.

And as usual, Violet brought her fab music collection and rocked the house.

Literally!

Theo had just about every type of pizza imaginable delivered hot and fresh by Queasy Cheesy.

Yep – Queasy Cheesy!

I was shocked to find out that Theo's family owns the one at the mall. As well as the other 173 locations in the national chain.

And get this!

As a special treat, his dad gave each one of us three FREE gift certificates for an all-you-can-eat Queasy Cheesy Pizza Fest.

OMG! I was SUPERhappy about that!

Because if I gave one Queasy Cheesy certificate to Mom, one to Dad and one to Brianna, I'd pretty much have ALL of my Christmas shopping done for next year!

Without having to spend ANY of my OWN money.

How COOL is THAT?

Anyway, I couldn't believe how quickly the time passed, and soon it was 10:00 p.m.

But we were having so much fun, no one wanted to leave.

I wasn't really the least bit worried because, according to my brilliant plan, my dad was patiently waiting for me somewhere nearby.

So of course I had a complete MELTDOWN when the doorbell rang and . . .

MY DAD HAD JUST
CRASHED MY PARTY!!
AAAAAAAAAAHH!!!!

The GOOD news (if you want to call it that) was
that my situation was so MASSIVELY HORRIBLE
that it COULDN'T possibly get any WORSE!

Or so I thought.

Theo's dad, Mr Swagmire, scratched his head and
looked even more confused than my dad. "Hmm?
Now, that's strange! All of the houses on this street
are 720 or above. But you're welcome to use our
phone to try to reach your daughter. Come in and
make yourself at home."

"Thank you. I appreciate your help. One quick
phone call should clear all of this up. . ." said my
dad.

That's when I decided it would probably be a good idea to grab the phone BEFORE my dad did.

But not to keep him from using it. I needed to call 911 to report a brutal crime that was about to occur.

Because when my dad finally figured out that he was wandering around LOST, on a cold, dark night, all because I'd given him a bunch of PHONEY information, he was going to KILL ME!!

The night had turned into a complete DISASTER!

My FRIENDS were down the hall.

My CRUSH, Brandon, was standing next to me.

My DAD was at the front door.

MAX THE ROACH was parked at the curb.

And I, NIKKI MAXWELL, was about to PEE my pants!

When Dad walked over to the phone to call me, I was so close I could have reached around the corner and touched him.

But I just stood there frantically holding my breath.

I was DOOMED! And any second now I was going to be SO BUSTED!

Or maybe . . . NOT.

I was SUPERrelieved when Theo came over and dragged Brandon away to show him his new video game system.

Just as Dad began dialling the phoney number, I spotted a telephone across the hall in the kitchen that was, luckily, out of his view.

I knew it was a crazy idea. But what did I have to lose?! I was already in way over my head.

So I quickly tippy-toed into the kitchen and snatched up the phone just before my dad finished dialling.

308

"Hi, Nikki! Boy, am I glad to hear your voice. I'm totally LOST! But . . . HOW did you know it was me?"

"Actually, I didn't! Er, I just, um . . . saw the caller ID?"

"That's strange! I'm not calling from home!"

"The caller ID said, um . . . Dad. And you know, it's totally a coincidence that YOUR name is Dad too. Because there are, like, millions of guys out there named Dad. Actually."

"Um, okay. Well, I can't find a house with the address you gave me. And right now I'm calling from a neighbour's house. I need you to find out the correct address."

"Well, Dad, you sound SO close by. Almost like you're in the next room or something. Hey, I bet if I looked out of this window right here by the phone, I just might be able to see—OMG! There it is! Dad! I see your VAN! It's parked about five houses down. Can you believe that? Wow!"

"Really! I guess I was waiting in the right place after all. That means I WASN'T lost!"

"Dad, why did you think you were lost? You just need to drive down the street five more houses. And if you give me a few minutes to say goodbye to everyone and grab my coat, I'll be right out."

"Okay, sweetie. I'll see you in a few minutes, then."

"Bye, Dad! Love you!"

I could NOT believe that our little conversation went so well.

Now, if Dad would just simply

1. hang up the phone

2. walk out of the house

3. get into his van and

4. drive further down the street

I WOULDN'T have to run away from home and join the circus.

I peeked from the kitchen as Dad thanked Mr Swagmire, shook his hand, and finally left.

Mission accomplished ☺!!

But then I turned around, and . . .

"Oh! Hi, Brandon!" I sputtered. "I didn't see you standing there. I was . . . on the dad with my phone. Er . . . I mean, on the phone with my dad."

I wondered how long Brandon had been standing there watching and listening.

"Is everything all right?" he asked.

"Yeah, I'm fine. Thankfully, my dad just left. HOME! He was here to pick — I mean — he's COMING to pick me up. . ." I stammered.

Brandon just kind of stared at me suspiciously and slowly nodded his head. "Really? Um, okay."

I could feel my cheeks getting warm and I started to squirm. "Well, I better get going. I don't want to keep my dad waiting."

"But I thought you said he just left home?"

"Er, he did. But he'll be here real soon. He's a superspeedy driver. You know, like those guys in

Formula One. Zooooom! That's my dad. Anyway, thanks for inviting me. Bye!"

"Do you have to go so soon? I just. . ." Brandon looked a little disappointed as his voice trailed off. "Okay, then. Thanks for coming, Nikki."

I turned and walked away as quickly as I could.

But I could almost feel Brandon staring at the back of my neck.

I hugged my BFFs, Chloe and Zoey, said goodbye to everyone, and thanked Theo for hosting such a great party for Brandon at his house.

That's when Marcy thanked me for inviting her.

"Thank YOU! For shutting down MacKenzie!" I laughed.

"No problem! If there's ever anything else I can do to help out, just let me know. I have no social life WHATSOEVER."

That's when a little lightbulb went off in my head.

"Actually, Marcy, there is! My Miss Know-It-All advice column has been keeping me pretty busy. Chloe, Zoey and I have been staying after school to work on them. I'd love for you to help out!"

"OMG! YOU'RE Miss Know-It-All!" Marcy gasped. "And you were right! I DID find some friends at this school."

So now Marcy will be hanging out with us during lunch and after school. She's a good kid!

As I stepped into the cold, crisp night, I felt happy and a little sad at the same time.

It was a blast hanging out with Brandon, and I liked him more than ever. But just when it seemed like sparks were about to fly between us, they abruptly fizzled.

It was quite obvious Brandon suspected something.

And me sneaking off to meet Dad didn't help
things. But I'd just DIE if anyone saw my roach
van. Especially Brandon ☹!

I casually strolled down the pavement.

But once I got past Theo's garden, I took off running towards the van like a madwoman.

When I climbed inside, Dad was still staring at my note and scratching his head.

"Hi, Nikki. It's really weird, but the house numbers around here don't seem to be in order," he mumbled.

"Don't worry about it, Dad," I said, feeling a little guilty I'd just led him on a wild goose chase.

Then he hesitated and looked SUPERanxious.

"So, let's just keep everything that happened tonight our little secret, okay?"

My mouth dropped open as I stared at him in disbelief.

SECRET?! Dad knew?!

But HOW?!

OMG! Had he seen me at Theo's house?!

"Well, if you tell your mom about me not finding the house, I'll never hear the end of it. She's always teasing that I get lost going to the mailbox," he explained.

I breathed a sigh of relief.

"Don't worry, Dad! Your secret is totally safe with me!" I gushed, and gave him a quick hug.

Then I slouched way down into my seat.

Even though it was pitch-dark outside, I didn't want to take a chance on anyone seeing me riding around with Max the Roach.

The fact that I had managed to survive Brandon's birthday party was a MIRACLE! But now I was worried that Brandon suspected something.

But I didn't blame him. I'm such a massive phoney, I wouldn't want to be friends with myself.

I guess I was just sick and tired of all the secrets and lies. I didn't know how much longer I could keep hiding who I really was. . .

The ONLY person in the ENTIRE history of mankind attending school on a stupid BUG EXTERMINATION SCHOLARSHIP!

WHY was my life so hopelessly CRUDDY?!

That's when I got a text message from Brandon: "I LOVE that kooky Crazy Burger hat and the gift certificates! Would you like to help me use them tomorrow for lunch? Please say YES!"

Brandon had just asked me out ☺!! To eat . . . but still! SQUEEEE!!

It wasn't a candlelight dinner at a romantic Italian restaurant, but Crazy Burger had the best gourmet burgers for miles around.

I texted him my answer right away: "YES! Should I meet you there?"

"Sure! But to be honest, I've been wanting to ride in your dad's funky, cool roach van for months!"

I had to read Brandon's text over, like, three times.

Then I totally lost it and burst out laughing.

My dad looked at me like I was INSANE!

All of these months I've been going insane trying to keep who I really am a big secret. And Brandon knew the real ME all along!

Only, I don't think he knows that I know about HIM!

Or DOES he??!!

All of the excitement and drama and unanswered questions about what we SECRETLY know and don't know about each other is enough to make my head spin.

Just thinking about it makes me feel a little nauseous. But in a really GOOD way!

And yes! I know I sound KA-RAY-ZEE!

But I can't help it.

I'M SUCH A DORK!!!
☺!!

Nikki Maxwell's

Guide to knowing if your crush likes you:
He wants to go with you to the biggest dance of the year.

(There's totally still time to ask him.)

(OMG – what if he doesn't say yes?!)

(OMG – what if he goes with MacKenzie?!!!)

Will Nikki go to the ball, or will she be a Dork-arella? Find out in *HOLIDAY HEARTBREAK...*

OMG! I'm suffering from the worst case of CRUSH-ITIS ever!

This morning I had these fluttery butterflies in my stomach that were making me feel SUPERnauseous ☹! But in a really GOOD way ☺!

I felt SO insanely happy I could just . . . VOMIT sunshine, rainbows, confetti, glitter and . . . um . . . those yummy little Skittles thingies!

I still can't believe my crush, Brandon, actually texted me last night after I left his birthday party.

And you'll NEVER guess what happened??!!

HE ASKED ME OUT TO CRAZY BURGER!! SQUEEE ☺!!

And yes, I know it's NOT like a real date or anything. But STILL!

I was SO elated, I blasted my FAVE music and danced around my bedroom like a MANIAC...

Hey! I was beyond FIERCE! I was an air-guitar—
playing, dancing machine!

After dancing in my room for an entire hour, I was so tired I could barely breathe.

That's when I collapsed into a wheezing, sweat-soaked mass of body odour and sheer exhaustion.

GASP!!
COUGH!!
HACK!!

A very HAPPY wheezing, sweat-soaked mass of body odour and sheer exhaustion.

ME, WITH A BIG FAT DORKY
SMILE PLASTERED ACROSS MY FACE!!

WHY? Because any minute now, Brandon was going to contact me so we could make plans to hang out at Crazy Burger.

SQUEEEEEE ☺!

So I snuggled into a comfy chair, stared at my phone and waited patiently for his call.

I WAITED . . .

And WAITED . . .

(2 hours later)

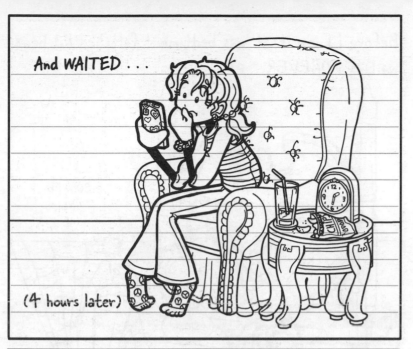

And WAITED . . .

(4 hours later)

And WAITED!!

(6 hours later)

Before I knew it, it was bedtime. I felt like I'd been waiting FOREVER. . . !!

ME, FLOPPED ACROSS MY BED, SULKING

But no call! No email! Not even a text message!
I even checked my phone to make sure the battery
thingy hadn't run down or something.

Unfortunately, my last call was from my BFFs, Chloe and Zoey. They had called me late last night with some REALLY juicy gossip.

Apparently, someone had showed up at Brandon's party unexpectedly to drop off a present for him shortly after I had left.

You'll NEVER guess who it was!

MACKENZIE !!

Okay, I'll admit it was really nice and sweet of her to do that. But she had totally overlooked one very important little detail . . .

SHE WASN'T INVITED! ☹!!

Which meant MISS THANG had basically CRASHED Brandon's party! Like, WHO does that?!

My BFFs told me that MacKenzie was twirling her

hair, giggling and flirting with Brandon like crazy. Then she got superserious and asked to talk to him PRIVATELY about something really important!

JUST GREAT ☹! Now I'm really starting to ~~worry~~ PANIC!

What if MacKenzie told him some awful lies about me so he wouldn't want to be friends anymore?!!

She's always talking about me behind my back and saying stuff like, "Nikki's a hopelessly insecure, fashion-challenged, diary-obsessed DORK!"

Which is so NOT true! Well . . . maybe it's a little true. Okay! Actually, a LOT true. But STILL!!

WHY did all of this have to happen just when Brandon and I were about to have our very first date-that-really-isn't-a-date ☹?!

PLEASE, PLEASE, PLEASE, PLEASE, PLEASE let Brandon call me tomorrow!!

SUNDAY, FEBRUARY 2

I've been awake now for

7 hours, 11 minutes, and 39 seconds

and Brandon STILL hasn't called ☹!!

I'm starting to worry that something really BAD happened to him.

I think he sincerely WANTED to call me.

And he sincerely TRIED to call me.

But he just COULDN'T!

Because maybe . . . he got, um . . . abducted . . . by . . .

ALIENS ☹!!

Hey, don't laugh!!

It could have actually happened. . . !!

"I CAN'T BELIEVE THIS IS HAPPENING! I DROPPED MY PHONE AND NOW I CAN'T CALL NIKKI!"

In spite of the fact that I was still suffering from a severe case of crush-itis AND having a really BAD day, my parents MADE me babysit my little sister, Brianna.

Just so they could go to a movie together! Like, how INSENSITIVE is that?! Sometimes I think Mom and Dad need to take a parenting class or something.

The last time I tried to talk to Brandon on the phone with Brianna around, it was a total disaster. She actually told him about my hairy legs and crusty eye boogers. It was SO humiliating!

Lately, Brianna has been totally obsessed with those diva hair salon shows on TV. And get this! She actually calls herself Miss Bri-Bri, Fashionista Hairstylist to the Stars!

I was shocked to see her sneaking into my parents' bathroom and stealing shampoo and perfume and stuff. It was like I had personally witnessed a MIRACLE!

Brianna was FINALLY trying to improve her very NASTY hygiene ☺!

WOO-HOO!

But later, when I peeked inside Brianna's room, I discovered she was MISSING!

And in her place was this strange little woman.

She was wearing fake diamond cat-eye glasses, a long scarf, four-sizes-too-big satin slippers and a kiddie painting apron filled with Mom's designer makeup collection.

I didn't know WHO the heck she was.

I wanted to scream, "Who are YOU? And what have you done with MY little sister?!"

But my gut told me to run away FAST and call the POLICE!

Then she smiled at me really big and said . . .

"BONJOUR, MISS NIKKI!
WELCOME TO SALON BRIANNA!!"

I was halfway down the hall before Brianna caught up with me. She grabbed my arm and dragged me back toward her room.

"Dah—ling! Where are you going?! Don't be skurd!" Brianna said in an awful fake French accent that sounded more like a six—year—old Arnold Schwarzenegger.

"You're playing with Mom's new makeup and perfume?! You DO realize she's going to KILL you when she gets home! Right?!" I scolded her.

"Never mind zat, dah—ling! You are Miss Bri—Bri's next appointment! Wee! Wee! Come! Come!" she said, pushing me into her ~~desk~~ salon chair.

Kidz Bop music was playing in the background. And she'd drawn the most hideous hairstyle posters and hung them on her wall to help set the mood of a trendy, upscale salon.

Those posters should've been a WARNING to me about Miss Bri—Bri's hairstyling abilities. I couldn't resist coming up with catchy names for each one. . .

"Don't worry, dah—ling," Miss Bri—Bri said. "I'm going to make you BOOTY—FUL! For your little friend Brandon. Yes?!"

For BRANDON?!!! I blushed profusely.

341

Hey! It was JUST a pretend makeover with
Miss Bri-Bri, Fashionista Hairstylist to the Stars!

What could possibly go WRONG?

"Okay. As long as it's ONLY pretend!" I grumped.

If I was lucky, this would keep Brianna occupied
until Mom and Dad got home. And it was way LESS
dangerous than us baking cookies and almost burning
down the house. AGAIN!

"YAAAY!!! My first customer!" ~~Brianna~~ Miss Bri-Bri
cheered. "Before I start, dah-ling, would you like
something to drink? Juicy Juice? Hawaiian Punch?
Chocolate milk?"

"Chocolate milk would be nice," I answered.

"Hans! Go get our customer, Miss Nikki, a glass
of le chocolate milk! Extra cold!" she commanded,
looking at the teddy bear in the chair next to mine.

The bear . . . I mean . . . Hans . . . didn't move.

"Well?!" She glared at him. "Don't just sit there! Go get zee milk for her. Now! PLEASE!!"

Then she turned to me and laughed uncomfortably. "Please excuse my assistant. Hans is new here. He speaks la French, but very little English."

I looked at the teddy bear, looked back at her, and raised an eyebrow. "Um . . . okay?" I replied.

"I know just what to do with your hair, dah—ling!" Brianna said as she draped a bath towel smock around my shoulders. "Now, just relax and let Miss Bri-Bri work her magic! Yes? Hans, would you please grab that magazine and give it to— Oh, never mind! I'll do it myself!"

Brianna handed me a trendy teen fashion magazine to read, just like in a real salon. I was impressed. Until I realized she had swiped MY new *Teen Thing* mag from my room. The little THIEF!!

But I had to admit, Miss Bri-Bri, Fashionista Hairstylist to the Stars, seemed to know her stuff. . .

ME, READING WHILE MISS BRI-BRI DOES MY HAIR

That's when I came across this very intriguing
article about — you guessed it — GUYS!!

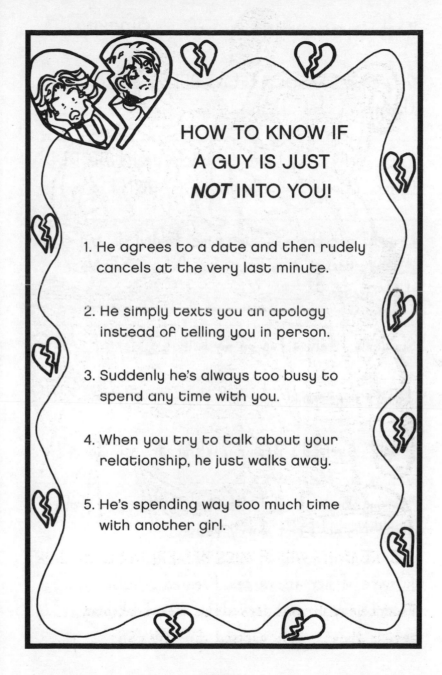

HOW TO KNOW IF A GUY IS JUST *NOT* INTO YOU!

1. He agrees to a date and then rudely cancels at the very last minute.

2. He simply texts you an apology instead of telling you in person.

3. Suddenly he's always too busy to spend any time with you.

4. When you try to talk about your relationship, he just walks away.

5. He's spending way too much time with another girl.

That magazine article was just . . . SHOCKING!

Only a guy who was a total LOSER would do those things.

I felt really lucky I didn't have to deal with "DDD" (Dysfunctional Dude Drama) in my OWN life.

I ripped out the magazine page, folded it, and stuck it in my pocket. You know, for future reference. Just in case.

Suddenly I felt a tug on my hair.

Then a huge yank!

"Ouch!" I yelped. "Brianna, WHAT are you doing?!"

"Making you booty-ful, dah-ling! Zere eez no problem at all! No, no! Don't worry, please!"

In spite of her assurances, I sensed a little uncertainty in that jacked-up accent of hers.

Next I felt another slight tug and then . . . SNIP!

A chopped-off braid landed in my lap!

I gasped!

Then, with a trembling hand, I picked up the braid and PRAYED that it belonged to someone else.

Like maybe Hans, that lazy, French-speaking teddy bear assistant!

"What is THIS?!" I yelled at Brianna as I stared at it in horror.

"Nut-ting! Nut-ting at all. I throw away! Yes?" She snatched the braid from me and tossed it over her shoulder. "There! All gone!"

"Brianna! Give me that mirror! Now! Or this game is SO over!" I screeched, my eyeballs bulging.

Brianna handed it to me and giggled nervously.

BRIANNA HANDS ME THE MIRROR

Well, I took one look in that mirror and . . .

OMG ☹!!

I don't have the words to describe how BAD my hair looked.

Maybe, um . . .

HIDEOUS-A-LICIOUS!

Which is, like, ten times worse than just plain ol' HIDEOUS!

I couldn't believe the HOT MESS I saw in that mirror.

I thought my eyes were going to rupture and bleed from being exposed to such awesomely wretched . . .

UGLINESS!!

AAAAAAH!!

(THAT WAS ME SCREAMING!)

And the back was even worse! Just as I had suspected, a large chunk of hair was missing. . .

↑
MISSING
HAIR CHUNK

I seriously considered crawling around on the floor until I found my severed braid.

Then I'd place it in a bucket of ice and rush to the nearest emergency room to see if doctors could somehow surgically reattach it. . .

"DOCTORS, PLEASE! YOU NEED TO DO
EMERGENCY SURGERY TO REATTACH
MY BRAID BEFORE MY, UM . . .
HAIR-FOLLICLE THINGIES . . . DIE!"

"My hair! My poor hair!" I sobbed. "Brianna,
I'm so mad at you right now I could just . . .
ARRRRRGGH!!"

"Dah-ling! Please! Calm down! This is a no-tears
salon! But tipping IS allowed!" Miss Bri-Bri grinned as
she held out her hand. "Got any loose change?"

She expected payment?!!

I was beyond DISGUSTED!

Sorry! But I'd had quite enough of Brianna and her:

1. phoney-baloney French accent.

2. ugly haircuts.

3. lazy, no-good assistant, Hans!

"Hair styled by Miss Bri-Bri is always booty-ful! I
take a PICTURE of your booty!" Brianna said as
she grabbed my phone off of her dresser and set it
to camera mode. . .

A blinding flash went off and I couldn't see a thing.

Which was lucky for Brianna! Because right then I was so mad I wanted to give HER a supercute and stylish haircut. With a chain saw!

"Nikki, is this the button you press to send stuff?" Brianna asked. "I wanna send this picture to Chloe and Zoey so I can get more customers!"

That's when I went from furious to LIVID! "Brianna, are you NUTS?! You'd better NOT send that picture of me to ANYONE!"

"Why not? I need more customers to get more money. How am I supposed to pay Miss Penelope to be my shampoo girl?!"

"Just give me back my phone!!" I screamed, and snatched it from her.

"Mommy says sharing is a good thing!" Brianna shouted and grabbed it back.

We yelled at each other and tussled over the phone for what seemed like FOREVER. . .

ME AND BRIANNA,
FIGHTING OVER MY PHONE

That is, until we heard the phone go *CLICK!* and then *BEEP!* I had a total meltdown right there on the spot!!

OMG, BRIANNA! YOU JUST SENT THIS HIDEOUS PHOTO TO EVERYONE IN MY CONTACTS!

OOPS!!

There's a saying that a picture's worth a thousand words.

Well, mine is worth a million laughs!

I looked like a PSYCHOTIC, HOMELESS, um . . . CLOWN who'd . . . accidentally stuck her finger in an ELECTRICAL SOCKET!

Chloe and Zoey immediately sent me "LOL" texts in response.

They were always texting me funny pictures.

But I was SUPERworried that after Brandon saw that photo, he'd be so freaked out, he'd NEVER want to hang out with me again!

He still hadn't called, emailed, or even texted me all weekend.

I was seriously contemplating whether or not to try and superglue that hair chunk back on or just part my hair differently to try to hide the bald spot when my phone chimed.

OMG!

I almost jumped out of my skin. It was a text from BRANDON!

Finally!!

SQUEEE ☺!!!

My heart was pounding as I read his text message.

I actually read it, like, three times before his very cryptic message finally sank in.

OH.

NO.

HE.

DIDN'T!!

I closed my eyes tightly and . . . groaned in despair . . . like a mortally wounded, um . . . gorilla or something. How could he do this to me?!!

I immediately recognised Brandon's behaviour from that magazine article "How to Know if a Guy Is Just _NOT_ Into You!":

1. He agrees to a date and then rudely cancels at the very last minute.

2. He simply texts you an apology instead of telling you in person.

I crossed off both #1 and #2 from the list.

Maybe Brandon was too embarrassed to be seen with a slightly goofy, majorly insecure girl who WASN'T a CCP (Cute, Cool & Popular) like MacKenzie.

Or maybe the thought of my dad's exterminator van with a plastic bug on it the size of a large hog had made him lose his appetite.

Permanently!

Suddenly I felt so . . . STUPID!!

What made me think Brandon would WANT to go anywhere with ME?!!

Anyway, for the past hour I've been working on a new Crush Rejection Equation to try and figure out what happened.

The calculations are SUPERcomplex. And who knows! All of my hard work on this equation might one day earn me the Nobel Prize in maths. . .

MY PHONE →

BRANDON PLUS NIKKI DIVIDED BY A RANDOM
TEXT MESSAGE EQUALS . . .
HEARTBREAK!

Why is all of this guy stuff SO confusing?!

I guess I could write in to my Miss Know-It-All
advice column and ask myself for romantic advice.

Especially since my two friends Chloe and Marcie
begged me to let them take over my column for the
entire month of February.

They're doing a special Miss Know-It-All Crush Crisis Love Advice column, which means I have the entire month off.

Anyway, here's my letter. . .

Dear Miss Know-It-All,

Why is love such a CRUDDY thing?

Help!

A Brokenhearted Dork

☹!

I'm still pretty bummed out over Brandon's text message.

I really wanted to give him the benefit of the doubt, but the magazine article wouldn't let me.

I planned to just pretend the whole Crazy Burger thing had never happened and TOTALLY ignore him.

However, when I arrived at school, the first thing I noticed was that ALL of the guys were acting really strange. Even the normally rowdy jocks were huddled together in small groups, quietly talking among themselves.

But mostly, everyone was staring nervously at some huge commotion down the hall.

WHAT was going on??! And WHERE were all the GIRLS?!

Okay, this was just too . . . WEIRD.

While all of the guys stood there gawking, I decided to go down the hall and investigate. . .

ME →

Practically every girl in the entire school was part of this huge crowd in line for tickets to the Sweetheart Dance.

Jordyn, the girl who sits behind me in geometry, showed me her tickets and excitedly filled me in. . .

"NIKKI, THIS IS THE MOST POPULAR DANCE OF THE YEAR! BUT MAKE SURE YOU GET YOUR TICKETS SOON BECAUSE THEY USUALLY SELL OUT IN A FEW DAYS!"

She was right about the dance being really popular. The line was so long that it flowed past the office, wrapped around the corner near the library and extended beyond the cafeteria door. It looked like the entrance to a sold-out Justin Bieber concert! But get this. . . !!

It was GIRLS ASK THE GUYS!

Of course, I totally FREAKED! Unfortunately, the ONLY guy I am even remotely interested in couldn't even stand to eat a burger with me ☺!

I was so NOT asking him to some Sweetheart Dance!!

All of this gushy sweetheart stuff was getting on my last nerve. So I decided to go to my locker and vent in my diary before my first class.

But THAT was a really BAD idea!

MacKenzie had bedazzled her locker with so many sparkly red and pink hearts, it practically blinded me. Even her lip gloss was red and glittery!

HOW in the world was I supposed to write in my
diary when all of HER very tacky BLING-BLING
was, um . . . BLING-BLINGING all over the place?!!

I couldn't believe what happened next. That girl wrinkled her nose and then sprayed her Pretty Poison designer perfume all over me, accidentally-on-purpose.

Like, WHO does that?! Finally, I just totally lost it.

"PLEASE, MacKenzie! Could you be more careful where you're spraying that stuff?"

"Sorry, Nikki! It's just that your odour is especially pungent today. And I don't have a can of disinfectant spray."

"Personally, I'd prefer disinfectant. What's the name of that perfume you're wearing? Flea-'n'-Tick Repellent?" I shot back.

Calling MacKenzie a mean girl is an understatement. She's a shark in lip gloss, skinny jeans and platform heels.

Suddenly she turned around and got all up in my face like spot cream or something. . .

"SO, NIKKI, ARE YOU GOING TO THE
SWEETHEART DANCE? OH, MY BAD!
THEY DON'T ADMIT ANIMALS!"

"Actually, MacKenzie, that stank you're smelling is
not me. It's coming from your mouth. You're obviously
suffering from a severe case of BLABBER-ITIS! Is
that stuff contagious?"

MacKenzie glared at me with her beady little eyes.
"Admit it, Nikki! You're just jealous because Brandon

liked the digital camera I gave him for his birthday
A LOT better than YOUR stupid gift certificates
to CRUDDY BURGER."

"It's not CRUDDY Burger. It's CRAZY Burger!"
I said, wondering how she even knew about it. Had
Brandon told her we were going to Crazy Burger
together to use his gift certificates?

"Whatever! Your gift was SO tacky! I got the
camera so Brandon can take pictures of me when I'm
crowned Sweetheart Princess. And I've already asked
him to the dance, so don't even think about it."

I just blinked my eyes in shock! MacKenzie had
already asked Brandon to the dance???!!!!

Did he say YES or NO?!! Or MAYBE? She had very
conveniently left out THAT little detail.

However, I had to admit, everything was starting to
make perfect sense.

When MacKenzie had asked to talk to Brandon in

private at his birthday party, it was probably to invite him to the Sweetheart Dance!

And if they were going to the dance together, there was NO WAY she'd want him hanging out with ME at Crazy Burger.

So he had sent me that text ☹!

I closed my eyes, sighed deeply and bit my lip.

Then an unexpected wave of anger rushed over me.

MacKenzie is NOT the boss of me! It's a free country! I can ask WHOEVER I want to the dance.

And yes, Brandon had just stood me up.

But STILL!

There was NO reason why I couldn't just totally HUMILIATE myself by ASKING him anyway. Right?!

WRONG!! If MacKenzie and Brandon want to be together, I'm NOT going to stand in their wa—

That's when MacKenzie rudely interrupted the deep conversation I was having with myself. "BTW, Nikki, just a friendly little reminder! Make sure you vote for ME for Sweetheart Princess on February fourteenth! Everybody else is going to. I'm SOOO popular!" MacKenzie gushed.

Then she flipped her hair and sashayed away. I just HATE it when that girl sashays!

I was really upset that MacKenzie was trying to undermine my friendship with Brandon. AGAIN!

What if I asked him to the dance too?! Then he'd be forced to choose!

TWO desperate girls and ONE guy! Just GREAT ☹!

Of course, this left me with one very obvious and compelling question.

WHY in the world would MacKenzie ask *ME* to vote for *HER* for Sweetheart Princess when it's so obvious that she *HATES* my guts?!

All of this is mind-boggling!! And my mind is so BOGGLED, I seriously need to talk to my BFFs, Chloe and Zoey.

They were the ONLY other girls in the entire school whose brains did NOT turn into MUSH today from Sweetheart FEVER!!

I'm already SICK of Valentine's Day, and it's still two weeks away!

☹!

TUESDAY, FEBRUARY 4

Okay, I was TOTALLY wrong about Chloe and Zoey NOT having Sweetheart Fever.

They're both so obsessed with the dance that their brains are way MUSHIER than all of the other lovesick, mushy-brained girls at school ☹!

Of course, this was a shocking discovery.

I first noticed it in gym class during our swimming section at the WCD High School pool.

We were supposed to be in the water warming up and doing laps for conditioning.

But Chloe and Zoey were SO excited about the upcoming dance that we spent the ENTIRE hour just hanging out on the side of the pool, gossiping about it.

Which was fine by me since I'm not that good at swimming anyway. . .

CHLOE, ZOEY AND ME, IN GYM CLASS
SWIMMING LAPS IN THE POOL
(WELL, SORT OF)

Even though they both wanted to go to the dance REALLY, REALLY badly, they had NOT got tickets yet.

And guess WHY?! THEY didn't want to go UNLESS I went TOO!

I was like, "Come on, GUYS! If you both want to go, you should just do it! I'm sure it'll be really fun and exciting!"

"But it wouldn't be the same without you, Nikki!" Chloe said sullenly.

"Come on, Nikki! We're BFFs. We're supposed to do EVERYTHING together!" Zoey whined.

That's when I totally lost my patience with those two and yelled at them. "Really?! So if I jumped off a cliff, then you two would do it also? And what if I accidentally got hit by a bus — would you want to get hit by a bus too? Come on, girlfriends! We're BFFs! Not CLONES! I think it's time for you to grow up and get a LIFE!"

379

But of course I said all of that inside my head so no one else heard it but me.

Even though they can sometimes be a little annoying, I would NEVER hurt their feelings on purpose. After all, they ARE my BFFs!

"Besides, I'm SURE you're DYING to ask your boo, Brandon, to the dance!" Chloe said, and started making kissy sounds.

"Yeah!" Zoey giggled. "Everyone saw you two making GOO-GOO eyes at each other at his birthday party."

Did I mention the fact that sometimes my BFFs can be a little SUPERannoying?

"We were NOT making goo-goo eyes at each other!" I whisper-shouted as I flushed with embarrassment.

"Were TOO!" Chloe and Zoey teased.

"Were NOT!"

"Were TOO!"

"Were NOT!"

"Were TOO!"

It seemed as if our silly little argument went on, like, FOREVER!

"Okay, already!" I said, finally giving in. "So maybe Brandon and I goo-goo-eyed each other once or twice. But it wasn't on purpose. Mostly." Then I quickly changed the subject. "But what I'M dying to know is who you'd like to ask to the dance. Come on, girlfriends! Spill it!"

Chloe and Zoey blushed profusely.

"Actually, I did have someone in mind. But since we aren't going, I guess that means you'll NEVER know!" Chloe said smugly, and gave me the stink eye.

"Same here!" Zoey said, and playfully stuck her tongue out at me. "For ME to know and YOU to find out!"

CHLOE AND ZOEY VERY RUDELY REFUSE
TO TELL ME WHO THEY'RE CRUSHING ON.

Did I mention the fact that sometimes my BFFs
are a MAJOR PAIN? But it was a NO-BRAINER!
They've been crushing on Jason and Ryan, two CCP
guys, for, like, FOREVER. DUH!!

Anyway, even though Chloe and Zoey were really
looking forward to the dance, the three of us
decided not to go.

I was actually kind of relieved, since I didn't have a date.

I decided not to tell them about the whole Crazy Burger fiasco and Brandon's text message. Or that he and MacKenzie were probably going to the Sweetheart Dance together.

To be honest, I wasn't all that sure about my friendship with Brandon anymore.

So I TOTALLY FREAKED when he came up to my locker today acting all nice and friendly. Kind of like nothing had ever happened between us.

He was like, "Hey, Nikki! Oh, by the way, about Crazy Burger. I just wanted to tell you—"

And I was like, "Really, Brandon. No problem at all. Just FORGET about it!"

Then he looked a little surprised and was like, "Wait, I really need to explain. I wanted to hang out with you last weekend. But things got a little crazy. After MacKenzie dropped by my birthday party, I realised that I—"

And I was like, "I know! You were superbusy. But I really don't have time to talk right now. I've got a lot of STUFF to do! SORRY! Sound familiar?!" Then I folded my arms and just glared at him with this aggravated look on my face like, WHAT?!!

And he stuck his hands in his pockets and just stared at ME with this perplexed look on his face like, *HUH?!!!*

It seemed like all of that glaring and staring went on, like, FOREVER.

Finally, Brandon shrugged. "Um, okay. I guess I better get to class. Later, Nikki."

Then he just walked away! Like, WHO does that?!

How could he leave right in the middle of a serious discussion about our friendship? It was like he didn't even care.

That's when the magazine article "How to Know if a Guy Is Just *NOT* Into You!" popped into my head again.

I took it out of my backpack and read it over. Then I crossed off another item on the list. . .

4. When you try to talk about your relationship, he just walks away.

Things had gone from BAD to WORSE!

But OMG! What Brandon did later that night was totally unexpected.

He sent me not one, but TWO more text messages!!

Did I get a sincere, heartfelt apology about that whole Crazy Burger fiasco?

NO! WAY!

* * * * *
FROM BRANDON:
&&&&&&kkkkkkkwwwbbbbbbbb@@@
8:12 p.m.
* * * * *
FROM BRANDON:
Sorry, Nikki! I just butt-dialled you. Please ignore.
8:14 p.m.
* * * * *

AARRGH !!

Back in November I put together a band called Actually, I'm Not Really Sure Yet (formerly known as Dorkalicious), and we performed in the Westchester Country Day Middle School talent show.

One of the grand prizes was a chance to participate in a reality TV show/talent boot camp called . . .

It's produced by the famous TV producer Trevor Chase, who was also a celebrity judge for our WCD talent show.

I was disappointed when MacKenzie's dance group, Mac's Maniacs, won and we didn't.

Hey, I just thought my band was FANTASTIC!

And apparently, so did Mr Chase. He said his boot camp was for amateurs and beginners. But he felt our band was already fairly polished and wouldn't benefit from it.

Of course that was a BIG compliment! But it gets even better.

He said he was interested in recording an original song that we'd written and performed, called "Dorks Rule!"

We're supposed to meet with him on Saturday, February 8. How COOL is THAT?!

So today after school we had practice at Theo's house.

It was always fun hanging out with Chloe, Zoey, Violet, Theo and Marcus. Although, things between Brandon and me were just plain . . . AWKWARD ☹!

He kept staring at me the whole time with this strange look on his face. Like I was a puzzle he was trying to figure out or something.

But the weird thing was that it seemed like everyone else had an extreme case of the giggles. I started to wonder what was in that hot chocolate we were drinking.

I was trying to conduct a serious meeting about the future of our band, and they just kept laughing and cracking jokes.

Well, everyone except Brandon. He just continued to stare at me, which made me SUPERnervous.

"COME ON, GUYS! STOP GOOFING AROUND!"

Anyway, our practice went really well. We totally ROCKED our song "Dorks Rule!"

MY BAND, PERFORMING "DORKS RULE!"

After practice, I noticed Chloe and Marcus, and Zoey and Theo, were actually FLIRTING with each other!!

That's when it occurred to me that they BOTH made really CUTE couples! The best part was that Marcus and Theo seemed to REALLY like Chloe and Zoey.

Unlike those two slimy CCP guys Jason and Ryan. It was quite obvious that they only hung around my BFFs to do MacKenzie's EVIL bidding. They had successfully manipulated Chloe and Zoey in the past.

But I am NOT about to let it happen AGAIN!

I don't know what that witch MacKenzie is cooking up in her cauldron. But she'd better hold on to her pointy little hat if she comes rolling up on me again! WHY? Because I'm so SICK of her and her two evil little flying monkeys, Jason and Ryan.

MACKENZIE AND HER EVIL FLYING
MONKEYS, JASON AND RYAN

That's when the most FABULOUS idea popped into my head.

Chloe and Zoey would absolutely DIE if I surprised them with tickets to the Sweetheart Dance!

And they TOTALLY deserve it too. They are FOREVER rescuing MY butt from one disaster or another.

Even though I'm not going to the dance, there's no reason why THEY can't go!

And Theo and Marcus would be the perfect dates for them!

SQUEEE ☺!!

Am I not BRILLIANT??!!!

After I got home, I texted them both and told them I had a GINORMOUS surprise for them. Of course they begged me to tell them what it is.

But I told them I'm going to give it to them tomorrow during fifth period since we all work together in the library as shelving assistants.

Chloe and Zoey are SUPERlucky to have ME as a BFF!

I STILL can't get Brandon's sad, slightly puzzled puppy-dog face out of my head.

Since he's been acting genuinely sorry about the whole Crazy Burger thing, just MAYBE I'll consider buying tickets for US, too!

☺!!

P.S. Assuming, of course, he's NOT already going with MacKenzie!

I was so excited about my BIG surprise for Chloe and Zoey that I could barely eat breakfast.

Thank goodness I had just enough money for six tickets saved up from babysitting Brianna and my allowance.

I begged my mom to drop me off at school ten minutes earlier than usual so I could buy the Sweetheart Dance tickets before Chloe and Zoey arrived.

As I rushed down the hall, I passed a bunch of girls who had obviously just purchased their tickets.

Several girls kissed their tickets, while others just stared and giggled hysterically. One girl twirled in circles and another jumped for joy.

OMG! It was like being in the hallway of a mental institution or something!

But the good news was, it looked like tickets were
STILL available! Woo-hoo!

However, this is what happened when I tried to buy mine . . .

I couldn't believe my ROTTEN luck!

"No more tickets are available?! Are you SURE?!"
I asked desperately.

"Since we're having a special catered dinner for the
dance, we had to turn in a figure for the number
of students attending one week before the event.
Unfortunately, our adviser placed the telephone call
with the final headcount five minutes ago. So we
can't sell any more tickets. Sorry!" said Brittany,
the cheerleading captain, as she pulled their poster
off the wall.

"Just GREAT!" I muttered.

Then I turned around and rushed straight down the
hall to the nearest girls' bathroom.

I locked myself in a stall and waited until the
bathroom was completely empty. Then, in a very
CALM and MATURE manner, I did what any normal
girl would do in my exact same situation. . .

I had a really good SCREAM 🙁 . . . !

400

Which, for some strange reason, always makes me feel a lot better ☺!

But now I had a whole NEW problem.

Chloe and Zoey were expecting this HUGE surprise.

And NOW I didn't have anything to give them!!

Which meant they were going to be SUPER-disappointed.

How CRUDDY would THAT be??!!

I dug through my locker, trying to find something to give them.

A mouldy peanut butter sandwich?

My favourite not-from-the-mall old hoodie?

An opened pack of tissues?

A half-used tube of lip gloss?

My situation was hopeless!

Maybe I could give them something really unusual.

For me, anyway.

Something that would require honesty, integrity and maturity.

Like maybe . . . the TRUTH?!

"I'm really sorry, Chloe and Zoey, but as a surprise, I tried to buy tickets to the Sweetheart Dance for you both, but they were sold out"?!

NO WAY!!

Unfortunately, honesty, integrity and maturity are NOT my strong points.

So instead, I decided to just fake it by giving them some junk from my locker. . .

SURPRISE! CHLOE AND ZOEY, AS A TOKEN
OF HOW MUCH I CHERISH OUR FRIENDSHIP,
I'D LIKE TO GIVE YOU THIS PACK OF
TISSUES AND TUBE OF LIP GLOSS,
BOTH ONLY SLIGHTLY USED!

Of course, they both thought I was nuts. They
looked at me, and then at their 'surprise', and then
at each other, and then back at me, and then at
their 'surprise' again, and then at each other.

Finally Zoey forced a smile and said, "Nikki! Um,
thanks. You . . . shouldn't have!"

But Chloe was NOT having it. "Yeah, Nikki. She's right! You really SHOULDN'T have! You're kidding, right?! Please tell me this isn't the big surprise you were telling us abo—" That's when Zoey gave Chloe a swift kick in the shin to shut her up.

"We totally love our gifts! Right, Chloe?" Zoey said, glaring at Chloe through a fake smile.

"I'll love them if it will keep you from KICKING me again!" Chloe grumbled under her breath, still rubbing her shin.

I plastered a fake smile across my face. "Um, you're both welcome! ENJOY!"

And YES! I was a total loser for tricking my friends like that.

And now I'm feeling REALLY guilty.

I can't believe I actually gave my BFFs slightly used TISSUE pack and LIP GLOSS!!

I mean, WHO does THAT?!

I'm such a TOTAL LOSER!

I wouldn't even want to be FRIENDS with MYSELF ☹!

Unfortunately, my day didn't get any better.

Once I got home, there was even more bad news waiting for me.

Trevor Chase had called and said he needed to reschedule for next month. He's in the process of producing a television special for Lady Gaga and was going to be in New York City for another three weeks.

So now my band and I WON'T be meeting with him on Saturday to discuss recording our original song.

My exciting career as a filthy-rich, world-famous POP STAR was over before it had even gotten started.

That's showbiz!

☹!!

I was a little worried when I saw a note from Chloe and Zoey on my locker this morning. . .

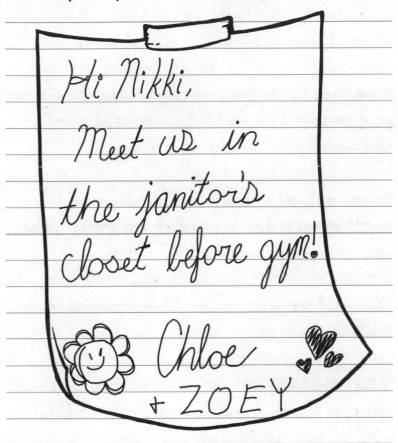

After giving them those crazy "gifts" yesterday, I figured they had decided that I was WAY too FLAKY to be their friend.

They were probably mad at me and demanding both an explanation and an apology for my bizarre behaviour yesterday.

And I didn't blame them one bit. I was still mad at MYSELF for what I did.

When I got to the janitor's closet, Chloe and Zoey were already there. But instead of being angry, they were SUPERexcited about something.

"Guess what, Nikki! Zoey and I decided to do something really fun. It's kind of a surprise!" Chloe said, giving me jazz hands.

"Yeah, and we waited so long that we almost missed out!" Zoey giggled.

"After the tacky surprise I gave you two, I'm almost afraid to see it!" I said, very relieved that they were not going to ditch me as a friend.

"Okay, now close your eyes!" Chloe said. And then they both shouted . . .

"SURPRISE!!"

When I opened my eyes, I was half expecting them to dump a bucket of water on me as a prank to repay me for those tacky gifts.

Then I noticed they were holding something in their hands . . .

TICKETS TO THE SWEETHEART DANCE ☺!!

My mouth dropped open. "OMG! Chloe! Zoey! You guys have tickets to the dance?! You BOTH decided to go? I'm SOOO happy for you!" I gushed. "Yesterday I tried to buy six tickets for us too. But they were sold out! That was actually going to be my REAL surprise!"

However, deep down I felt a little sad, because I really wanted all of us to go to the dance together. Our romantic dream of going on a triple date would have FINALLY come true!

But it wasn't like I was jealous of them or anything.
I mean, how juvenile would THAT be?!

"Wow! YOU actually tried to buy tickets for US?!"
Zoey exclaimed. "Well, Nikki. . ."

WE BOUGHT TICKETS FOR YOU!!

OMG! I was SO shocked and surprised when they
both handed me my very own tickets to the
Sweetheart Dance.

Chloe had already asked Marcus and he said YES!
And Zoey had already asked Theo and he said YES!

So now I just have to get up enough nerve to ask
Brandon! And PRAY he hasn't ALREADY agreed to
go with MacKenzie.

I have to admit, I've been giving him a hard time.
And every time he's tried to explain what happened
or apologise, I've pretty much shot him down. But
it's mostly because I'm really frustrated that things
aren't working out the way I had hoped they would.

So on Monday I plan to make the extra effort to
try and patch things up between us.

The Sweetheart Dance is going to be AWESOME!
And Chloe and Zoey are the best friends EVER!

SQUEEEEEE!!! ☺!!

I had just got home from school when I got another
text message from Brandon. . .

* * * * *

FROM BRANDON:

Busy at Fuzzy Friends bathing a smelly, long-haired dog and thought about you ☺.

4:57 p.m.

* * * * *

Okay, I'm really happy that Brandon was thinking about me and all. But do I really remind him of a smelly, long-haired dog?!!!

* * * * *

FROM NIKKI:

Hi Brandon. Thanks! I think . . .

4:59 p.m.

* * * * *

GRRRRRR!!

OMG!! Did I just growl like a DOG?!

I have to admit, Brandon always seems to be superbusy lately.

If it's not Fuzzy Friends, it's the newspaper or some big photography project.

It's like he doesn't have time for me anymore.

I grabbed my backpack and pulled out that magazine article, "How to Know if a Guy Is Just *NOT* Into You!"

And as I had suspected . . .

3. Suddenly he's always too busy to spend any time with you.

It was another match!

I crossed #3 off of the list.

NOT good!

Okay, now I'm starting to worry that our relationship is *DOOMED!*

☹!!

The last thing I wanted to do was take Brianna to the Kandy Kingdom playland at the mall. But Mom had invited some ladies over for her book club and asked a certain someone to take Brianna out so she wouldn't wreak havoc at home.

This "someone" agreed to do it, but his secret plan was to hang out with friends at the bowling alley and dump Brianna at the mall with her poor, unsuspecting older sister.

Of course, I totally lost it and yelled, "DAD, THAT WAS A REALLY JERKY THING TO DO TO ME!! YOU SHOULD BE ASHAMED!" But I just said it inside my head, so no one else heard it but me.

I sat on a bench in front of Kandy Kingdom and tried to write in my diary. I watched Brianna slide down from the castle tower, jump into the moat filled with balls and bounce in the royal dungeon until my eyes glazed over.

OMG! I was SO bored I wanted to grab one of the giant plastic lollipops and knock myself unconscious to put an end to my suffering. . .

BRIANNA

← ME

To make matters worse, the place was decorated with zillions of HEARTS!

Which, unfortunately, reminded me that the Sweetheart Dance was ONLY a week away and I STILL needed to get up the courage to ask Brandon to go.

JUST GREAT ☹!

I was about to go and grab that giant lollipop, when I saw our neighbor lady, Mrs Wallabanger.

"Hello, Nikki, dear!" she said cheerfully. "What a pleasant surprise to see you here! How are your parents?"

"Hi, Mrs Wallabanger. BOTH of my parents are doing fine. How about YOU?"

Mrs Wallabanger's smile quickly faded. "You say they BOTH have the FLU? Goodness gracious!" She shook her head in pity. "I hear there's a nasty bug going around right now."

In spite of her hearing aid, Mrs Wallabanger was still VERY hard of hearing. She usually misunderstood about 90% of everything I said.

So most of the time I just went along with whatever she said and didn't try to correct her. Although she's a bit eccentric and very feisty, she's basically a nice person.

"Well, you tell your mother I'm going to bring over some of my famous chicken soup, all right, dear?"

"Uh . . . okay," I answered awkwardly.

"Oh! And before I forget, I want to introduce you and Brianna to my grandson," she said.

That's when I noticed the cutest little boy standing behind her. He was about the same age as Brianna.

He saw me looking at him and bashfully hid his face. . .

MRS WALLABANGER, INTRODUCING
ME TO HER GRANDSON

"Brianna!" I motioned for her to join us. "Come say hello to Mrs Wallabanger's grandson."

"What grandson?" she asked, looking around. "Is he invisible?"

"Girls, I want you to meet Oliver," Mrs Wallabanger said. "Don't be shy, Oliver. Nikki and Brianna won't bite."

I grabbed Brianna firmly by her shoulders. I don't bite. But with her, you can never be too careful. Oliver saw Brianna and came out of hiding.

"Hi there, Mrs Wallabanger's grandson!" Brianna said excitedly. She gave him a toothy grin and held out her hand to shake his.

But he just looked at her and stared at her hand in amazement. Suddenly he pulled something out of his pocket and placed it over his hand. It was a tattered gym sock. It had several small holes and was covered with dirt stains.

An oversized pair of googly eyes had been sewn onto the sock, and a large button nose was dangling by a loose thread.

"I'm Oliver, and my friend Mr Buttons thinks your hand smells like Cheetos," he said, holding up his sock puppet.

"That's 'cause Miss Penelope and me had some for lunch," she replied, and licked sticky orange dust from her fingers. "Mmm . . . cheesy! Wanna taste?"

She shoved her slobbery hand in Oliver's face.

"GROSS!" He wrinkled his nose and pushed her hand away. "GIRLS GOT COOTIES!"

"Well, you have way more cooties than me, you BIG MEANIE!" Brianna yelled back.

Mrs Wallabanger looked totally confused.

"Now, what's all of this talk about GIRL SCOUT COOKIES and BEANS-'N'-WEENIES?"

"Um, actually, Oliver and Brianna were just having a, um, friendly little discussion about their favourite foods," I lied.

"Well, Nikki, dear, could I ask you to do me a big favour? I'd like to make a quick stop by RadioShack to see if they have some hearing-aid batteries. I like to keep a few extra on hand because without them I can't hear a thing. Would you mind watching Oliver until I return?"

"Sure," I answered. "Just take your time. Brianna and Oliver can get to know each other better."

"Thank you. You're such a sweetheart!" She smiled and pinched my cheek. "I'll be back in two shakes of a lamb's tail."

"Brianna, be nice to Oliver, okay?" I said. "Why don't you two go play together?"

"I don't wanna play with that weirdo!" she shouted. "Look! He has a puppet on his hand! Besides, Miss Penelope's my best friend, and I only play with HER!"

"Well, I don't want to play with YOU, either!" Oliver huffed. "Mr Buttons is the bestest, smartest friend in the world! And he's an astronaut, too!"

"Well, Miss Penelope is a superhero like Princess Sugar Plum. And she keeps the world safe from the evil tooth fairy!" Brianna bragged.

Oliver's eyes widened, and he looked like he'd just seen a ghost.

"Did you just say the t-t-tooth fairy?!" he stammered. "Once I swallowed my tooth so she wouldn't come after me. That fairy lady is CRAZY!"

"You did that TOO?!" Brianna asked in surprise.

The two of them chatted on and on about the tooth fairy, dinosaurs, Princess Sugar Plum and chocolate cake for what seemed like forever.

And get THIS!

Pretty soon Miss Penelope and Mr Buttons joined in on their very weird conversation.

The four of them were acting just like BFFs!

OLIVER, BRIANNA, MR BUTTONS AND MISS
PENELOPE, HAVING A FRIENDLY CHAT TOGETHER

All of the giggling and puppy love was utterly adorable!
Even though it involved two VERY weird little kids.
And their even weirder talking hand puppets.

If they started having play dates together on a regular basis, I'd have obnoxious imaginary friends, migraines, broken furniture, kitchen fires and nervous breakdowns TIMES TWO! No . . . FOUR! I broke into a cold sweat just thinking about it.

"I'm back!" Mrs Wallabanger announced. "It was so kind of you to watch my grandson for me. Enjoy the rest of your day, girls. Now come along, Oliver."

Oliver ran up to his grandmother and took her hand.

"Bye, Miss Penelope!" ~~Oliver~~ Mr Buttons yelled as Oliver waved his little sock-puppet hand.

"Bye, Mr Buttons!" ~~Brianna~~ Miss Penelope screeched with her very big mouth.

After Mrs Wallabanger and Oliver left, I gave Brianna an evil grin. . .

BRIANNA AND OLIVER,
SITTING IN A TREE,
K-I-S-S-I-N-G!!

"STOP IT OR I'M TELLING MOM!" she yelled at me. She was blushing profusely, and I couldn't stop laughing.

427

It was SWEET revenge for all of those times Brianna had embarrassed ME in front of Brandon!

"If I didn't know better, I'd say somebody is having her first crush!" I teased.

"Not me!" Brianna snapped. "But Miss Penelope might like Mr Buttons a teeny-weeny bit because they both love chocolate cake. She told me not to tell anyone, so you have to promise to keep it a secret!"

"Okay. I promise," I said, and gave her a big hug.

So maybe the thought of Brianna having a crush isn't *that* nauseating.

I'm a romantic, after all.

I can already picture their future wedding. Brianna would be dressed in a designer Princess Sugar Plum gown and Oliver would be wearing a clunky astronaut suit. . .

BRIANNA AND OLIVER'S WEDDING

The "kiddie gourmet" wedding feast would include gummy bear appetizers, spaghetti hoops, chicken nuggets, crackers, Hawaiian Punch, and a five-tiered chocolate cake with bubble-gum filling.

How CUTE would THAT be?

Hey, even little PSYCHOS like Brianna need love too! ☺!

I'm already DREADING school tomorrow.

Why?

Because we have a floating skills test in swimming class.

Hey, if a human was meant to float, we'd be made of plastic. And instead of having a belly button we'd have a little nozzle thingy so we could be pumped full of air, just like a tyre. I'm just sayin'!

Whenever I try to swim in the deep end of the pool, I pretty much sink right to the bottom.

Like a really heavy rock.

But that's not the worst part!

Do you have any idea of the very gross stuff that's lying on the bottoms of swimming pools?!

It's like an underwater lost-and-found down there. . .

ME, LOOKING AT ALL OF THE JUNK
AT THE BOTTOM OF THE POOL

What I really need is a swimming-class excuse
form that other kids and I can use to get out
of swimming class. . .

SWIMMING-CLASS
EXCUSE FORM

FROM: _____
(YOUR NAME)

TO: _____
(NAME OF SWIMMING INSTRUCTOR)

RE: Medical Excuse for Swimming Class

It is with
- ☐ great sorrow
- ☐ a really bad headache
- ☐ food stuck in my teeth
- ☐ a funky foot odour

that I inform you that I am unable to participate in today's swimming class. Last night I discovered that I'm severely allergic to

☐ my mom's meat loaf.

☐ my little brother's boogers.

☐ most crawling insects.

☐ water.

After swallowing just a tiny amount, I became really

☐ nervous

☐ dizzy

☐ constipated

☐ confused

and accidentally fell

☐ into the bathtub

☐ down the stairs

☐ in love

☐ into a snake pit

and totally busted my

☐ liver.

☐ tailbone.

☐ nose.
☐ baby toe.

Due to the massive trauma I suffered, I
suddenly and unexpectedly went into
    ☐ a medley of show tunes.
    ☐ a closet to hide from the tooth fairy.
    ☐ a fit of involuntary hiccuping.
    ☐ my sister's room to yell at her.

I was rushed by ambulance to the emergency
room, where the doctor told me I was lucky
to be alive. Apparently, exposure to the high
concentration of
    ☐ spit
    ☐ bacteria
    ☐ disease
    ☐ belly-button fluff

found in pool water could be deadly and cause
both a serious infection and a severe case of

☐ abnormally hairy legs.

☐ irritable bowel syndrome.

☐ compulsive chicken dancing.

☐ projectile vomiting.

Of course I am

☐ totally devastated

☐ surprised and shocked

☐ dazed and confused

☐ completely baffled

by this awful news. As a health precaution, my doctor has ordered me to avoid pool water for at least the next

☐ week.

☐ month.

☐ year.

☐ decade.

Thank you for understanding my health situation and being so amazingly

□ sympathetic.

□ ugly.

□ gullible.

□ stupid.

Sincerely,

_____

(YOUR SIGNATURE)

Am I NOT brilliant?!!

☺!!

NOTE TO SELF: THE SWEETHEART DANCE IS IN FOUR DAYS ☺!! ASK BRANDON ASAP!

Last night I dug around in the garage and found a big box of Brianna's old water toys that had been put away back when she was a toddler. Hey, I was desperate!

But the good news is that I found the cutest little floating-toy thingy that fit around my waist perfectly.

As long as I didn't try to breathe.

And packed in the same box was a SUPERold swimsuit that belonged to my grandma when she was a little girl.

I thought I looked pretty cute walking out to the pool for swimming class.

Until Chloe gasped, Zoey covered her eyes and everyone else stared.

SIERRA THE SEA HORSE AND I GET
READY FOR MY FLOATING SKILLS TEST.

MacKenzie just looked me up and down like she had never seen a swimsuit with LEGS. Or Sierra, a hot-pink Princess Sugar Plum Baby Sea Horse floating toy with purple hearts on it!

I mean, WHERE has that girl been all of her life?

Under a ROCK?!!

Then MacKenzie batted her eyes at me all innocent-like and made a very snarky and insulting comment in front of the entire class.

"Um, excuse me, Nikki. But the class for Water Babies meets tomorrow at four p.m., NOT today."

Of course everyone snickered.

I could NOT believe that girl had the nerve to publicly insinuate that I was a Water Baby!!

"Gee thanks, MacKenzie, for the info on the other class!" I said really sweetly. "Now why don't you go and jump into the deep end of the pool, swallow twenty-seven gallons of water, and EXPLODE!"

And of course my gym teacher didn't help matters any. She said I couldn't get into the pool with my sea horse because floating toys were NOT allowed.

But I didn't see that rule posted on the wall. It only said:

WCD POOL RULES

1. NO running!

2. NO eating!

3. NO horseplay!

4. NO peeing in the pool!

Anyway, I must have had a really big breakfast or something, because when I tried to take it off, that stupid sea horse was STUCK! Even Chloe and Zoey couldn't pry it off of me. . .

CHLOE AND ZOEY, TRYING TO HELP
ME GET OUT OF THAT SEA HORSE

And because I could hardly breathe I started having these really WEIRD hallucinations. I saw myself:

In bio class sitting next to Brandon while wearing the sea horse.

Going to the Sweetheart Dance wearing the sea horse.

Graduating from high school wearing the sea horse.

Moving into my college dormitory wearing the sea horse.

Getting married wearing the sea horse.

And giving birth to my first child wearing the sea horse.

OMG! It was like I was going to be STUCK wearing the sea horse the rest of MY LIFE!

That's when I just totally lost it and started SCREAMING hysterically!

Or due to a lack of oxygen, maybe I was just HALLUCINATING that I was screaming hysterically. I really couldn't tell for sure since I was very confused.

That's when my gym teacher called the janitor and told him to come ASAP because she had an emergency situation.

He actually had to cut the sea horse thingy off of

me with these giant metal clippers. Which of course made me supernervous.

One little accidental SNIP and I could have lost an arm or leg or something.

Hey, it could happen! I'd ALREADY lost a braid to Brianna just eight days ago.

Anyway, the good news is that after the janitor finally got that thing off, I started breathing again.

OMG! I felt SO much better after that sea horse fiasco was over!

But the surprising thing was that my gym teacher actually gave me a passing score on my floating skills testing for "Good effort!" Mainly because she said she'd had enough DRAMA for one day and DIDN'T want me in the pool endangering MY life, HER life, or the lives of other STUDENTS in the class.

I was SUPERhappy things turned out so well! ☺!

Anyway, I still had to figure out how I was going to ask Brandon to the Sweetheart Dance.

I had no idea how all of the other girls at my school were brave enough to ask their crushes to the dance.

I guess the major difference is that I'm a spineless coward and just the thought of Brandon possibly saying no totally freaked me out.

I decided to take the direct approach: Track him down in the newspaper office. And just . . . ASK him.

I mean, how hard could it be?

EXTREMELY ☹!!

I had a dry mouth, shaky knees, and a stomach full of rabid butterflies.

And that was from just merely thinking about it.

But apparently, Brandon and the rest of our photography staff were on a two-day field trip touring a local community newspaper. So my only option is to talk to him about the dance when he returns on Wednesday.

I STILL can't believe I actually passed my floating skills test!

WOO-HOO!

☺!!

NOTE TO SELF: THE SWEETHEART DANCE IS IN THREE DAYS ☺!!

I just LOATHE shopping for Valentine's cards with Brianna. It's the same DRAMA every single year.

"But I just gotta have the Princess Sugar Plum valteen cards!" Brianna whined.

Mom had dropped Brianna and me off at the main entrance of the mall while she hunted for a parking space.

"It's V-A-L-E-N-T-I-N-E! Not valteen!" I grumbled.

"If I don't get my Princess Sugar Plum cards, I will cry once upon a time in a faraway land, forever and ever, the end!" she whimpered.

"Well, unless you want me to drop you off at the mall's lost and found, you'd better NOT cry forever and ever!" I muttered.

"ACTUALLY, I *FOUND* THIS LITTLE GIRL
THROWING A TANTRUM IN THE MALL. . . ."

"Anyway, it's just a silly card that kids in your class will throw away the second they open it! So what's the big deal?!" I grumped.

"I want my Princess Sugar Plum valteens! NOW!" Brianna cried.

We searched for those cruddy Princess Sugar Plum valentines all afternoon. And nine stores, five tantrums and one migraine headache later, we STILL hadn't found any. Every single store was sold out!

At least the mall was prepared for the onslaught. Sales clerks at every store were strategically stationed by their Valentine's display holding boxes of tissues for the kids who burst into tears once they found out that the Princess Sugar Plum Valentine's Day cards were all sold out.

It was totally disgusting how most of the stores had taken complete advantage of the situation and set up huge displays with other Princess Sugar Plum products. . .

It was quite obvious they were hoping the traumatised little brats would buy an assortment of the forty-nine other Princess Sugar Plum products instead.

There was Princess Sugar Plum bubble bath, body lotion, shampoo, toothpaste, vitamins, Band-Aids, sweets, pretend glitter makeup, bubble gum, cereal, breakfast bars, peanut butter, dolls, board games, fashions, dog food etc.

Basically, you name it, they had it.

Somewhere on a remote island there's probably a secret factory where fat little purple elves with pointy little shoes, sugar plum hair and creepy, beady little eyes crank out Princess Sugar Plum junk twenty-four hours a day, seven days a week. Kind of like that Willie Wonka guy and his chocolate factory.

Of course, when Brianna didn't find the Princess Sugar Plum valentines, she quickly morphed into a wailing, slobbering, snot-nosed wreck.

But what I couldn't figure out was how the sales clerks could be so calm and peaceful in the midst of total chaos!

There were little girls crying, screaming, yelling, screeching, shrieking and squealing everywhere.

How could they just stand there smiling calmly through all of that high-pitched, eardrum-shattering noise while a couple of hundred five-year-olds threw simultaneous tantrums?

I was impressed.

Until I saw their secret weapon.

EARPLUGS!!!

Yes!

Those SNEAKY little scoundrels!!

The clerks were all wearing earplugs to protect their hearing AND their sanity!!

WAAA! I WANT
PRINCESS SUGAR
PLUM VALTEENS!

WEARING
EARPLUG
THINGIES
↓

TISSUES

← BRIANNA

Anyway, Mom and I were exhausted from shopping,
and Brianna was an emotional basket case.

In the car on the way home I came up with a
BRILLIANT idea!

454

"Brianna, what do you think about me making your Princess Sugar Plum valentines instead? I'm a pretty decent artist, and I'm sure you'd love 'em."

Brianna immediately stopped crying and looked at me suspiciously, like I was trying to sell her some swampland in Florida — really cheap!

"But if YOU make them, they won't be REAL Princess Sugar Plum valteen cards!" she sulked.

That's when Mom winked at me. "Brianna, dear, I have a wonderful idea! How about while Nikki is making your cards, you can eat a big, yummy bowl of Princess Sugar Plum cereal for dinner?!"

Brianna's eyes lit up. "Princess Sugar Plum cereal! FOR DINNER?! THAT would be FUN!" She giggled.

But suddenly Brianna's mood darkened and she started to pout again.

"But, Moooom! I just ate the last booowl of Princess Sugar Plum cereal this morning. And we

455

don't have any more miiiilk," she cried pitifully.

Mom quickly spun the car around by doing a U-turn right in the middle of the street as I held on for dear life. SCREEEEECH!! (That was our tyres!)

"Then we'll just stop at the grocery store and you and Nikki can run in and get some cereal and milk! How does that sound?" Mom asked cheerfully.

"Well . . . okay, I g-guess." Brianna sniffed glumly.

Once we were inside the store, I held Brianna's hand so she wouldn't wander off or get into any trouble. Then we headed for the cereal aisle.

"Hmmm! Let's see. . ." I muttered to myself as I tapped my chin. "Princess Sugar Plum cereal with tooty-fruity marshmallows, Princess Sugar Plum cereal with princess fairy dust, Princess Sugar Plum cereal with glitter sprinkles, and finally, Princess Sugar Plum cereal with a free mini glow-in-the-dark tiara. . ."

ME, TRYING TO FIGURE OUT WHICH CEREAL
TO BUY WHILE WATCHING BRIANNA (SORT OF)

There were so many choices I couldn't make up my mind. "Brianna, which cereal do you want?" I asked as I turned around.

That's when I discovered she had disappeared into thin air!

Although, it WASN'T the first time. I broke into a cold sweat as memories of the time I lost Brianna at the *Nutcracker* ballet flooded into my brain.

"<u>NOOOOO!!!</u> Not AGAIN!" I shrieked as I frantically ran down the aisle. "BRIANNA. . .!!"

Suddenly I spotted her!

She had stacked a pile of assorted grocery items on the floor and climbed up on top of them.

Then, balancing dangerously on her tippy toes, she was reaching desperately for an item on the top shelf of a big colourful display. This is what happened. . .

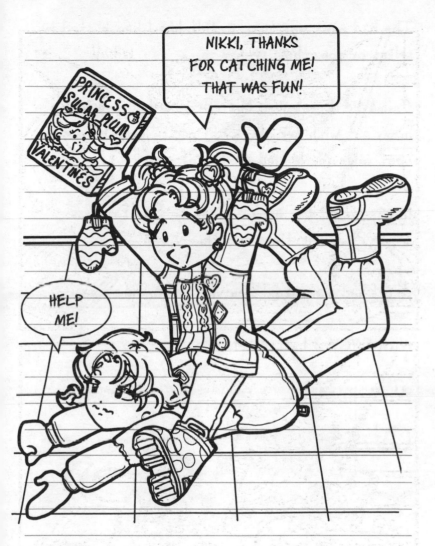

Well, there was good news and bad news.

The good news was that Brianna wasn't hurt.

The bad news was that it felt like I had busted my spleen or something.

Or maybe it was just that Brianna had kicked me in my gut with her chunky Princess Sugar Plum snow boot when she landed on top of me.

In any event, the annual quest to find Princess Sugar Plum valentines was finally over.

And I had managed to survive yet another year.

With ONLY a busted spleen.

Woo-hoo!

☺!

WEDNESDAY, FEBRUARY 12

NOTE TO SELF: THE DANCE IS IN TWO DAYS ☺!!
ASK BRANDON!! IT'S NOW OR NEVER!!

Today everyone was buzzing about who was going to
be crowned Sweetheart Princess.

Students can vote for any eighth-grade girl.
However, the girls who wanted it really badly (like
MacKenzie) were putting up posters. The entire
student body votes during school on February 14,
and the winner will be announced later that night
at the dance.

According to the latest gossip, everyone was
pretty sure MacKenzie was going to win. Especially
MacKenzie!

OMG! That girl is so hopelessly VAIN!

All day she was acting supernice to everyone and
giving out sweet hearts and free fashion advice to
bribe people to vote for her.

Although, I have to admit, her posters are
SUPERCUTE...!

MACKENZIE'S
SUPERCUTE →
POSTERS

I ALMOST wanted to vote for her MYSELF! NOT! ☺!!

Anyway, TODAY was the big day!

During bio I was FINALLY going to ask Brandon to go to the Sweetheart Dance with me.

OMG! I was a nervous wreck!

And yes! I realised there was a possibility he might already be going with MacKenzie. But at this point I had nothing to lose.

I gulped down my lunch. Then I rushed to the girls' bathroom and practised what I was going to say to him in the mirror . . .

"Brandon, I know this is kind of last-minute and everything, but I would really love it if you would take me to the Sweetheart Dance!"

In the bathroom, everything went PERFECTLY!

But when I actually tried to ask Brandon, I got totally distracted by all of the stuff that was going on in class. . .

SO, BRANDON . . . I KNOW THIS IS KIND OF LAST-MINUTE AND EVERYTHING, BUT I WOULD REALLY LOVE IT IF YOU WOULD TAKE . . .

OMG! That quiz was a complete DISASTER!! We were supposed to draw the Krebs cycle, and I totally KNEW the correct answer.

However, I was so FREAKED out by the whole asking-Brandon-to-the-Sweetheart-Dance fiasco that I totally blanked out and couldn't remember a thing. So I just drew the first thing that popped into my head...

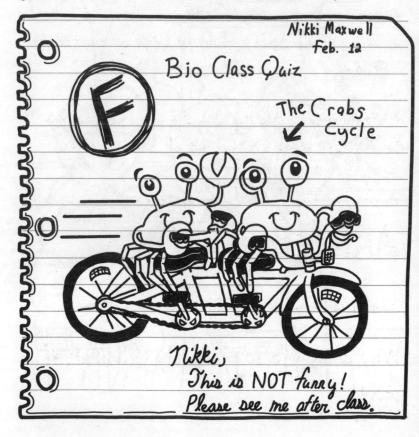

Nikki Maxwell
Feb. 12

Bio Class Quiz

The Crabs
Cycle

Nikki,
This is NOT funny!
Please see me after class.

Unfortunately, my teacher did NOT appreciate MY creativity, humour, or artistic talent.

When I talked to Ms Kincaid after class, she told me I was in bio, not ART class. Then she warned me that if I got another grade below a C or goofed-off in her class again, she was sending a note home to my parents.

Of course they would totally overreact and take away my phone AND ground me until my eighteenth birthday.

Thank goodness Ms Kincaid allows us to drop our lowest test score at the end of the semester.

Anyway, I STILL have to ask Brandon to the dance!!

ARRGHH!!!

That was me pulling my hair out in frustration.

Why is my life so massively CRUDDY?!

!!

Yesterday I was so upset about Brandon and that stupid bio quiz that I planned to go straight to my room and have myself a big pity party.

Brianna was in the kitchen humming to herself and working on her Princess Sugar Plum ~~valteen~~ cards. . .

That's when the most FABULOUS idea popped into my head!

I had totally embarrassed myself trying to ask Brandon to the Sweetheart Dance.

But what if I gave him a Valentine's Day card instead?

Then I could WRITE a little note inside inviting him to the Sweetheart Dance!!

It would be cute, sweet, and romantic!

SQUEEE ☺!

How could he say no to that?!!

I scavenged the house for cool stuff I could use for his card and found glitter, satin ribbon, red foil wrapping paper, lace, rhinestones and gel pens.

Then, blasting my favourite Taylor Swift tunes for inspiration, I created a beautiful, one-of-a-kind, personalised valentine just for Brandon...

ME, MAKING A CARD FOR BRANDON

The final step was to write a deep, heartfelt poem inspired by our friendship and mutual respect for each other. Like . . .

ROSES ARE RED,
VIOLETS ARE BLUE,
I'D REALLY LOVE TO GO
TO THE SWEETHEART
DANCE WITH
YOU!!

Yes, I know!

My poem is cheesier than two large pizzas.

Taylor Swift makes writing mushy songs about your boyfriend look really easy.

Anyway, this morning I went to school ten minutes early so I could give Brandon my card before classes started.

But it wasn't until second period that I FINALLY spotted him at his locker talking to Theo!

I didn't have a choice but to go into stalker mode and secretly follow him around, waiting for the perfect moment to give him the card.

But that moment NEVER came. Someone was always hanging around or talking to him. I didn't know the guy was so popular.

Although I was still pretty traumatised from that pop quiz fiasco yesterday, one thing was very clear. Cornering Brandon in bio class was going to be my ONLY chance at attending the Sweetheart Dance!

I got to class superearly and just sat there clutching my card, waiting for him to arrive. I was a nervous wreck!

And having the extra time to think just made me worry about all of the things that could go wrong AFTER he read my poem.

I mean, what if Brandon said NO? Or laughed at me? Or just . . . PUKED?!

OMG! I was a sweaty, paranoid . . . WRECK! I felt like people were staring at me and whispering about me. . .

ME, NERVOUSLY WAITING FOR BRANDON
SO I COULD GIVE HIM MY CARD

When Brandon finally arrived, I thought I was going
to pee my pants.

475

"What's up, Nikki?!" he said, brushing his hair out of his eyes and giving me a crooked smile.

I just stared at him. I opened my mouth to say hi, but no words came out.

"Um . . . are you okay?" he suddenly asked, looking concerned. "You look a little, um . . . frazzled!"

"Actually, Brandon . . ." I finally blurted out really loud, "I just wanted to give—"

"BRAAAN-DON! Wasn't that pop quiz yesterday just AWFUL?" MacKenzie asked, rudely interrupting me. "I thought I failed for sure. But lucky for me I squeaked by with a B+. So, Nikki, what did YOU get on the quiz, hon?"

Then she smiled at me and batted her eyes all innocent-like.

I wanted to slap that smile right off her face.

But before I could answer, MacKenzie turned her

back to me and started gushing to Brandon about how much she was looking forward to seeing all of the great photos he'd taken with that new camera she'd given him for his birthday.

I could NOT believe that girl was ignoring me right to my face like that. And get this! She kept blabbing her big fat mouth right up until our teacher arrived.

Which totally RUINED my chance to talk to Brandon BEFORE class. And if MacKenzie had her way, she'd HOG all of his attention and totally RUIN my chance to talk to him AFTER class TOO!

I was sick and tired of her little mind games.

So that's when I decided I'd just give Brandon my card DURING class! Hey, I sat right next to him!

And MacKenzie couldn't do a thing to stop me.

Because our class had performed poorly on our pop

quiz yesterday, Ms Kincaid planned to spend the entire hour at the board diagramming the Krebs cycle while we took notes.

OMG! Her lecture was SO boring I thought my brain was going to melt and ooze out of my ears. . .

"The citric acid cycle — also known as the Krebs cycle — is a series of chemical reactions used by all aerobic organisms to generate energy through the oxidisation of acetate derived from carbohydrates, fats and proteins into carbon dioxide. In addition . . ."

I stared at Brandon for what seemed like FOREVER waiting for him to look in my direction. But he was busy taking notes.

That's when I took my pencil and gently poked his arm.

At first he looked slightly startled, then a little confused.

I pulled the card out of my notebook and mouthed the words "For YOU!"

He blinked in surprise and then pointed at himself, as if to say "For ME?!"

I nodded my head. "Yes!"

As I watched Ms Kincaid out of the corner of my eye, I quickly shoved the card in Brandon's direction.

However, I think that supercute smile of his must have affected my nervous system and messed up my hand-eye coordination or something. Because the valentine slid right past him, glided across the floor, and landed centimetres from Ms Kincaid's left foot!

I wanted to jump out of my seat and try to grab it before she saw it.

But someone right behind me started to cough.

Really loudly.

And because it was such an obviously FAKE cough, I guessed that it was MacKenzie.

Distracted by the noise, Ms Kincaid turned around.

I pretended not to notice the big glittery red valentine lying on the floor right in front of her. But it didn't matter because everyone else in the room was staring at it like it was a four-metre-long two-headed flesh-eating snake.

"Okay, people. I'm up here trying to teach you this stuff! And someone has decided to disrupt the class by handing out valentines a day early?!!"

Everyone snickered.

"So, who does THIS belong to?" she asked as she reached down and picked up the card.

The room was so quiet, you could hear a pin drop. Neither Brandon nor I felt morally obligated to offer a confession.

He kept HIS mouth shut because if I brought the card to class, it belonged to ME (not HIM).

And I kept MY mouth shut because if I'd just given the card away, it technically belonged to HIM (not ME).

Unfortunately, my cover was quickly blown. Probably because the back of the card had big letters that said: "From Nikki" DUH!!

"Miss Maxwell, I think this belongs to you!" Ms Kincaid said, glaring at me.

"Um, it kind of fell out of my notebook. Accidentally," I muttered.

"Really? So you weren't passing notes in class?"

"Actually, I wouldn't really call it a note?" I mumbled. "It's more of a . . . card."

The class snickered again.

Since you think your card is more important than the Krebs Cycle, I'm sure you wouldn't mind me sharing it with the entire class, right?

HAPPY VALENTINE'S DAY, BRANDON!

"Actually, I—I was hoping you wouldn't share it with the class?" I stammered.

More laughter. OMG! I was SO embarrassed. I wanted to dig a really deep hole right in the middle of the floor, crawl into it, and . . . DIE!

Brandon's cheeks were flushed, and he looked really nervous.

Ms Kincaid read the card silently, crossed her arms and stared at me.

Then, choosing to spare Brandon the massive embarrassment, she turned, marched across the room and tossed my valentine onto her desk.

"Nikki, please see me after class!"

I could feel everyone's eyes on me. MacKenzie, now miraculously cured from her coughing affliction, had this smug little look on her face.

Brandon shrugged and mouthed the word "Sorry!"

But I just stared blankly straight ahead.

I could NOT believe that MacKenzie had totally set me up! AGAIN!! I was so mad I could SPIT!!

And now I was going to get a note sent home to my parents and possibly even an after-school detention.

Finally the bell rang and bio was over.

Brandon actually looked kind of upset. "I'm really sorry about what happened, Nikki! I'll just wait for you right outside the door until you're done talking to the teacher, okay?"

"Don't worry! It was just a stupid card. I'll be fine. Really!" I said, trying to muster a smile. "The last thing you need is a tardy."

"I guess you're right. I just feel bad since you made that card for me." Suddenly his face brightened. "Hey! I'm going to hang out at Fuzzy Friends after school today. The bakery across the street makes some mean cupcakes! Why don't you stop by? It'll be my treat! Besides, we haven't really talked much since my birthday."

"Yeah, that would be very cool, actually!" I blushed.

"But I'm supposed to watch Brianna after school today. I'll text my mom and ask if I—"

"MISS MAXWELL!" Ms Kincaid interrupted. "Whenever you're done chatting, I'll be here WAITING . . . !"

"Sorry!" I said to Brandon, rolling my eyes. "I'll see you later. Maybe."

"Later. Hopefully!" Brandon smiled and gave me a thumbs-up. Then he headed for the door.

I shoved all of my stuff into my backpack and slowly walked up to my teacher's desk.

"Um, you wanted to see me?" I muttered. I was expecting the worst.

"Nikki, I've noticed you've been really distracted lately. Yesterday you drew a cartoon on your quiz and today you were disrupting class by giving out valentines instead of taking notes. Is everything okay?"

I shrugged my shoulders. "I'm okay, I guess. It's just that the Sweetheart Dance is tomorrow. I planned to ask Brandon yesterday, but we had that pop quiz. Then today you confiscated my card before I could give it to him. So things are just . . . cruddy!" I explained, trying to ignore the large lump in my throat.

Suddenly Ms Kincaid smiled and shook her head.

"When I was your age, I thought I'd NEVER survive middle school! But I did, and so will YOU. Here!" she said, handing my valentine back to me. Then she winked at me. "Good luck!"

I just stared at her with my mouth open. I was so shocked, I didn't know what to say.

"Thank you! I can't believe you just . . . ! Thank you!" I sputtered.

"Now, I'm warning you, Miss Maxwell. No more funny business in my class, or you're going to be doodling crabs AND giving out valentines in DETENTION."

I did my Snoopy "happy dance" all the way to the library. Inside my head!

My Plan A had failed. But now I had a Plan B!

I would meet Brandon at Fuzzy Friends after school. Then, while we shared a yummy cupcake, I'd give him my valentine.

SQUEEE ☺!!

He'd say YES! And by this time tomorrow my BFFs and I would be just hours away from our very first dates.

A triple date! Just like we'd dreamed of!

I texted my mom, and she said I could hang out at Fuzzy Friends, but only for forty-five minutes since it was a school night and I had homework.

Finally school was over! It was hard to believe that in just ten minutes it was going to be official.

I'd actually be going to the Sweetheart Dance with Brandon! SQUEEE ☺!!

I was at my locker getting my coat when I got two texts barely a minute apart. I thought they were from my mom. But I was pleasantly surprised to see that they were from . . . BRANDON!

However, I gasped in shock when I read them . . .

* * * * *
FROM BRANDON:
Hey MacKenzie,
What's up! Wasn't bio crazy today?
3:07 p.m.
* * * * *
FROM BRANDON:
Sorry, Nikki! My bad. Wrong #.
3:08 p.m.
* * * * *

OMG! I had a meltdown right there at my locker!

HOW COULD BRANDON

ACCIDENTALLY SEND A TEXT

MEANT FOR MACKENZIE TO ME?!!

I don't know if I was more angry or disgusted!
It seemed like Brandon was ALWAYS talking to
MacKenzie or working on some random newspaper
project with her.

And now it was quite obvious he was TEXTING her on a pretty regular basis too!

All while inviting ME to hang out at Fuzzy Friends and eat cupcakes with him??!! I mean, WHO does that?!!

I reached into my backpack and dug out that wrinkled magazine article, "How to Know if a Guy Is Just NO T Into You."

I read it over, then crossed off the last item left on the list:

5. He's spending way too much time with another girl.

I sighed and blinked back my tears. I felt so STUPID!

Brandon was NOT interested in me at all.

And according to the EXPERTS, he'd done all FIVE of the things on the magazine checklist! I'd carefully documented each and every one. . .

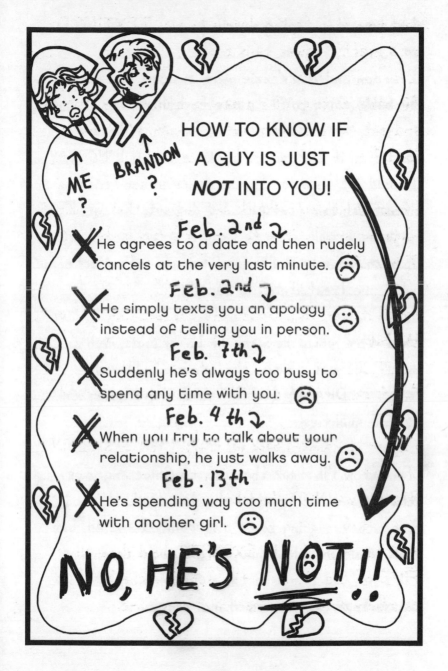

I had to stop fooling myself.

Brandon and MacKenzie were an item and were probably going to the dance together.

And even if they weren't, there was still NO WAY I could ask Brandon to the dance after receiving those last two texts!

How could he be really good friends with MacKenzie when she treated ME so badly?

And WHY would he want to be friends with her?! She was a mean, spoiled, manipulative, vain . . . DRAMA QUEEN! And those were her BEST qualities!

Tomorrow I'll break the news to Chloe and Zoey that I won't be going to the dance with them. I know they're going to be disappointed and all, but this whole Brandon thing is NOT working out.

I just hope they'll understand.

It's really sad losing a good friend like Brandon to MacKenzie. And the last thing I want is to lose my BFFs, too.

Then I'd be all alone at this school again.

I sighed deeply and slammed my locker door shut just as MacKenzie and Jessica brushed past me, giggling.

"OMG! Jess!" MacKenzie gushed. "Guess who just texted me?!"

She showed her phone to Jessica. Then they both squealed in excitement like two baby pigs or something.

I didn't want to fight with MacKenzie.

I didn't want to go to the dance with Brandon.

I didn't want to disappoint my BFFs.

All I REALLY wanted to do was rush home and have a really good CRY!

But first I had to stop by the girls' bathroom.

Only, it wasn't for the most obvious reason.

I sniffed and wiped away a tear that had trickled down my cheek.

Then I ripped Brandon's valentine into tiny pieces and flushed it down the toilet!

I had pretty much accepted the fact that I WASN'T going to the Sweetheart Dance. But I still felt disappointed, hurt and just plain miserable.

I must have been pretty traumatised by the whole thing, because I had the most horrible nightmare!

It was the night of the Sweetheart Dance, and I was at home putting dishes in the dishwasher and feeling kind of depressed about my life.

Suddenly my fairy godmother appeared and waved her magic wand. She turned my heart pj's into a beautiful evening gown and my bunny slippers into glass slippers.

Then she waved her wand again and turned Brianna's Princess Sugar Plum Magical Flying Car (with real working headlights) into a life-size limo and Brianna's Baby Unicorn into a chauffeur.

OMG! It was like I was Cinderella or someone!

And when I arrived at the Sweetheart Dance, Brandon was dressed like a prince and standing there waiting for me. We danced the night away and had a wonderful time together. It was SO romantic!

Then, at the stroke of midnight, MacKenzie was crowned Sweetheart Princess and my fairy tale turned into a horror story.

My gown and glass slippers turned back into my pj's and bunny slippers. And my limo and chauffeur turned back into the Princess Sugar Plum Magical Flying Car (with real working headlights) and Baby Unicorn.

OMG! I was SO embarrassed to be at the school dance in my pajamas with Brianna's toys. Everyone was laughing at me. Even Brandon, Chloe and Zoey!

But this was the really scary part. Suddenly MacKenzie turned into this huge monster with pointy teeth, and she started growling and chasing me around the dance. I barely escaped by galloping away on Baby Unicorn. . .

GRRRRR!

← MACKENZIE

It was probably the WORST nightmare I'd ever had in my entire life.

I woke up in a cold sweat.

But this is the crazy part!

Even though I was wide awake and staring at the ceiling, I could still hear MacKenzie (or something) growling.

GRRRRRRRRRRRRR!

GRRRRRRRRRRRRRRR!

GRRRRRRRRRRRRRRR!

And it seemed to be coming from outside.

I rushed to my bedroom window and cautiously peeked out, half expecting to see a glammed-up monster in a tiara terrorising the neighbourhood.

OMG! I couldn't believe my eyes. . .

IT WAS A TOTAL BLIZZARD OUTSIDE!!

Overnight, we'd had a whopping tweny centimetres of snow!!

And the growling sound I'd dreamed about was actually Dad's snowblower.

ALL of the schools in the area were closed, including WCD Middle School.

That's when it hit me. . . . OMG! Our Sweetheart Dance was probably cancelled as well!!

I felt so sorry for my BFFs and all of the other girls at school.

I'm sure they were SUPERdisappointed!

I usually enjoy when school is cancelled due to snow. But today I just felt kind of numb.

So as a special treat to try and cheer myself up, I decided to make . . .

HOMEMADE DOUBLE-CHOCOLATE FUDGE ☺ . . . !

501

BRIANNA!! WHY ARE YOUR HANDPRINTS IN MY DOUBLE-CHOCOLATE FUDGE?!

Luckily, I was able to cover up Brianna's handprints by sprinkling those cute little Valentine heart sweets over the top of the fudge.

BTW, I called Chloe and Zoey to get an update on the Sweetheart Dance. They had good news and bad news! The bad news was that the dance had in fact been cancelled due to the snowstorm. However, the good news was that it's rescheduled for Friday, February 28. Of course, they were disappointed since they were all geared up to go to the dance TONIGHT! But I reminded them that the new date is ONLY two weeks away!

Anyway, after lunch Brianna and I gave Mom and Dad their Valentine's Day cards and some of the fudge I'd made. Of course they LOVED everything!

I was a little shocked to receive a goofy text from Brandon: "HAPPY VALENTINE'S DAY!! Sitting here eating your box of chocolates and thinking of you ☺!"

In spite of the blizzard outside, the Category 1 hurricane inside (also known as Brianna) and my very dark and stormy love life, I actually managed to survive Valentine's Day! I just wish I had some magical glue that could fix all of the broken hearts in the world!!

Today I agreed to watch Mrs Wallabanger's adorable little grandson Oliver for a couple of hours while she played bingo at the senior centre.

Okay! I admit I was wrong! I should NOT have teased Brianna about having a crush on Oliver last week.

And I don't blame her for STILL being a little mad at me about that silly K-I-S-S-I-N-G poem.

But I never imagined she'd go hide in a closet and refuse to play with him. Especially after they got along so well when they played together at Kandy Kingdom in the mall.

Trying to coax Brianna out of the closet was a major headache. "Come on, Brianna! Why don't you come out and play with Oliver? It'll be fun!"

Oliver smiled and nodded his head. "Brianna, do you wanna play Princess Sugar Plum Monster Truck?"

Finally Brianna slowly opened the closet door and peeked out.

BRIANNA, PEEKING OUT OF THE CLOSET

I couldn't believe Brianna was acting like such a little drama queen!

She knew good and well that if Oliver wasn't visiting, I'd snatch her butt out of that closet so fast she'd have a permanent wedgie.

Brianna rolled her eyes at me and finally stomped angrily out of the closet.

That little brat didn't appreciate the fact that I'd spent fifteen minutes setting up the family room with assorted toys, games and stuffed animals!

I'd even managed to find some dinosaurs, astronauts and wild animals for Oliver, thanks to Princess Sugar Plum's Journey to Dino Island, Blast-Off Voyage to Mars and Swinging Safari Adventure.

But in spite of a room full of toys, Brianna and Oliver just sat there staring at each other like strangers.

"Hey, Oliver! Look at this cool T. rex!" I said enthusiastically. "ROAR! ROAR!"

"And, Brianna, why don't you show Oliver your Princess Sugar Plum spaceship with real-life blast-off sound effects! ZOOOOOOM!"

"No way!" Brianna grumped. "Boys have COOTIES!"

Oliver looked sad and sighed. Poor kid! I felt really sorry for him. Then Brianna got really personal and started dissing MY babysitting skills.

"Nikki! As a babysitter, you STINK! If Miss Penelope was watching us, we'd have lots of fun!"

"Fine!" I said. "Then let HER do it! She'll see how hard it is to watch a little brat like you."

"Fine!" Brianna yelled at me. "You're . . . FIRED!"

That's when Brianna brought out Miss Penelope.

A smile spread across Oliver's face as he quickly pulled his tattered Mr Buttons sock puppet from his pocket. Within seconds Miss Penelope was showing Mr Buttons Brianna's Princess Sugar Plum spaceship.

"I'm an astronaut, and I've been all over the galaxy! Wanna see my moon dust?" Mr. Buttons asked.

"You actually have REAL moon dust?!!" Miss Penelope exclaimed.

~~Oliver~~ Mr Buttons reached into Oliver's pocket and dumped a small pile of sand and rocks on the floor. . .

MR BUTTONS SHOWS OFF HIS MOON DUST

"COOL!" Miss Penelope gushed in amazement.

I couldn't believe my eyes! Soon Miss Penelope and Mr Buttons were having so much fun laughing, playing, and running around that Brianna and Oliver joined in too.

The ~~two~~ four of them took a trip to Mars and had a conversation in an alien language. Then they hunted for the tooth fairy in the jungle while riding on dinosaurs.

Since Miss Penelope had both of the munchkins under control (Brianna was right, she WAS a pretty good sitter!), I decided to chillax by having a snack and writing in my diary.

Everything was going great until I heard Oliver crying. Apparently, Mr Buttons was missing. Brianna insisted that he had been KIDNAPPED by the tooth fairy!

Oliver was SUPERupset. "I w-want Mr B-Buttons! He's my b-best f-friend!" he wailed.

Soon Brianna and Miss Penelope started to cry too. "Mr Buttons is g-gone f-forever!"

It looks like I'll have to finish this diary entry later. Right now I have a babysitting emergency on my hands!!

I've heard how people can end up emotionally scarred for life simply by losing their favorite security blanket or toy as a little kid.

Which probably explains why a lot of the kids at my middle school are so MESSED UP!

But what am I supposed to do in a situation like this? Call 911 and report a missing dirty sock named Mr. Buttons?!

☹!!

(TO BE CONTINUED . . .)

Now, where was I (tapping chin and thinking) . . . ?

Okay . . . Mr Buttons was missing! And Oliver, Brianna and Miss Penelope were having a simultaneous meltdown.

We looked EVERYWHERE! And still couldn't find that stupid sock. I knew socks had a nasty habit of disappearing in the dryer. But I had no idea how one could just vanish into thin air.

"Nikki! You're the babysitter!" Brianna screamed. "Do something! And do it NOW!"

I was like, Oh. No. She. DIDN'T!! "Really?! So I'M the babysitter now that Mr Buttons is LOST and everyone is CRYING?!" I yelled at Brianna. "Personally, I think this is all Miss Penelope's fault. Tell HER to go find Mr Buttons!"

But since I WAS the mature, responsible older sister, I decided to take matters into my own hands.

After rummaging through my sock drawer, I found an old mismatched sock with ruffles and lace. I grabbed a black marker and drew on a face. Then I stapled on some wool for hair, dabbed on some cherry-red lip gloss, and *BAM!!* A new puppet was born. I called her Maxine. Mainly because she was as UGLY as Max the Roach. (Max is a two-metre-long hideous-looking plastic bug bolted to the top of my dad's bug extermination van.)

Although, with the big hair, long eyelashes, fancy lace and ruffles sock outfit, clueless expression and five thick layers of lip gloss, she bore a striking resemblance to . . . *NEVER MIND*. I rushed back into the family room to introduce Maxine to Oliver.

"Oliver, please don't cry!" Maxine pleaded in a squeaky voice. "Everything will be okay. I promise!"

"Wh-who are you?" Oliver sniffed.

"I'm Mr Buttons's older sister. My name is Maxine. Nice to meet you!"

MAXINE

"Wow! You're Mr Buttons's SISTER?!" Oliver giggled as he wiped away his tears.

Brianna must have felt a little jealous or something because she just glared at Maxine and frowned. "Um . . . WHY do you have fluff all over your face?" Brianna asked.

"Yeah, and your hair looks funny too," Miss Penelope scoffed, looking her up and down.

"Hey, back off, girlfriend!" Maxine said, rolling her eyes at Miss Penelope. "At least I HAVE hair!"

So, maybe Maxine WAS a little fluffy. Sorry, but I was NOT about to destroy a good pair of socks. And WHY would Miss Penelope get all snotty and insult another puppet when SHE was a puppet too?! Was I the only person who found all of this disturbing, bizarre and a wee bit creepy?

Maxine continued. "I'm here to help you find Mr Buttons. But don't worry about that guy. He's a prankster and he's probably just playing hide-and-seek!"

Oliver's face brightened. "You think so?"

"Don't listen to her!" Brianna fumed. "I think he's been KIDNAPPED by the TOOTH FAIRY!!"

"I have a great idea, Oliver!" ~~Maxine~~ I said. "Why don't you hang out with Maxine while I finish looking for Mr Buttons. Okay?"

"That would be fun!" Oliver giggled.

I handed Maxine to Oliver. Then I went from room to room in search of Mr Buttons. When I returned, Brianna and Oliver had plastered over a dozen Kidnapped, Missing and Wanted posters all over the family room in their desperate attempt to find that puppet.

Brianna was about to tape a poster to a pillow on the couch when she suddenly gasped in surprise. "Hey, look! It's Mr Buttons!! The tooth fairy kidnapped him and stuck him behind this pillow?!" she exclaimed.

"Mr Buttons! Mr Buttons!" shouted Oliver. "I'm so glad to see you!"

We all gave Mr Buttons a great big group hug.

Just then the doorbell rang. It was Mrs Wallabanger.

"Hi, Mrs Wallabanger," I said, thankful she hadn't arrived five minutes earlier.

"Hello, Nikki, dear. How are my little gangbusters doing?" she asked cheerfully.

"They're GREAT!" I answered. "We played some games and even went on a BIG make-believe ADVENTURE!"

Suddenly Mrs Wallabanger frowned.

"What was that?! You think I've gained weight and need to get a wig and dentures?!" she asked, highly insulted.

"NO! Actually, you look beautiful! Just the way you are," I tried to reassure her.

As Oliver was leaving, he gave me a great big hug.

"Nikki! You're the best sitter me and Mr Buttons have ever had!"

"Thanks, Oliver! Both Maxine and I will be looking forward to you visiting again."

He took a few steps down the sidewalk, holding his grandmother's hand. Then he abruptly turned around and raced back to the door to give Brianna a hug too.

"Thanks for finding Mr Buttons," he whispered. "He made this especially for you!"

Oliver reached into his back pocket and handed Brianna a wad of red construction paper.

Brianna unfolded the paper to reveal the most
beautiful crinkled-up, lopsided Valentine's heart I
have ever seen in my entire life . . .

Both Brianna and Miss Penelope had these big goofy
smiles on their faces as they waved goodbye.

"Bye, Oliver! Bye, Mr Buttons! Come back soon!"

AWWWWWWW ☺! That whole scene was so cute and sickeningly sweet, I almost couldn't stand it.

Yes, Oliver was a little weird. And misunderstood. But he was such a good kid! Mrs Wallabanger was lucky to have him as a grandson.

That's when it hit me that Oliver reminded me a lot of, well . . . he-who-shall-remain-nameless.

Anyway, I was really happy that Brianna had found a new friend she had so much in common with.

I just hope Oliver won't change when he gets older. Like, you know . . . some people.

I almost forgot! Speaking of new friends, I now have a roommate . . . MAXINE!!

She's moving in to my sock drawer.

☺!!

Due to the snowstorm on Friday, today was unofficially Valentine's Day at WCD!

Chloe, Zoey and I traded valentines. And I gave them some of my homemade double-chocolate fudge, which they LOVED!

I noticed Brandon staring at me in the hall this morning. It seemed like he wanted to say something, but I just totally ignored him.

And in bio I noticed he had what looked like a valentine or something stuck in his notebook. I assumed it was probably from MacKenzie. Or maybe even FOR MacKenzie.

But I didn't bother to hang around after class to find out. As soon as the bell rang, I grabbed my stuff and ran out of there like my hair was on fire!

And speaking of MacKenzie, I know that girl HATES my GUTS! But never in a million years did I think she would actually stoop so low as to try to DROWN me!

In gym today my teacher announced that we'd be learning about swimming safety and the buddy system.

Okay, I'll admit it. One of my most embarrassing secrets is that I'm NOT a very good swimmer.

Just imagine how cruddy I feel when Brianna is confidently doggy-paddling around in the deep end while I'm nervously wading in the kiddie pool!

Talk about HUMILIATION ☹!

"Okay, class!" our teacher began. "I hope everyone read over the handout on swimming safety I gave you last week. Because today we're going to discuss what to do if your swim buddy gets in trouble. I'm going to need two volunteers."

MacKenzie and I immediately gave each other the evil eye! Just the mere thought of us working together as partners was beyond repulsive.

I think our teacher must have seen our reactions and decided that making us wear the school's smelly, saggy, scratchy regulation swimsuits was NOT enough torture.

"Let's see. How about . . . MISS MAXWELL . . . and MISS HOLLISTER?"

OUR GYM TEACHER, FORCING
MACKENZIE AND ME TO BE
SWIMMING PARTNERS

MacKenzie and I both rolled our eyes and groaned.

I immediately started feeling a little nauseous and I hadn't even swallowed any of the nasty, germy pool water yet.

"Okay! Let's do some role-playing. Miss Hollister, you'll be the swim buddy on the shore. And Miss Maxwell, you'll be the swim buddy struggling in the water."

Well, one thing was for sure. I wouldn't have to do a lot of acting to be totally convincing in THAT role.

"Actually, I was w-wondering if you maybe could pick someone else?" I stammered nervously. "I'm really not that good of a swim—"

"Come on, Miss Maxwell, hustle! In the pool! NOW!" she yelled at me like I was there trying out for the Olympic swimming team or something.

So I took a running leap, grabbed my nose, and did a cannonball into the pool. . .

SPLASH!

OMG! I hit the water like a brick. It literally knocked the wind out of me. I coughed and wheezed as I paddled for my life.

"Okay, Miss Hollister, imagine you're at the beach and you notice your swim buddy struggling in the water. What do—"

"Wait," MacKenzie interrupted. "Which beach is it?"

"I don't know . . . ANY beach!" the gym teacher snapped impatiently. "That doesn't matter."

"I know! How about . . . the HAMPTONS?!" MacKenzie said excitedly.

"Fine! A beach at the Hamptons! And you're worried your swim buddy might be in trouble. What would you do?"

"What would I do? Wow! That's a hard one. Well, for starters, I probably WOULDN'T go to the Hamptons! We vacationed there last year, and there were WAY too many tourists," she answered smugly. "Hey! Put ME on a Brazilian beach! With an air-conditioned cabana, raspberry-melon iced tea, and lots of cute surfer boys!"

"You're completely missing the point! This is about water safety!" the gym teacher said, flustered.

How DENSE could that girl be?

"Hurry up and answer the stinkin' question, MacKenzie!" I yelled. "I can't paddle much longer!"

MacKenzie scratched her head and gave the gym teacher a long, blank stare.

"Um, is this, like, a multiple-choice question or something?" she asked, twirling her hair. "I've heard the beaches in Hawaii are to die for!"

"Getting! Stomach! Cramps!" I panted. "HEEELP!!"

"Hollister, you're supposed to be aware of your swim buddy at all times!" the gym teacher yelled. "YOUR swim buddy is possibly in TROUBLE! Now go jump in the water and save her!"

"Who? ME?! I DON'T think so!" MacKenzie replied coolly. "I just curled my hair this morning."

"WORST! (glug) . . . SWIM BUDDY! (glug) . . . EVER!!!" I gurgled, choking on more water.

Then my head went under. I can't remember what

happened after that. I guess I blacked out and my teacher jumped in to rescue me. That's what I was told, anyway. However, what I DO remember is waking up on the tile floor next to the pool.

I was surrounded by a bunch of snickering classmates, a not-so-happy gym teacher and my BFFs.

ME

That's when I felt something weird around my waist.

And when I looked down, I discovered I was wearing a yellow doughnut-shaped inner-tube thingy with baby ducks on it.

It wasn't NEARLY as cute as the sea horse my teacher had flat-out refused to let me wear in the pool just last week.

Go figure!

"You're keeping that thing on for the rest of the class today. Got it, Maxwell?" my gym teacher said drily. "If you're having that much trouble swimming in one metre of water, you're going to need all the help you can get."

"Wait a minute!" I exclaimed. "Are you saying I almost drowned in only ONE metre of water?!! That's barely up to my shoulders! I thought for sure I was in the deep end!"

My teacher sighed and shook her head.

OOPS! My BAD ☹!!

Then she launched into another one of her stern lectures.

"Listen up, people! Water safety is serious business! The buddy system is _NO_ joke! Lives are at stake! To ensure that everyone completely understands these concepts, tomorrow I'll be giving you a written test! Sorry! But after what just happened here today, I really don't have a choice," she said, and glared at MacKenzie.

Every kid in the class groaned this time, including me.

Our teacher continued. "Please read over the handout I gave you. You really need to learn this stuff. Any questions?"

I could tell the entire class was pretty ticked off, based on the dirty looks MacKenzie was getting.

"Hey, don't blame _ME!_" MacKenzie shrugged and batted her eyes all innocent-like.

Then she whipped around and pointed her finger right in my face . . .

It's all HER fault! Blame the
DORK IN THE DOUGHNUT!

I could NOT believe that girl just threw me under the bus like that.

AND I definitely didn't appreciate her little "dork in the doughnut" comment!

If MacKenzie hadn't sat there very STUPIDLY planning her next beach vacation while watching me DROWN, we wouldn't be having a written test.

In GYM, of all classes.

It was all HER fault!

But of course MacKenzie is Miss PERFECT!

And all of the CCPs were rolling their eyes and whispering about ME!

The "DORK in the doughnut"!

UGH! I give up!

Next time . . .

Just let me DROWN!

☹!!

AAAAAAAAAAAAAAHHH!

(That was me screaming!)

I was totally FREAKED out by what I saw in the halls when I got to school this morning.

It was surreal! I felt like I'd walked into one of my worst nightmares. I wanted to just call my parents and go home.

WHO did this to me?!!! And WHY?!!!

Only three other people at school knew about it.

"It" being that horribly embarrassing photo that my bratty sister, Brianna, accidentally texted to the ENTIRE world.

Okay! Well, maybe NOT the entire world.

Just CHLOE, ZOEY and BRANDON!

Just looking at that photo gives me a migraine...

Chloe and Zoey were really upset and have pinkie
sworn to me THREE times that they had NOTHING
to do with it. And I really want to believe them.

So that leaves . . . BRANDON. But WHY would he
do this? Or give my picture to someone who would?

Anyway, this is what I saw when I arrived at school
this morning. . .

"VOTE NIKKI MAXWELL FOR SWEETHEART PRINCESS!" POSTERS WERE EVERYWHERE!

But the most humiliating thing is that everyone thinks I plastered those hideous posters around the school because I WANT to be voted Sweetheart Princess.

When in reality, I DIDN'T put up the posters! And I DON'T want to be voted Sweetheart Princess! Okay, so maybe I wouldn't mind all that much if it actually happened.

But come on! I'm the biggest loser in the entire school. Like, WHO would even vote for me?!

And even if there WAS the possibility of getting a few random votes from students, I'm sure my very creepy picture made them change their minds.

This little STUNT had MacKenzie Hollister written ALL over it! I would give anything to know how MacKenzie got her grubby little hands on my photo.

Thank goodness my BFFs were there to help me rip the posters down.

It took us, like, FOREVER!

ME, CHLOE AND ZOEY TEARING
DOWN THOSE HIDEOUS POSTERS

Why in the world would MacKenzie do this when she knows I'm not going to the dance? Maybe she's just trying to rub it in my face that I don't have a date. I'm so sick of her little mind games!

Then, to make matters worse, I got a text from Brandon during lunch.

* * * * *
FROM BRANDON:
You looked kind of freaky in that picture.
But you're STILL my friend :-p!
12:36 p.m.
* * * * *

It's going to take me YEARS of intense therapy to get over all of the traumatic experiences I've had in middle school just this past week!

AAAAAAAAAAAAHHHHH!!

(That was me screaming AGAIN!)

!!

Today in swimming class we had a skills test on diving.

"Now, class, the object of this skills test is to measure your ability to dive AND retrieve the objects from the bottom of the pool as quickly as possible," our teacher explained. "You'll be diving for seven plastic rings."

Come on! What's the point? What are we training for? A dolphin show or something?! Why doesn't the teacher just sell tickets to see us perform and throw us fish as a reward when we do a good job? I'm just sayin'!

But get this! I couldn't believe there was no ambulance or some elite emergency team here to rescue us.

You know, like the ones you always see on the sidelines at our football games.

Didn't it dawn on our teacher that we might need CPR or maybe even oxygen?

Or how about one of those supersized rescue-hook thingies to pull us out of the water in the event of an emergency?

MacKenzie was next in line to take her skills test. When the teacher yelled "DIVE!" MacKenzie dove into the pool, barely making a splash. Within seconds she had scooped up all of the rings and was back out of the pool with the fastest time in the entire class.

She waved and blew kisses to everyone like she had just won a gold medal in the Olympics or something.

That girl is so VAIN!

However, I was not the least bit intimidated.

Dad had purchased everything I needed for my skills test from a yard sale last summer. . .

ME, READY TO DIVE IN MY SCUBA GEAR

Anyway, when my teacher hollered "DIVE!" I jumped in and grabbed all the rings in record time. Even faster than MacKenzie!

My gym teacher congratulated me on my remarkable performance. But then she got an attitude about the whole thing and gave me a . . .

big fat D ☹!

I was so DISGUSTED!

"Sorry, Miss Maxwell," my teacher said. "But you're diving for plastic rings, NOT sunken treasure! No scuba gear is allowed!!"

Apparently, it was against the pool rules. But HOW was I supposed to know THAT?!

The only sign about rules I saw said . . .

WCD POOL RULES
1. NO running!
2. NO eating!
3. NO horseplay!
4. NO peeing in the pool!
5. NO floating toys!

There was nothing on that list that said . . .

NO SCUBA GEAR!

That's when I totally lost it and yelled at my teacher. "Sorry, lady, but I'm NOT some humpback whale capable of diving to the deepest, darkest, most dangerous depths of the pool. I NEED my mask, wet suit, regulator, tank and scuba fins. Besides, the water is so deep my eyeballs could pop out. And I could die from decompression sickness.

"Worse yet, YOU didn't even bother to have an ambulance here just in case I needed to be rushed to the hospital! So let me see YOU dive to the bottom of the pool without having a massive stroke or something!"

But I just said that in my head, so no one else heard it but me.

That diving skills test was SO unfair! I should definitely get a do-over!! I'm just sayin'!! ☹!!

I'm really starting to worry about my grade in swimming. If I get lower than a C as a final grade, my teacher will request a meeting with my parents.

OMG! What if I end up losing my bug extermination scholarship and can't attend this school any longer?

And as if I don't already have enough problems, I noticed Brandon staring at me in the halls today. He actually tried to talk to me in bio, but I totally ignored him.

AGAIN!

But then things got even weirder!

I was working in the library and minding my own business, and guess who just popped in like he owned the place or something??!!

BRANDON ☹!!

I know! I couldn't believe it either!

Anyway, he asked if he could talk to me, and I said yes, but right then I was really busy putting away books.

Then he said, "Well, I'll help you put them away, and then we can talk while we're working."

And I said, "Actually, you CAN'T help me because you don't know where the books are supposed to go on the shelves."

That's when he suggested that HE could help by handing ME the books so I could place them on the shelves.

He was being very nice, sweet and helpful, and getting on my LAST nerve all at the same time!

So he was handing me books, and I was putting them on the shelves.

Which made me SUPERnervous because he kept kind of . . . staring at me.

BRANDON KIND OF STARES AT ME WHILE WE'RE PUTTING AWAY LIBRARY BOOKS.

Finally he cleared his throat. "Nikki, I just wanted to let you know that I felt really bad about you getting in trouble in bio for trying to do something nice for me."

"Like I said before, it wasn't that big of a deal!"

"Well, it was to ME. So I want to do something nice for you."

"Actually, that's not necessary. It was just a stupid card!"

"I don't think it was stupid."

"Well, I do!" I shot back.

Brandon stared at the floor. "Anyway, I thought maybe we could hang out at Crazy Burger this Saturday. I know the last time I mentioned it, you said you didn't want to go because you were SUPERbusy!"

I could not believe he actually said that to me!

Not the part about hanging out at Crazy Burger. But that part about me NOT wanting to go to Crazy Burger because I was SUPERbusy.

"WHAAAT?! No way! Brandon, YOU said you couldn't go to Crazy Burger because YOU were SUPERbusy!"

"HUH?! No, Nikki! YOU told ME you were too busy and couldn't go. It was at your locker. I wanted to go, but that Saturday and Sunday didn't work out."

"Actually, you kind of stood me up," I said.

"No, I didn't. When I tried to explain what happened, you shut me down."

"That's NOT what happened. I was trying to talk to YOU and you just walked away!"

Lately, whenever we tried to have a conversation, we ended up fighting. Brandon and I just stared at each other in frustration. . .

For some strange reason, we were having major communication problems.

I knew in my gut that something was wrong! But I didn't have the slightest idea what it was or how to fix it.

Finally Brandon sighed and brushed his hair out of his eyes.

"Okay. So, how about Crazy Burger on Saturday? At six thirty p.m. If you're not too busy," he said, giving me a crooked smile.

"Okay, sure! If YOU'RE not too busy!" I said, smiling back at him.

Then we both kind of stared at each other and blushed.

All of this smiling, staring and blushing went on, like, FOREVER!

So, it was official. Brandon and I were hanging out at Crazy Burger on Saturday.

I couldn't wait to tell Chloe and Zoey the exciting news.

But I didn't have to. . .

Chloe and Zoey were secretly spying on us the entire time?!

I could NOT believe my BFFs would stoop so low as to do something like that to Brandon and me!

Especially during a very private and personal conversation about our friendship.

Chloe and Zoey are always sticking their big fat noses in my personal business. But it's mostly because the two of them really care about me.

I have to admit . . .

They're the best friends EVER!!

☺!!

I'm still so excited about Crazy Burger that I barely got any sleep last night.

Of course I couldn't wait to see Brandon in bio.

SQUEEE ☺!

We blushed, smiled and made goo-goo eyes the ENTIRE hour. I could see MacKenzie and Jessica staring at us and whispering like crazy. But I didn't care.

To be honest, I don't remember a single word my teacher said about today's lesson. But it was the BEST. CLASS. EVER!

I'm SO happy Brandon and I are FINALLY getting along again. I just hope spending time together at Crazy Burger will help strengthen our friendship.

But right now my immediate problem is that I don't have the slightest idea what to wear on our first date.

I don't want my outfit to be too dressy, but not too casual, either. It needs to be . . . PERFECT!

I just stood there staring inside my closet for what seemed like FOREVER! But unfortunately, I didn't see anything that was PERFECT ☹!

ME, LOOKING FOR THE PERFECT OUTFIT!

I was DESPERATE! So I decided to take DRASTIC action.

I knew it would be dangerous because of the risk of exhaustion. But I didn't really have a choice.

I was going to TRY ON all of my clothes superfast and mix and match tops and bottoms until I came up with a SUPERCUTE outfit! Also known as a . . . TRY-ON-A-THON!

When the smoke finally cleared, my TRY-ON-A-THON was a HUGE success!

I came up with the most FAB OUTFIT ever . . . !

ME, MODELING MY FAB OUTFIT!

Now all I have to do is get through the meal
WITHOUT:

1. dropping my hamburger in my lap.

2. accidentally squirting ketchup on Brandon.

3. laughing so hard that soda dribbles out of my nose.

MUST.

NOT.

FREAK.

OUT!

☺!!

OMG! Today's the big day! Brandon and I have a date at Crazy Burger in just a few hours!!

SQUEEE ☺!

By the time I showered, did my hair, and got dressed, it was 6:15 p.m. and time for my mom to drive me to the restaurant.

I was a nervous wreck!

I had sat next to Brandon in bio, like, forever. But the thought of sitting next to him at Crazy Burger was more scary than those *Friday the 13th* movies that my parents refused to let me watch.

"Hi, Nikki!" he said, smiling. "It's cool that we're FINALLY getting to hang out here."

I quickly checked behind me just to make sure he wasn't talking to someone else named Nikki.

"Hi, Brandon!" I said, blushing profusely.

For the next five minutes, we just sat there nervously sipping our sodas and staring at each other with these big, dorky grins plastered across our faces. It was SO romantic! Well, kind of.

It felt like the butterflies in my stomach were having a big party. And some of them must have flown up to my brain, because I could barely think straight.

Brandon seemed more quiet than usual too.

Then I picked up the paper thingy from my straw and started wrapping it around and around my finger while I tried to think of something funny, witty, or interesting to say. I came up with . . .

"Hmm, I wonder what stuff is in that ketchup?"

That's when Brandon picked up the ketchup bottle and started reading off all of the ingredients. "Well, it says tomato concentrate, distilled vinegar, corn syrup, salt, spice, onion powder and other ingredients."

I grabbed a piece of the straw paper thingy and made a giant spit wad and shot it right out of my straw, and it landed on the table in front of Brandon's glass. *SMACK!*

Brandon was surprised that I knew how to make spit wads.

Then he took a few sips of his soda.

But when his straw made those loud slurpy noises, like *SKURR–SKURR*, he coughed nervously and almost knocked over his glass.

Then we stared at each other some more. Next I took the salt shaker and poured salt into my hand and made these little miniature mountains while Brandon watched.

Suddenly his stomach started making these loud grumbling sounds, probably because he was hungry or something.

"OMG! Brandon, your stomach sounds just like a jet engine!" I teased. You should have seen the look on his face. I thought he was going to DIE of embarrassment!

Then, finally, our burgers came . . .!

OMG! They were crazy delicious! Soon our nervous
jitters went away and we actually had an intelligent
conversation.

He gave me an update on Fuzzy Friends, his work for the school newspaper and his photography projects.

I told him about losing a hair chunk at Salon Brianna, Mrs Wallabanger's grandson and the horrors of swimming class.

We both laughed until our sides hurt. It was amazing how Brandon was just so . . .

FUNNY and NICE!

Then things got SUPERserious. He said he felt awful when he heard that someone had plastered those crazy posters of me around the school. He said he's ALLERGIC to mean people!

We both agreed that MacKenzie was probably behind it.

I really wanted to ask him if he had any idea how she'd got her hands on that photo since Brianna had only emailed it to Chloe, Zoey and him.

But I was sure he would have been highly insulted and disappointed that I'd accuse him of helping MacKenzie pull a nasty prank like that. So I decided NOT to mention it right then.

Somehow, we ended up talking about the Sweetheart Dance.

"So, are you going?" I asked.

"No. But I would if the right person asked me."

"Does that mean the wrong person asked you?"

"Yeah, MacKenzie actually came to my birthday party and asked me. But I told her no. Since then she's been hanging around, trying to get me to change my mind. She even offered to have her dad make a sizable donation to Fuzzy Friends if I'd go with her. Hey, we need the money badly, but . . ." His voice trailed off.

I started playing with the straw paper thingy again as my mind raced.

So MacKenzie had asked Brandon to the dance?!

And he turned her down?!

I was SUPERhappy AND relieved to hear that news.

Now I could ask him to the dance!

If I could just muster up the courage.

"Well, maybe someone else wants to ask you but she's afraid you might say no," I said, blushing.

"Really?!" Brandon blinked in surprise. "Actually, I'd probably . . . no, definitely say YES! Like, IF she actually asked," he said, staring at me.

That was my cue!

Brandon was basically asking ME to ask HIM to the dance!

"Well . . . um, about the dance. I wanted to ask you . . . if you . . . um, think, er . . . WE . . . will have another

BLIZZARD?! We got a whopping twenty centimetres of snow last time!" I babbled like an idiot.

STRIKE ONE!

Brandon continued to stare at me. "Nope. Do you want to ask me anything else?"

"Actually, there IS something I'd like to ask."

"Okay . . ."

"So, would you . . . like to, um, have DESSERT??!! I hear the red velvet chocolate cake at this place is to DIE for!"

Brandon smiled and nodded his head. "Sure, Nikki! That sounds great!"

I wanted to kick myself. STRIKE TWO!!

"Um, Brandon, there's j–just one last thing I want to ask you . . ." I stammered nervously.

"Wait. Let me guess!" Brandon teased. "You want to know if . . . I want ice cream?"

"No! Not that!" I replied.

"Hot fudge on the side, with whipped cream?"

"NO!" I giggled.

"I know! Those little sprinkle thingies!"

"NOOO!" I shouted.

"Then, WHAT . . . ?!" Brandon asked in mock frustration.

"I want to know if you'd . . . you know . . . go to the Sweetheart Dance with me!" I blurted out, blushing profusely.

Suddenly Brandon got this SUPERserious look on his face and started fidgeting with his straw. Okay, now I was really nervous. Maybe asking him was a big mistake.

"Actually, Nikki, there's just no way I could—"

"That's fine! Really!" I interrupted. "I totally understand. I asked you at the last minute and everything!"

I gave him a weak smile. But deep down inside I felt so hurt I wanted to burst into tears.

"Actually, Nikki, there's just no way I could say NO to you!" Brandon said as he brushed his hair out of his eyes and gave me that crooked smile.

That's when I blushed again and smiled at him.

And then he blushed and smiled at me. All of this blushing and smiling went on, like, FOREVER!

So not only did I have a really great time at Crazy Burger, but now . . .

I'M GOING TO THE SWEETHEART DANCE WITH BRANDON!!

SQUEEE ☺!!

I am SOOO excited!

ME, DOING MY SNOOPY "HAPPY DANCE"!!

I can't wait to call Chloe and Zoey and tell them the FANTASTIC news!

Although, there's a slight chance my BFFs already know, if they were at Crazy Burger hiding under our table SPYING on us. AGAIN!

I guess we'll be able to go on a TRIPLE DATE together after all. Just like we'd planned!

SQUEEE!!! ☺!!

OMG! This is going to be SOOO romantic!!

ME, HOLDING MY HEART AND
SWOONING MASSIVELY!!

It's hard to believe that I'm actually going to the Sweetheart Dance with Brandon.

SQUEEE ☺!!

I think Chloe and Zoey are even more excited about it than I am. They've already called me a dozen times and I just told them the news an hour ago.

The dress code is formal attire, which means girls get to wear floor-length dresses! You know, like Cinderella and all of the Disney Princesses.

How COOL is THAT?!

Chloe and Zoey already have their dresses.

But being the great friends that they are, they agreed to meet at the mall to help find the perfect one for ME.

Anyway, I must have tried on fifty dresses. . .

Or too FRILLY!

Or too FUNKY!

We came back from the mall empty-handed.

Of course I was pretty bummed out.

It didn't help matters that we ran into Jessica, and she saw me shopping for a dress. And since she's MacKenzie's BFF, that means she's going to BLAB all of my personal business.

But the good news is that there are STILL four more shopping days until the dance!

I'm pretty SURE I'll find the perfect dress.

Somewhere!

I mean, how HARD could it be?!

☺!!

Okay, I'm starting to PANIC! Mom said she would take me shopping for a dress on Wednesday. But that's only two days before the dance!! She said if we can't find a new dress, I can just use the ~~very ugly~~ silver and seaweed-green bridesmaid dress from my aunt Kim's wedding.

Mom, are you KA-RAY-ZEE?! I REFUSE to go to the Sweetheart Dance looking like some kind of MUTANT FISH!

Sorry, Mom, but this is a formal dance — NOT a COSTUME party!

Anyway, after dinner I got the sweetest text from Brandon.

577

SQUEEE!! I think hanging out at Crazy Burger really helped our friendship.

* * * * *

FROM BRANDON:

Hi Nikki,

Looking forward 2 going 2 the dance with U. Good luck finding a dress that will actually make U look beautiful!

7:39 p.m.

* * * * *

Wait a minute!! Did he just say . . . ?!

Now I REALLY need to BURN this DRESS!

☹!

Today in gym class we were having timed swimming races against each other.

For some strange reason, whenever I try to swim more than six metres, my legs cramp up and get stuck in really weird positions. I look kind of like one of Brianna's old Barbie dolls with TWO broken legs. And once my legs are all messed up, I start to panic and rarely make it to the other end of the pool.

But mostly I was SUPERworried because this race was going to be 50% of our swimming grade ☹!

Our gym teacher blew her whistle. *TWEET, TWEET!!* "Next group, please take the starting line!"

It was finally time for MY race to begin.

Chloe gave me a big hug and jazz hands for good luck. Zoey gave me a hug too and recited another of her inspirational quotes, this time from John Lennon . . .

"'When you're drowning, you don't say "I would be incredibly pleased if someone would have the foresight to notice me drowning and come and help me," you just scream!'"

I was like, "Thanks a million for that, Zoey!"

I think that quote was supposed to encourage me. But quite frankly, it scared the SNOT out of me! You just SCREAM?!! What kind of advice is THAT?!

Oh! And did I forget to mention that I was swimming against MacKenzie and three CCPs?

"So, Nikki! I see you're going to attempt to swim today without your scuba suit or ridiculous floaty toys." MacKenzie sneered.

Her friends snickered. I just rolled my eyes at that girl. I wanted to say something. But right then my knees were so shaky I was more worried about accidentally falling face-first into the water before the race even got started.

Our teacher stood on a podium to begin the race. "Swimmers, take your mark. Get set . . ." *TWEET!*

← ME

ME, TRYING NOT TO FALL FACE-FIRST INTO THE WATER

I dove into the water and began swimming frantically.

Although we had just got started, I could already clearly see I was way behind.

Yep! Dead last! It was so HUMILIATING ☹!

To make matters worse, I was slowing down and my leg muscles were starting to cramp up.

Finally I stopped swimming and started to doggy-paddle.

MacKenzie was in the lead, and the three other girls were close behind her. I wanted to give up!

That's when I looked over my right shoulder and caught a glimpse of a dark shadow slightly behind me. Actually, it looked a lot like a . . . shark's fin?!

I took another look and . . . YES! It WAS a shark's fin, just several metres away. I couldn't believe my eyes!

OMG! I think I actually peed in the pool!

And judging from the size of its fin, that thing was GIGANTIC! Out of sheer terror, I started swimming as fast as I could.

A shark in the pool?! How in the HECK did that get in here? I wondered as I swam for my life. I came up with three possible theories.

It could have been living in the Westchester County sewers like those alligators, pythons and other scary creatures we hear about in the news.

Or if it was in the drainage system, it probably got too big for the pipes and burst through the drain and into the pool.

Or maybe it escaped from the Westchester Zoo and was swimming down the creek behind our school when it decided to stop off at the pool for a quick LUNCH!

One thing was for sure. I had no intention of becoming its next MEAL.

You know, yummy Nikki Nuggets dipped in chlorine.

I must have had a surge of adrenaline or something because I kept swimming faster and faster until I reached the end of the pool.

Then I jumped out and zipped right past my teacher, screaming at the top of my lungs . . .

SHARK! SHARK!
RUN FOR YOUR LIFE!

MACKENZIE, TRYING TO FIGURE OUT
HOW I BEAT HER TO THE FINISH LINE

Hey, there was no way I was going to hang around poolside. Sharks swim ashore, attack their prey and then drag them back into the deep to be eaten!

At least, that's what they do in movies and on TV!
And personally, I wasn't taking any chances. So I
kept running until I got to the very top of the
bleachers. Only then did I check behind me to make
sure that shark hadn't followed me up there. Hey, it
could happen!

That's when I heard my gym teacher make an
announcement over the loudspeaker. "May I have
your attention, please? I'd like to congratulate
Nikki Maxwell. She not only won first place in the
swimming race, but she set a new school record
for the fifty-metre swim. That's an A+ for you,
Miss Maxwell. Job well done! Please come and pick
up your award certificate."

I cautiously walked back down to the pool, where
Chloe and Zoey gave me a big hug.

"Did you not see that humungous shark in the
water?" I gasped.

"All we saw was you give MacKenzie a good beatdown
in that race!" Zoey gushed.

"OMG! You won by a mile!" Chloe giggled. "You were out of the pool before she even finished."

"But I could have sworn I saw a SHARK!"

My BFFs walked to the other end of the pool and returned with something big and shiny with a huge fin. Only, it DIDN'T have pointy teeth.

"THIS is NOT a SHARK, Nikki!" Chloe said.

"Um . . . try plastic SCUBA FIN!" Zoey giggled.

"Sorry, guys! But it looked like a shark to ME!" I muttered.

OMG! I was SO embarrassed.

Anyway, after winning the race and then getting fifty extra-credit points for breaking the school record, I ended up earning an A as the final grade in my swimming class!

That stupid class had been kicking my butt all month. I never would have thunk this could happen.

Woo-hoo! I was beyond HAPPY!

And now the coach actually wants me to join the girls' swimming team.

How CRAZY is THAT??!!

☺!!

Today after school, Mom and I went shopping to try and finally find a dress for the Sweetheart Dance. First we went to the dress section of Forever Sixteen, but the clothing racks were empty and there wasn't a single dress in sight.

A pile of broken clothes hangers littered the floor. It looked just like the aftermath of an elephant stampede!

Then we went to five more stores, and all of them were in the same condition.

"No place in this ENTIRE mall has a dress?" Mom asked, clearly frustrated. "I can't believe that! Let's try finding a sales clerk."

We were at a fancy department store, and we finally found a sales clerk hiding behind the checkout counter. In the fetal position!

"Excuse me, ma'am," Mom said to her. "We're looking for a dress. Could you help us, please?"

"D-d-dress?!" the sales clerk gasped in horror. "Did you just say . . . DRESS?! AAAAHHH!!!" she screamed hysterically and dashed out of the emergency exit door.

What I didn't realise was that thousands of

desperate middle school and high school girls had
descended upon the mall and turned dress ~~shopping~~
hunting into a brutal gladiator sport. . .

Back home, Mom suggested again that I wear that "adorable" ~~mermaid~~ bridesmaid dress.

EWW!!

Clearly, she has a bad memory, because that thing is HIDEOUS!

Sorry, Mom, but vomit green is NOT my colour.

And that dress is impossible to walk in! It's so tight around my legs that it looks like a giant fish tail.

While the other bridesmaids walked gracefully to the "Wedding March" song, I flopped my way down the aisle like a human-sized catfish or something!

Those rug burns were pure agony!

It was getting late and I was running out of time!

The last thing I wanted to do was to traumatise

Brandon by showing up at the dance looking like a
MUTANT FISH GIRL or something.

Right now I'm SO frustrated that I'm seriously
considering just NOT going to the dance.

Why is my life so hopelessly

CRUDDY?!

☹!!!

I had an unexpected visitor after school today! I was in my room doing my French homework when suddenly I was rudely interrupted . . .

"There you are, Miss Nikki! I, Miss Bri-Bri, Fashionista and STYLIST to the Stars, have been looking all over for YOU!" Brianna exclaimed. "Come quickly, dah-ling! Miss Bri-Bri must style you before her next appointment!"

"Don't take another step toward me, or you'll be sorry!" I screamed. "I have a French book in my hand, and I'm NOT afraid to use it. Last time you TOTALLY ruined my hair! Are you even a licenced professional?"

"But all of that was my assistant's fault. I fired Hans. Now come! Miss Bri-Bri shall make you booty-ful! Yes?"

"NO WAY! Miss Bri-Bri can go jump in le LAKE! I'm still mad at you!"

"Zen I shall make it up to you. Miss Bri-Bri pinkie promises! Or she'll eat a thousand boogers!"

WHAT kind of promise was that?! I was pretty sure Miss Bri-Bri ate boogers anyway! On the other hand, whatever dress she had to offer me couldn't be any uglier than the one I already had.

I didn't have much to lose! Well, other than another hair chunk. But that was a risk I was willing to take for the dance. And for Brandon!

"Okay, Brianna! I'm going to give you ONE more chance! So don't screw this up!" I warned.

"Dah-ling! We have much work to do! Please follow my new assistant, Miss Penelope."

Miss Penelope waved at me and then grabbed my arm and led me down the hall.

She was wearing lots of rings and bracelets, glittery nail polish, hot-pink lip gloss and drawn-on cat-eye glasses that matched Brianna's.

"Dah-ling! Here we are! Welcome to BOUTIQUE BRIANNA!" Miss Bri-Bri announced, taking me into the upstairs bathroom. "Miss Bri-Bri has designed a gazillion booty-ful dresses for very famous and important people, like Princess Sugar Plum, Selena Gomez, Beyoncé, and Mrs Claus! And I have created zee perfect dress for you, dah-ling! Miss Penelope, please show Miss Nikki to zee dressing room," she ordered.

Suddenly Brianna raised her hand to her ear, whispered something to Miss Penelope, and then frowned.

"What was zat, Miss Penelope?" she asked. "You are on zee phone with Dora zee Explorer and Boots zee Monkey? You say Boots needs new boots? Very well, dah-ling! Pencil him in before my six o'clock appointment with SpongeBob!"

Brianna turned to me and smiled apologetically. "Please excuse zee interruption, dah-ling. Miss Penelope's up to her knuckles in phone calls and paperwork. Now, where were we? Oh yes! Zee dress for YOU!"

She walked up to the bathtub and pulled back the shower curtain. SWISH . . . !!

"NOW, MISS NIKKI, PLEASE STEP INTO YOUR DRESSING ROOM!"

I was really shocked to see a clothing bag with my name on it hanging inside the "dressing room".

But I was afraid it might be a trick.

"Hmm . . . You want me to step inside?" I eyed her suspiciously. "Why? Is this a prank? Did you put a shark in there or something?!"

"Of course not! My boutique has a no-shark policy, dah-ling!" Brianna replied, slightly offended.

"All right, already!" I muttered under my breath as I climbed into the tub.

Brianna closed the curtain behind me. SWISH!

"I'll check back with you in a few minutes, dah-ling. As soon as I finish up with Sasha and Malia Obama."

Although the clothing bag looked new, I expected to find Brianna's ratty old hot-pink Barbie robe inside.

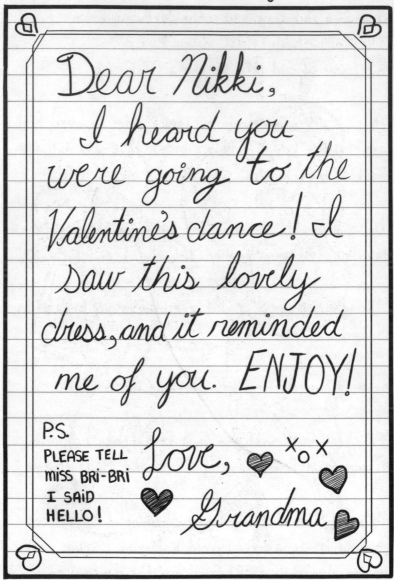

Dear Nikki,

I heard you were going to the Valentine's dance! I saw this lovely dress, and it reminded me of you. ENJOY!

P.S.
PLEASE TELL
MISS BRI-BRI
I SAID
HELLO!

Love,

Grandma

I was right! Brianna WAS up to something!

That delusional little SNEAK had contacted
Grandma and arranged a wonderful surprise . . .
The most BEAUTIFUL dress EVER!!

It was absolutely PERFECT for the dance. I couldn't
wait to show my BFFs.

SQUEEEEE!!!

All of the CCP girls will be so JEALOUS!

I paid Miss Bri-Bri for her "services" with a bag of Skittles.

"See, dah-ling?! Miss Bri-Bri made you a very BOOTY-FUL dress! Yes?!"

"Miss Bri-Bri TOTALLY ROCKED!" I giggled.

"Then we can forget zee little haircut problem?!"

"Forgotten!" I said, and gave ~~Brianna~~ Miss Bri-Bri a big hug.

Then I excitedly rushed off to my room to try on my new dress.

☺!!

Today the entire school was buzzing about the dance. Students excitedly lined up between classes to vote for Sweetheart Princess. The latest gossip was that MacKenzie was going to win by a landslide.

I avoided voting entirely. It was just a reminder of MacKenzie's nasty prank, which I was trying very hard to forget.

I still didn't have the slightest idea how she got her hands on that Salon Brianna photo. Maybe it was my imagination, but in every class it seemed like kids were staring at me and whispering ☹!

So I just zoned out and spent the entire day staring at the clock and counting down the hours until the Sweetheart Dance ☺! 10, 9, 8, 7, 6, 5, 4 . . . !

Before I knew it, school was over and the dance was starting in less than an hour. I took one last look at myself in the mirror.

On the inside, I felt SUPERinsecure. But on the outside, I looked like a real princess. . .

Well, MINUS the scrawny arms and shoulders ☹!

Mom's new *Get Toned in 20 Minutes DVD* was a total rip-off. I had used it for forty minutes after school to tone up my arms, but they STILL looked EXACTLY the same. What's up with THAT? Mom definitely needs to get her money back!

For some reason, I was having a severe case of the last-minute jitters. I felt super self-conscious about EVERYTHING.

I sighed and popped a Tic Tac into my mouth. Then I stuffed my phone into my purse, grabbed my coat and headed downstairs.

Suddenly my phone chimed. I was pretty sure it was a text from Chloe and Zoey letting me know they were on their way to pick me up.

There was just NO WAY I was going to risk public humiliation by riding in my dad's ROACH MOBILE! It was MY brilliant idea to have Zoey's mom drive us there and Chloe's mom drive us home!

But surprisingly, the text wasn't from Chloe or Zoey.

It was from BRANDON! SQUEEEEEE ☺!!

I guessed that he was probably sending me a message telling me he couldn't wait to see me or something. You know, like in all of those romance novels. SQUEEEEEE ☺!!

Swooning massively, I held my breath and read his pre-Sweetheart-Dance text message out loud:

I blinked in disbelief and read it again. This had to be some kind of mistake!

Obviously, some other dude named Brandon had just decided, at the very last minute, to "TEXT DUMP" his poor unsuspecting date!!

And then sent it to ME by accident!

NOT ☹!!

I felt like I had been hit in the stomach. By a bowling ball.

WHY would Brandon do this to me?!!!

Okay. Maybe because he was SICK! But STILL! What harm is a little flu bug between really good friends?!!

Since the dance was such a big deal, I was hoping he would have gallantly ignored his fever and nausea and just showed up with a barf bag or something.

If I had the flu, I would have done that for HIM!

Hey! If I had been hit by a bus, I would have come to the dance in a full-body cast with some SUPERcute matching earrings!

This was the last straw!

I felt like I was on a crazy emotional roller coaster, plummeting into a deep, dark bottomless pit. And I wanted off!

I knew I couldn't blame Brandon for getting sick! But why did he wait until the very last minute?!

And why did he drop the bomb on me in a very tacky text message instead of apologising profusely in person? Or at least in a phone call?!

It was like he wasn't thinking about my feelings at all!

Deep down in my gut, I suspected that Brandon was not sick at all. He had probably taken

MacKenzie up on her Fuzzy Friends cash offer.

And after changing his mind about going to the dance with me, he wasn't brave enough to tell me to my face.

I was stupid and delusional to think we'd ever become good friends. I really hated to admit it, but MacKenzie was right ☹!

I dragged myself back to my room, slammed my door shut and collapsed on my bed.

Then I sobbed hysterically into my pillow.

OMG! I felt beyond HORRIBLE. My heart was actually hurting.

I had been lying there for what seemed, like, FOREVER, when suddenly I heard footsteps and two familiar voices outside my door.

I closed my eyes and groaned. Oh, CRUD! I'd forgotten to call Chloe and Zoey . . . !

They burst into my room like a hurricane.

"Nikki! Your favorite BFFs are here!" Zoey squealed happily. "Are you ready?"

"Don't be TARDY for the PARTY!" Chloe shouted, and gave me jazz hands.

I slowly sat up on the edge of my bed, sniffed and dabbed at my tears.

My BFFs immediately froze and stared at me in shock with their mouths hanging open.

"OMG! Nikki! What's wrong?!" they both shrieked.

"I'm n–not going to the d–dance!" I muttered. "Brandon just texted me. He says he's . . . SICK!"

"WHAT?!" they gasped.

That's when I totally lost it and burst into

TEARS. . .

I FEEL AWFUL! I CAN'T BELIEVE BRANDON
JUST STOOD ME UP LIKE THIS!!

I had a complete and massive meltdown. Chloe and
Zoey both hugged me. They were about to cry too.

"I'm really sorry," I sputtered, "but you're going to
have to go to the dance without me." Then I blew
my nose rather loudly. _HONK!_

Chloe and Zoey looked at each other and then looked at me.

"Sorry, Nikki. But we're not going to leave you here like this!" Zoey said, squeezing my hand.

"We care about you! So either we're ALL going to the dance, or we're ALL staying here," Chloe said softly.

"I'll be fine," I protested. "You both have dates. Theo and Marcus are nice guys, and they don't deserve to be stood up. It feels really . . . BAD!"

"Nikki, if you don't want to go, we understand. We'll just call the guys right now and tell them the situation," Zoey said, picking up her phone.

"Please! You're both just making me feel worse!" I yelled. "I want to be ALONE! Just GO AWAY!"

That's when Chloe and Zoey stared at me in disbelief. I think I must have really ticked them off or something because they were not smiling.

"Sorry, Nikki! But we're NOT going to let you have a nervous breakdown over some dude not taking you to a stupid dance!" Chloe fumed.

"So cry yourself a river, build a bridge and get OVER it!" Zoey said, rolling her eyes.

I could NOT believe my BFFs weren't being more sympathetic about my situation. Hey, I was heartbroken and in real pain! Hadn't I earned the right to be a melancholy drama queen?

Note to self: Get a new CRUSH. And some new BFFs!

Even though I was mad at Chloe and Zoey for not joining my pity party, I had to admit they truly cared about me. They were willing to miss the Sweetheart Dance! AND their first dates! I mean, WHO does THAT?!

I sniffed and blew my nose again. *HONK!!*

"Okay, guys! You win! I'll go to the dance. Against my

will. But I'm NOT going to have fun! And you CAN'T make me!" I grumped.

Chloe and Zoey screamed happily and squished me in a hug sandwich.

"You are NOT going to regret this!" Zoey giggled.

"We're going to have a BLAST together!" Chloe squealed.

"I. Can't. BREATHE!" I croaked, gasping for air.

After prying myself out of their hug, I went to the bathroom to wash my face and freshen up for the dance.

OMG! I looked HORRIBLE!

My hair was a mess and my face was streaked with black tears from my mascara.

I looked like a zombie bride or something. . .

SNIFF!
SNIFF!

However, thanks to Chloe and Zoey, I was starting
to feel like maybe it WASN'T the end of the
world. Most important, I was NOT going to let
Brandon turn me into a snivelling puddle of SNOT
and TEARS!! Well, not for more than fifteen
minutes, anyway.

When we arrived at the Sweetheart Dance, I was surprised to see pretty much the entire student body there.

I barely recognized our drab cafeteria. It had been turned into a Queen of Hearts fantasyland. Dozens of red hearts hung gracefully from the ceiling while bunches of pink, red, and white helium balloons floated gently around the room like miniature clouds. The walls were strung with hundreds of tiny red and white lights that reflected off a giant mirror ball in the centre of the room.

All of the girls wore gorgeous formal dresses that rivaled the dresses at any high school prom. I saw sparkles, glitter, sequins and pretty much every colour of the rainbow.

However, my most favourite dress was my OWN ☺!

Marcus and Theo were there, patiently waiting for Chloe and Zoey. I couldn't tell who was more nervous, my BFFs or their dates. But as soon as they spotted each other, everyone was all smiles.

OMG! They were SO adorable! It was totally worth coming to the dance just to see them together.

"We saved six seats. Right near the wing-dings table!" Theo said, leading the way.

"OMG! I LOVE wing-dings!" I said excitedly.

Dealing with all of that drama and emotional turmoil had pretty much sapped my energy and left me famished. I was STARVING!

It looked like I had a date for the dance after all. I was going to spend most of the evening with a huge plate of yummy wing-dings. Woo-hoo ☺!

Chloe and Zoey glanced at Theo and then whispered to each other.

"Um, Theo? Actually, we'll only need five seats. Brandon's sick. So Nikki will be hanging out with us tonight," Chloe explained.

Theo and Marcus looked at each other and then at us.

"Brandon's sick? Are you sure?" Theo asked.

"YES!" Chloe and Zoey answered tersely.

"But I just saw him five minutes ago. Did he leave or something?" Marcus asked.

"WHAT?!!" Zoey shrieked.

"NO WAY!!" Chloe screeched.

"OMG! Brandon is actually HERE?!" I gasped. "Are you SURE?!"

Theo and Marcus looked at me like I was crazy.

"Yes, we're sure," they replied.

"I can't believe it! WHAT is HE doing here?!" I sputtered.

Theo shrugged. "I think talking to MacKen—"

"MacKenzie?! But he's NOT supposed to be here!" I spat.

"He isn't?" Marcus asked.

"NO!" Chloe and Zoey shouted.

"I can't just sit here and pretend like nothing happened!" I fumed.

Basically Brandon had stood me up so MacKenzie could pay HIM to take HER to the dance.

Right then he was the last person I wanted to see.

"But the table is close to the w-wing-dings! Just like Zoey asked!" Theo stammered.

"I think I want to go home," I said, panicking.

Theo looked worried. "Please don't leave, Nikki. I can find us a new table! Maybe near the punch instead of the wing-dings?"

"Actually, Theo, this has absolutely NOTHING to do with wing-dings," Chloe snapped.

"It doesn't?" Theo blinked.

"Brandon told Nikki he was SICK!" Zoey huffed.

"Well, um . . . maybe he IS sick. We didn't really ask him how he was feeling," Marcus muttered.

Suddenly a wave of anger swept over me. "I can't believe Brandon actually lied to me. I need to see this with my own eyes!"

"Okay. Then Zoey and I will come with—" But before Chloe could finish her sentence, I turned and marched across the dance floor.

It was crowded and very dimly lit.

But finally my eyes adjusted to the darkness. Everyone was up dancing to the latest tunes by One Direction and the Wanted. Suddenly I saw the answer to my question just in front of me. Theo and Marcus were right! Brandon WAS, in fact, there . . .

. . . WITH MACKENZIE ☹!!

Blinking back my tears, I quickly turned and walked away before Brandon spotted me.

I brushed past Marcus, Theo, Chloe and Zoey, and then ran out the door and down the hall.

"Nikki! WAIT!" my BFFs called after me.

But I just ignored them.

I rushed straight to the bathroom furthest from the dance and locked myself in the last stall. No one would find me in there. I just wanted to be alone.

Brandon had LIED to me!

He wasn't sick at all. I guess I wasn't pretty or popular enough for him.

Why didn't he just tell me he wanted to go to the dance with MacKenzie? I leaned against the cold stall door as my thoughts raced.

I could feel hot tears trickling down my cheeks.

Just great ☹! The last thing I needed right then was my face covered with black tear stains.

I angrily tugged at the roll of toilet paper and just stared blankly as the paper rolled off.

I was buried knee-deep in paper, but I didn't care.

I grabbed one end and dabbed my eyes and cheeks.

Then I blew my nose.

HONK!!

Suddenly the bathroom door creaked open.

"Do you think she came all the way over here?" Chloe asked.

"It's possible. All of the bathrooms near the dance are pretty crowded," Zoey answered.

"Hey, I think you're right," Chloe said. "Look under that stall. Only Nikki would use that much toilet paper!"

624

They whispered to each other, then knocked on my stall door. I opened it a few inches and peeked out.

"GO AWAY!" I said glumly.

"Nikki, we are SO sorry about all of this! We had no idea Brandon was here," Chloe said.

"Hey! It's not your fault that Brandon is a lying rat!" I fumed.

"You need to forget him! The sooner the better!" Zoey said.

Of course I choked up again when I heard that.

"We're only telling you this because we care about you," Chloe said. "Just breathe, okay? Can I get you anything? A bottled water? Are you hungry?"

How could I possibly think about food when my whole world was crashing in on my head? "Actually, I want to go home now. I'm going to call my mom."

"We totally understand," Zoey said sadly. "This whole evening has been a nightmare!"

"Well, the least we can do is go grab you some wing-dings to take home with you. We'll be right back," Chloe said.

Actually, a huge plate of wing-dings sounded pretty good.

"Thanks, guys. I could eat a horse," I muttered.

I was alone in the bathroom again with nothing but my jumbled thoughts.

What had turned Brandon into such a JERK that he would text-dump me less than an hour before the Sweetheart Dance?

MacKenzie!

Her plan had totally worked. Brandon had ripped out my heart, threw it in the dirt and trampled all over it. Just like she wanted! And now they were probably flirting with each other during a slow dance!

UGHHH!!!!

I picked up my phone to call my mom but was interrupted by a loud commotion. Chloe and Zoey came storming back into the bathroom.

"Nikki!" Zoey shrieked. "You are NOT going to believe this! Brandon just walked up to us and asked us where you were. He says he's been waiting for you!"

"What?!" I poked my head out of my stall. "Are you kidding me?!"

"OMG! I was livid!" Chloe fumed. "So I said to him, 'You can keep waiting until heck freezes over! You're just a phoney, backstabbing slimeball who is supposed to be at home SICK!'"

"And get this! He said he didn't have the slightest idea what we were talking about!" Zoey said.

"How could he just LIE right to our faces like that?" Chloe ranted. "That's when I said really sweetly, 'Okay, Brandon, maybe a refreshing drink will help clear up your foggy memory!'"

"OMG! You actually said that to him?" I gasped. "Then what happened?"

"I had to grab the Karate Kid before she dumped a cup of punch over his head and gave him a beatdown," Zoey said, glaring at Chloe.

← CHLOE, THE KARATE KID

"Hey! Give me a break!" Chloe shot back. "I was trying to get a drink and he just happened to be in my way! Anything I almost did to him was purely accidental."

"Chloe, just calm down! You're not making this any better," I scolded.

"You know what would make ME feel better? How about I 'accidentally' sock Brandon in the stomach?"

"Chloe, you can't just walk up to a person and sock him in his stomach," Zoey said. "There are laws against that!"

"Okay, then. How about I punch him in the nose?! Or give him a kick in the butt? He totally deserves that and more!"

"Chloe! This is a middle school dance, not the HUNGER GAMES!" I yelled. "I want to go HOME. Not to JAIL!"

Finally she regained her composure. "Sorry, Nikki!

I just temporarily lost it," she said quietly.

But I'd already had enough.

"Listen, guys! This is NUTS! I need to get out of here. I'm going to call my mom and have her pick me up. But the last person I want to see or talk to is Brandon."

"Yeah, and he definitely doesn't want to see ME!" Chloe said, making a fist and cracking her knuckles.

"Okay, Nikki. Chloe and I will go out and make sure the coast is clear. Then you can make your getaway. We'll be right back."

I glanced at myself in the mirror. I was a mess. But I put on two layers of lip gloss and gathered up all of my stuff, including my courage.

I was SO ready to leave that smelly stall.

Chloe and Zoey almost broke down the door rushing back into the bathroom.

"Nikki, you're not going to believe what just happened!" Chloe screeched.

I rolled my eyes. "Please don't tell me you punched Brandon."

"Actually, I DIDN'T. But I REALLY, REALLY wanted to!" Chloe growled.

"We just saw Brandon again!" Zoey panted. "He says he wants to talk to you!"

I started to panic. "NO! I can't talk to him right now! You guys didn't tell him where I was, did you?!"

"Of course not!" they answered.

"I've tried really hard to be friends with Brandon. And after Crazy Burger, I thought we'd finally worked things out. But I give up! He has made me cry, upset my best friends, ruined the Sweetheart Dance, killed what little self-respect I had and, and, um . . . driven me temporarily INSANE!"

"Nikki, don't say that about yourself," Zoey said quietly. "You're NOT insane!"

"JUST LOOK AT ME! Not only do I look like a zombie bride, but I'm having a complete meltdown. In a bathroom stall! While buried in a roll of toilet paper!"

"OMG!" Chloe quipped. "You ARE insane!"

"We're really sorry, Nikki! We shouldn't have made you come to the dance against your will," Zoey mumbled.

"Don't be sorry," I replied. "It's good that I finally learned the truth about Brandon. I just wish he had the decency to tell me himself, face-to-face."

"I WOULD if you'd let me!" said a voice outside the bathroom door.

"BRANDON?!" I sputtered. "OMG!"

"I didn't tell him you were hiding out in here! I swear!" Zoey whispered to me.

"Don't look at me!" Chloe whisper-shouted. "I don't talk to pathological liars!"

"Actually, I just followed Chloe and Zoey over here," Brandon said. "Nikki, will you please come out so we can talk?!"

"There's nothing to talk about," I shot back. "Just leave me alone. You should have just told me you wanted to go to the dance with MacKenzie and saved me a lot of heartache."

"Nikki, YOU asked me to this dance. I think you owe me an explanation for why you decided to stand me up!" Brandon said.

"What?! I didn't stand YOU up! You stood ME up! But I don't want to talk about any of this. You're supposed to be home sick with the flu! Remember?" I yelled through the bathroom door.

"Okay, fine! If you're not coming OUT, then I'm coming IN," Brandon said.

Chloe, Zoey, and I were speechless.

"NO WAY! He CAN'T be serious!" I finally gasped.

We stared at the door in disbelief as it slowly creaked open and Brandon peeked in.

His face was flushed, and he looked totally bewildered.

I could NOT believe he'd actually come inside the girls' bathroom to talk to me.

"I can't believe I'm actually inside the girls' bathroom. But I really need to talk to you!" he muttered.

Chloe and Zoey were about to protest.

But I think Brandon looked so utterly embarrassed that they felt kind of sorry for him.

"If anyone catches me in here, I'll probably get detention for a month!" he said, looking around nervously. "Anyway, I really apologise for coming in here, but I'm desperate!"

"Actually, Chloe and I were just leaving," Zoey said.

"I'M not going anywhere," Chloe said, folding her arms. "There's no way I'd miss any of THIS! I wish

I had a bucket of popcorn and some gummy bears."

"Chloe! Let's go!" Zoey said sternly.

She grabbed Chloe's arm and dragged her through the door.

"OW! That hurt!" Chloe complained, rubbing her arm.

Chloe turned around and shot Brandon a dirty look. "Hey, dude, you better watch your step. We'll be standing right outside this door. Listening!"

"Um, Chloe, don't worry. I'll be just fine. Really!" I assured her.

Once Brandon and I were alone, my heart started pounding and my palms got sweaty.

"Nikki . . . you've been acting kind of strange ever since my birthday," Brandon said. "But I don't understand why."

"ME?! YOU'VE been acting strange lately," I

said, trying to swallow the lump in my throat. "And those text messages! They've been just . . . CRUEL!"

"Text messages? What text messages?!"

"Don't pretend you didn't send them!" I glared at him. "They came directly from your phone. At first I didn't want to believe you gave MacKenzie that crazy picture of me, but now I'm starting to wonder. If you don't want to be friends with me anymore, just say so!"

"Nikki, it seems like YOU don't want to be friends with ME. One minute you're fine and the next minute you're mad at me. This whole month has been crazy! I thought maybe it had to do with the Sweetheart Dance or something."

My phone chimed and I pulled it out of my bag.

It was yet another text message from Brandon.

"See? This is EXACTLY what I'm talking about. I'm

really tired of your texts. Seriously!" I said,
pointing to my phone.

ME, PUTTING BRANDON ON BLAST
BECAUSE I'M SICK AND TIRED OF
HIS SORTA WEIRD AND SLIGHTLY
OFFENSIVE TEXT MESSAGES

"Um, Nikki! You have a problem. I've been HERE in the GIRLS' BATHROOM talking to YOU for the past three minutes."

"I have a problem?! Really? You're the dude sneaking into the GIRLS' bathroom! Obviously, YOU have a problem!! Have you considered counselling?"

"Nikki! How could I have just sent YOU a TEXT?! Did you see me do it?" he asked.

"Huh?" I muttered, staring at my phone.

Okay, now I was totally confused.

"Then WHO just sent me this text?!"

I opened the message on my phone and read it out loud: "I'm so sorry about the dance. But I just coughed up what looked like a big slimy greenish booger and thought of you!"

Then I handed my phone to Brandon so he could read the text that had come from HIS phone.

He read the message scowled and shook his head.

"So that text is supposed to be from ME?" Brandon asked. "Come on! Do you think I would actually talk about something as crass and juvenile as boogers? And when have I EVER used a smiley face? I'm really sorry you had to go through all of this, Nikki."

"Well, if these texts aren't from you, then WHO is sending them? And WHY are they coming from YOUR phone?"

"I don't know. But what I do know is that I COULDN'T have sent them because I lost my phone a month ago! It's been missing since my party. Since Theo's brother has a phone just like mine, we thought maybe he'd accidentally taken it back to college or something."

A wave of relief washed over me.

So Brandon had NOT been sending all of those crazy text messages for the past month! Maybe we could actually salvage our friendship after all.

"Well, that makes me feel a lot better. But why didn't you just tell me you lost your phone?"

"Because you never gave me a chance. I missed going to Crazy Burger with you the first time because Theo and I were searching all over the place for my phone. I tried to apologise and explain everything that next day at school, but you blew me off," he said.

"Okay, so maybe part of the misunderstanding was MY fault. I'm sorry. But why were you hanging out with MacKenzie just now?"

"You're right. I was talking to MacKenzie earlier tonight. But she came up to me, not the other way around. She told me you were home sick with the flu and wouldn't be coming to the dance."

"Wait a minute! I got a text message right before the dance saying the exact same thing! That YOU had the flu and couldn't make it!"

"You're kidding! So you thought I was just NOT going to show up?" Brandon asked.

"To be honest, I didn't know what to think! I wanted to stay home, but Chloe and Zoey dragged me here. And when I saw you here with MacKenzie when you were supposed to be home sick, I got a little upset!"

"A little?!"

"Okay! I TOTALLY lost it!!" I admitted.

"Well, I knew you'd never just stand me up like that! That's why I asked Chloe and Zoey if you were here. Zoey gave me the stink eye and Chloe went nuts and tried to dump a cup of punch over my head. It was scary!"

"I'm really sorry. That was probably my fault. I guess they were mad at you because of all the things I'd said about you."

"Well, I'd feel a lot safer if you told your BFFs to back off. Anyway, I'm really glad we talked. Now maybe things can get back to normal."

"Yeah, but we still don't know who is behind those text messages or how they got your phone," I said. "Although, I think I have a hunch who's probably responsible."

"Me too. My phone seemed to disappear around the

same time MacKenzie left my party that night.
But we need proof she has it."

We just stared at my phone and racked our brains.
And the more times we read that nasty text message,
the more angry and frustrated we became . . .

That's when the most brilliant idea popped into my head.

It was the perfect prank and would expose the culprit.

And all I had to do was send a very simple text message. To . . . BRANDON!

* * * * *
FROM NIKKI:
Hi Brandon,
I know you were happy about MacKenzie's generous offer to help Fuzzy Friends. But I think buying her that diamond necklace from Tiffany & Co. as a thank you gift was a bit much. Anyway, I went ahead and gift-wrapped it like you asked me. But I placed it in #1573 (behind the school), which is exactly where it belongs.
Sorry ☹!
8:17 p.m.
* * * * *

Now all we had to do was wait patiently for the perpetrator to take the bait.

Brandon smiled at me. "Nikki, you're an evil genius. So, now that we've squashed all the drama, are you and I . . . cool again?"

"Sure! We're cool!" I said, blushing.

"Great. Let's get the heck out of here. Friends don't let friends hide out in the girls' bathroom!"

Then we both laughed really hard at Brandon's joke.

Chloe, Zoey, Brandon and I walked back to the dance together and joined Theo and Marcus at our table.

When I told my BFFs about the mysterious text messages and Brandon's lost phone, they could hardly believe it.

Anyway, we pigged out on wing-dings. And the fancy catered dinner was fabulous too.

I couldn't believe an evening that had started out

so horribly wrong had turned out to be so . . . wonderful!

But mostly I was SUPERhappy that we were all finally getting along again, just like old times.

Okay! I had learned my lesson. I would NEVER, EVER doubt Brandon's friendship again, I told myself.

"Oh, Brandon! There you are!" MacKenzie squealed. "I've been looking all over for you!"

She was really surprised to see me sitting there. "OMG! Nikki!" She sneered. "What are YOU doing here? I thought you were home sick. You're obviously coming down with something! Your face looks like death on a STICK! I hope it's not contagious."

I just rolled my eyes at that girl.

"BTW, I have a little surprise for you. Apparently, a few of your so-called friends have been handing out copies of that hideous picture of you behind your back. I just wanted to let you know. Hey, with friends like those, who needs enemies? Anyway, I thought I'd give you this one to hang in your locker!" Then she shoved a poster right in my face. . .

"We ripped down the posters YOU put up! No real friend of mine would do that to me!" I shot back.

"Oh, really?" MacKenzie said, and stared right at Brandon! "I guess you never know who you can trust! Right, Brandon?"

"MacKenzie, you're such a liar! Brandon would never do something like that!" I argued.

Brandon looked really uncomfortable and glared at MacKenzie. But I noticed that for some reason, he avoided looking at me. Why was he acting so . . . guilty?

MacKenzie laughed. "He was giving them out to people right under your nose!"

"Brandon, WHAT is she talking about?" I was starting to get upset all over again.

"I had absolutely nothing to do with the posters that were plastered up last week. But MacKenzie's right. I have to admit, this one is mine . . ." Brandon said, hanging his head.

I stared at him in shock! Just when I had decided to trust him again, he was acting like a total JERK!

"How could you do this to me?" I cried. "The last thing I need is dozens more of those pictures floating around the school!"

"Dozens?! Marcus and I helped Brandon hand out at least three hundred of them. That picture is too hilarious!" Theo laughed. "Everybody wanted one."

"Marcus, how could you?!" Chloe exclaimed in shock.

"Theo, that's just CRUEL!" Zoey said, shaking her head in disgust.

I stood up abruptly to leave. "Sorry! I've had enough! I'm out of here!"

"Wait, Nikki. We're coming with you," Chloe said.

"Let's go get our coats," Zoey huffed.

"Wait, just let me explain!" Brandon pleaded.

"There's NO excuse for what you did!" I scolded, blinking back tears for what seemed like the fifth time tonight. "It wasn't funny!"

Suddenly the house lights came on and Principal Winston took the stage.

"Okay, students! May I have your attention, please? It's time to crown our WCD Sweetheart Princess."

"OMG!" MacKenzie shrieked. "They're about to announce the Sweetheart Princess. I'm pretty sure I won. Anyway, I gotta go. They're going to need me onstage. LATER, HATERS!" Then she sashayed away. I just HATE it when that girl sashays!

Mr Winston continued. "First I'd like to thank our maths teacher, Mrs Sprague, for counting all of the ballots earlier today. Now I am very proud and honoured to announce that our new WCD Sweetheart Princess is . . ."

MacKenzie Hollister, I grumbled inside my head. It's ALWAYS MacKenzie Hollister!

"NIKKI MAXWELL!! CONGRATULATIONS!!"

OMG! I could not believe my ears! I just stood there in total shock with my mouth hanging open.

If Chloe and Zoey hadn't been holding on to me, I would have fallen right over.

How could this have happened? And why would anyone vote for me, the BIGGEST DORK in the entire school?

That's when Brandon brushed his shaggy hair out of his eyes and gave me a crooked smile. Then he turned the poster over and handed it to me . . .

OMG! My eyes almost popped out of my head! It said nice stuff about ME. Only no one had bothered to tell ME about it. Or my BFFs, Chloe and Zoey. Finally it all made sense why kids had been whispering about me at school today.

"Would Nikki and her date please come up to the stage?" Mr Winston asked. "We have a special gift for you, young lady!"

As the entire student body cheered (well, everyone except MacKenzie, who was staring at her phone), Brandon and I made our way to the stage.

It felt like I was in a dream. I carefully opened a white box and inside was the most beautiful tiara I'd ever seen!

OMG! Brandon was the perfect escort.

He even helped me with my tiara.

Okay, he placed it on my head totally lopsided!

But STILL! It's the thought that counts.

After that, each couple at the dance got to pose for a really nice keepsake picture. It felt like we were at a senior prom or something. . .

CHLOE AND MARCUS ☺!

ZOEY AND THEO ☺!

And last but not least . . .

ME AND BRANDON ☺!!

I thought all of our photos came out SUPERcute!

Then, thanks to Jordyn, we FINALLY learned the identity of the mysterious person who had stolen Brandon's phone and sent me those messages . . .

OMG! LOOK OUTSIDE!

Soon the lights went down and the disco ball lit up for a slow dance.

Brandon kept staring at me with this strange look on his face. Then he nervously cleared his throat.

"Wow, Nikki! I've been wanting to tell you that you look . . . um, totally . . . !!" Brandon's mouth opened but no words came out. I guess he was speechless.

"Thank you," I gushed. "And I wanted to say that you look beyond awesome!"

"Thank you!" Brandon said shyly. "So . . . uh . . . do you wanna . . . ?" He nodded toward the dance floor.

"Sure. I'd love to," I answered, and took his hand.

We danced, laughed and spoke to each other in what probably sounded like gibberish for the rest of the evening. But we understood each other perfectly.

It was the most sweetly AWKWARD and insanely BEAUTIFUL moment of my entire LIFE!

It was like I was a princess in my very OWN fairy tale.

And Brandon was my handsome prince and a very cool friend. I was finally having my dorkily ever after and I wanted this moment to last forever.

Suddenly I remembered that most of my favourite fairy tales ended with the prince and princess sharing a romantic KISS!!

So of course I TOTALLY FREAKED during our very last dance! And guess what happened?!! OMG! I was so nervous I thought I was going to pee my pants. Which, BTW, wasn't the first time, and definitely NOT the last!

I can't wait to share ALL of the exciting details! SQUEEE!!

TOMORROW!!

Sorry! I'm SUCH a DORK!
☺!!

Rachel Renée Russell is an attorney who prefers writing tween books to legal briefs. (Mainly because books are a lot more fun and pyjamas and bunny slippers aren't allowed in court.)

She has raised two daughters and lived to tell about it. Her hobbies include growing purple flowers and doing totally useless crafts (like, for example, making a microwave oven out of lolly sticks, glue, and glitter). Rachel lives in northern Virginia with a spoiled pet Yorkie who terrorises her daily by climbing on top of a computer cabinet and pelting her with stuffed animals while she writes. And, yes, Rachel considers herself a total Dork.